Believe

Varun Gwalani

FROG BOOKS

First published in India 2013 by Frog Books
An imprint of Leadstart Publishing Pvt Ltd
1 Level, Trade Centre
Bandra Kurla Complex
Bandra (East) Mumbai 400 051 India
Telephone: +91-22-40700804
Fax: +91-22-40700800
Email: info@leadstartcorp.com
www.leadstartcorp.com / www.frogbooks.net

Sales Office:
Unit: 122 / Building B/2
First Floor, Near Wadala RTO
Wadala (East) Mumbai 400 037 India
Phone: +91-22-24046887

US Office:
Axis Corp, 7845 E Oakbrook Circle
Madison, WI 53717 USA

ISBN 978-93-82473-81-7

Book Editor: Sharmila Ramnani
Design Editor: Mishta Roy

Typeset in Book Antiqua
Printed at Repro India Ltd, Mumbai

Price — India: Rs 195; Elsewhere: US $8

Dedication

This book is dedicated to my parents for always letting me be who I am and pursue my dreams.

About the Author

Varun Gwalani is an 18-year old resident of Mumbai, studying Arts in Jai Hind College. He's been an avid reader all his life. Some of his favourite authors include Paulo Coelho, J.K. Rowling, George Orwell and O.Henry.

Varun has always dreamed of being an author with the ability to tell a story that will fascinate and engage the reader. Over a period of three years, he has written a collection of over fifty short stories.

This is his first published work. For feedback and queries, you may connect with Varun at gwalanivarun@gmail.com

Contents

Prononciation Guide

Levion-*L-eh-vie-un*

Leviite-*Lee-vite*

Levitis-*Lee-vite-is*

Natis-*Nay-tis*

Natism-*Nay-tism*

Sinome-*Sin-om*

Prologue

The light was growing. The sun was rising in the east, bringing with it the glow of morning. At first, all the light went around the hill to the east, but then it rose higher and bathed the structure on top of the hill with a soft radiance. Then it rose higher and the Eye on the structure's tower was thrown into prominence as if some enormous intelligence was suddenly making itself known.

One golden ray of light went through the window and landed right in the middle of the face of the girl watching this beautiful phenomenon. She lifted her hand and observed with a feeling of wonder at the way the light touched her skin, illuminating it and warming it gently. She smiled to herself and watched the scene with the same content smile.

The door to her room opened, as she knew it would. She didn't turn. Her mother saw that she was awake, smiled as well and said, "You've got to be up for school in two minutes, Victoria."

Victoria nodded absently. Her mother leaned down and gave her a kiss on the head. Victoria turned and hugged her around the neck. "Love you, mom," she said.

Her mother put her arms around her as well and then stood up saying laughingly, "Okay, you can have five minutes."

Victoria smiled wider and turned to look out the window again.

When she was ready for school, she walked to the table to eat breakfast with her family. Her brother, she remembered, had already gone to school for an early class. She hugged her parents and kissed them on the head before sitting down. As soon as she had seated herself, she picked up her fork and knife and started eating her omelettes voraciously. Her parents smiled knowingly at her enormous appetite and went back to their food.

"I heard you were top of the class in Maths again, my dear. Congratulations," her father said to her.

She looked up from her food long enough to blush and mumble, "It was nothing, easy test."

"Rubbish," her mother said with a wave of her hand. "You're just being modest. I'm sure tests in almost every subject haven't been 'easy'. You're a smart and talented girl. You'll go far."

Victoria finished up her food and stood up, her face a deep red. "You're my parents; you have to say that. Anyway, I'm going to be late for school. See ya!" She took her bag on one shoulder and ran off.

Her parents smiled at each other. "That girl is so full of life and cheerfulness!" her mother remarked.

"Yet so determined and focused," her father added, taking the other's hand. "We've raised a fine girl."

They went back to their breakfast, feeling happy with themselves as parents.

****

Even before her parents could complete their discussion about her, Victoria had already met a bunch of girls and was walking with them to school. She was on the fringes of the group, listening intently to the conversation about crushes and clothes. There were points when she wanted to ask something or make a comment, but she stayed silent because she was too shy to say anything.

The impromptu leader of the group, perhaps sensing this, turned to her and asked kindly, "You look like you have something on your mind, Victoria."

Victoria, caught off guard, blushed and looked away. "Oh, it's nothing."

There was excited murmuring and *ooing* from the crowd. "Victoria liiiiiikes someone," one girl said teasingly. The other girls said encouragingly, "Tell us, Victoria, tell us!"

"Well," Victoria, sufficiently embarrassed, started, "I think that Mike is kind of cute." Her blush deepened.

There were squeals and chatter all around. "Oh, you mean Howard's friend?" "He *is* cute." "I saw him the other day and..." "He was arguing with her, wasn't he?" "He was upset..." "I've heard he's kissed her..." "Already?!"

Seeing that this talk was upsetting Victoria, the leader cut through, "Let's not talk about that girl. I'm certain she's not going to be with him much longer."

This seemed to placate Victoria and the group. After a minute, a girl asked Victoria, "So, do *you* want to kiss him?"

There were squeals and giggles as Victoria blushed deeper than ever. "Not now," she said, embarrassed. "Maybe after a while."

Though there were giggles, most of the girls nodded in agreement.

Eventually the conversation moved to other topics and they reached school.

****

After the final bell had rung, she stayed back in class to ask the teacher a few questions and then decided to spend some time there to finish her homework. After she was done, she left school alone. It was late afternoon and everyone was either at work or at home, taking a nap to pass the hot hour. Victoria walked, humming to herself as she went. She reached the square and saw Mr. Andrew Cutter on the other side. He was a lean, tan, middle-aged man.

She smiled and walked towards him to greet him. Usually he seemed in very good shape, but at that moment he seemed a bit unsteady. They reached the middle of the square together and her greeting died on her lips as he collapsed. She rushed to him and bent down towards him. She held his head with both her hands and noticed that his face was green. She was about to call for help when his eyes bulged and he started coughing blood. In fright she involuntarily dropped his head which hit the ground hard.

This caused him to cough harder, and his nose started bleeding too. His eyes bore into Victoria's, pleading for help, but she didn't know what to do. Suddenly his whole body started trembling and finally his eyes grew even wider, and finally the life went out of them.

Victoria stood there staring for a few seconds, before she vomited near the dead man's head. She took a look at him again and then fainted in the pool of vomit and blood.

As she was falling, however, her eyes turned upward, above the golden legs on the pedestal in the square, above the roofs of the houses and onto the great Eye, which pierced her very soul, and gave her some comfort in the darkness.

Chapter 1

Author in a Bar

This story takes place in a world, the name of which is not important, far away from ours, but with many similarities, other than the fact that we are more technologically advanced than them. The story is restricted to only a very small area, so knowledge of the rest of the world is not necessary for it to fulfil its purpose.

****

It was a bar, the kind of bar where ordinary people came to drink away their sorrows until they were drowning in a haze of liquor-induced darkness, which simply added to the natural dimness of the place; or to "pick up girls" which involved charming a girl sufficiently so that she would go home with you or on a date with you. After all, the girl of your dreams might be at the bar, just waiting for you to come and sweep her off her feet after dozens of guys have made passes at her.

The girl in green seemed to stand out among the relative eyesore around her. She looked around, knowing exactly what she wanted: some fun. She considered herself somewhat of an expert at spotting people who wanted exactly that as well. She liked observing people; she fancied herself to have great insight into human nature and prided herself on her ability to know what people were like.

She surveyed the crowd. At first, she didn't see anything special, but then she noticed him.

This man was different. He stood out like a king among his subjects. His clothes and his manner reeked of money. He seemed like the kind of man who had been around it all his life. Then why was he in such a place?

She walked over. He was a good looking guy of average height. His well-fitted shirt revealed a good physique underneath, though he tried not to accentuate it. He had dark hair and blue eyes. She couldn't shake the feeling that his face looked familiar, but she just couldn't remember from where. He seemed to be wholly intent on a point in space directly in front of him. His unshaven face made him look more like a drinker but she had a feeling this man was different, and she felt drawn in by his air of mystery.

She sat down next to him and ordered a drink. His concentration broke and he gave the once over look. He saw a good-looking girl of average height in the low-cut green dress that matched the colour of her eyes. Then he had a sip of his drink and returned to the point in space.

The girl was not to be discouraged. She ran her hand through her long, thick black hair and then extended it.

"Hey; Samantha."

The man seemed to have been expecting this; he smiled a small smile, shook the girl's hand and said, "Tom."

Samantha smiled. Her drink arrived. She had a sip, turned to him and said, "So what's a guy like you doing in a place like this?"

Tom laughed a little and said, "That line ever work for you?"

Samantha smiled and said, "Very rarely use it. Because most of the time it's not true. You don't seem like the kind that would be seen in places like this."

"So I see you go to places like this and try your lines on random guys a lot," said Tom, turning away from her and back to his drink in what felt like an air of dismissal. But Samantha persisted.

"I guess you think I'm just a random girl roaming around trying to have sex, which I probably am, but that doesn't mean I'm not good at it. I can tell you some reasons why you're here."

Tom had a sip of his beer, but inclined his head a little, which indicated he was listening.

"Well, you have a prominent tan line but no ring, which means that your wife is either dead or divorced. This place means something very special to you and your memory of her, which is why you've come back to relive it or...recapture it."

Tom smiled out of the corner of his mouth. His expression indicated that he still wasn't too convinced. Samantha noticed this and offered to go on but Tom raised a hand and said, "How do you know I'm not just some guy who just wants a meaningless one-night stand?"

"You could be, but that would be to fill the hole caused by the loss of your wife."

He shrugged and said, "Could be." Then he paused and asked her, "So, you read a lot?"

"Yeah," she said, thrown off guard by his sudden question. "Why?"

"Only you can ask the questions around here?" he asked, raising an eyebrow.

Samantha shook her head, slightly confused. She just couldn't get a grip on this guy. And the feeling that she had seen him somewhere still lingered.

"So what do you do?" she asked.

"I channel my thoughts and imagination which I conjure up by using words in meaningful arrangements. This results in the formation of visual images in the mind and consequently I am able to convey my thoughts to a wide segment of people." He paused and said with a small smile, "I'm a bestselling writer."

"Ah," she said. That smile was the chink in the armour. "I'm sure you're a great writer," she said.

Tom raised an eyebrow at her and said, "Why? Just because I fit the 'silent, moody, brooding author' look? I must be good! Well let me tell you, that's just a cliché. Clichés are boring." He paused. "And trust me, I'm anything but boring." He tried to give a 'suave' smile, but it turned out to only appear weird. *He's definitely not used to this,* Samantha thought. He finished the rest of his drink and said, "And you might have read it, but I doubt anyone has ever grasped what I really want to say."

She was about to say that a misunderstood author sitting in a bar was kind of cliché, but then decided against it. It was painfully clear that he was uncomfortable in this situation, even though he was trying very hard not to appear so. Finishing her drink, she realized that she was getting tired of all talk and no action. Time to see if he was a lost cause or not. "So why don't we finish this at my place?"

The man shook his head. Samantha shrugged and was just about to get up when he held up a hand. He ordered another drink, drank it in one go, got up and said, "Now let's finish this at your place."

****

Samantha lay on the bed, staring at the ceiling and gasping. That had been really good and she had no regrets bringing this odd man home. But somehow, she felt that he was holding back; this was confirmed when she looked over at him. He was panting slightly, but his expression was slightly pained.

She sat up and put her hand on his shoulder. "Something wrong?" she asked, not really expecting a response.

He shrugged and said softly, "This was a mistake." He got up and seemed to be surveying the room for the first time. Samantha could understand that soon as she had shut the door behind her, he had done away with the pleasantries of waiting and had started kissing her furiously. The rest was pretty simple.

The bedroom, like the rest of the house, was Spartan. Tom walked over to the small writing table below the bookshelf. Then he looked over her books, the one luxury she seemed to allow herself.

"I thought this would be good for me, a rebound, I mean. I guess you never really can let go of sadness."

That last line seemed familiar to Samantha. She shrugged off the feeling and said, "So I see I was right; you are grieving."

He didn't say anything, but continued looking at the books on the bookshelf.

"Sex makes you talkative, but not by much," she muttered. She looked at him again. He seemed to have paused at a certain book.

"Anything that interests you?" she asked.

He took out a book and showed it to her. "Is this a good book?"

She looked at the book he was holding up. It was *We Are All Alone* by Conner White. She made a face. "That book," she said with slight contempt in her voice, "is one of the most well written pieces of trash I have ever seen. I just bought it out of curiosity after the book caused some stir. The author is so negative, the ideas he is trying to convey through his words are ones you would generally expect from a man who is lifeless and devoid of hope, yet his writing style is so...compelling that you feel like reading it, and that's probably the only reason it sells." She took a breath and continued, "You know, he could really write something good with his skills, but he's wasting it."

On hearing her words, Tom's face became expressionless. On seeing him with the book in his hand, something clicked in Samantha's mind. She got up and said in a shocked voice, "You! You're Conner White!"

The man shrugged and replaced the book on the shelf. "I remember you from a book signing or something in a bookstore I was passing through. You look different..." Then she paused as if she was remembering something before she exclaimed, "Your wife died recently!"

Tom/Conner shrugged again and turned to her before saying, "Why so shocked? I told you I was an author."

"Well...it's just that..." she stuttered, at a loss for words. "You don't look like an author...or a negative person."

He raised an eyebrow and stepped closer, "So you weren't convinced. You thought I was just idly boasting. Why don't I look like an author? Is it my lack of glasses? Is it my good looks? Is it because I was so good in bed?"

She shuddered and stepped back. She took the sheet and wrapped it around her. The very fact that she had sex with Conner White fully seeped in and she shuddered again. Suddenly she felt as if her whole body had been infected with a surge of negativity which had been injected by this man. Finding out who he was had completely changed how she saw him.

"I still don't understand why you seem so upset," he said, looking calm. "What I write is just my opinion; who is to say yours is right? I'm allowed to write my opinion. You think you're some expert on assessing human behaviour? That little ring observation was one which any amateur could have made. You didn't believe that I was an author although it was staring you in the face and you were so surprised to learn that I was a negative person. Guess you misread me."

Samantha seemed to be gaining confidence. She said in an angry tone, "I'm upset because you're one of the people responsible for spreading hopelessness and sadness in the world. Your books actually try to *convince* people that there's no hope left! You tell people to stop believing in their loved ones and everyone around them! Your works are so depressing they've actually driven people to suicide! You're a killer!"

Conner blinked and said, "That isn't true."

Samantha became furious. "Yeah, I bet that helps you sleep at night while others are going without sleep wondering how they can survive in a world you made them believe in! She pointed at the door and said angrily, "Get out of my house!" Conner quietly moved away. As he was dressing, Samantha said, "And I didn't misread you. You're just an egoistic man who thinks he's better than others; you want to put others down so that you can feel superior!"

Conner finished dressing and exited the apartment. As the door slammed behind him, he put his head in his hands and thought, *If only it were that simple.*

Chapter 2

Stopping By the Woods

That was it.

That was the breaking point.

Staring at that blank page for over 3 hours, rewriting every word that came to his mind until it reached the point where it all had to be erased; that had gotten to him like nothing else could. Through grief and joy, infamy and solitude, his writing had never failed him; it was the one thing that had always come through for him somehow or the other.

But now, even that one skill of his was leaving.

He banged both hands on either side of the desk on which the typewriter was placed and got up angrily, his chair toppling backwards to the floor. He stormed out of the room and into the garden, where he kicked a football onto the wall repeatedly. He went to the gym and started working on the punching bags with rage and inefficiency just like a drunken man attacking a lamp post after slamming into it and apparently getting insulted by it.

He imagined the punching bag as a myriad of opponents; the only problem was that (like the rest of us) his main opponents were ones with no physical form, so he made them manifest in different forms - death, bad luck, sadness - all were imagined as maniacal beasts with horns, wings and an assortment of mythical body parts, which had to be vanquished by his hand, lest they cause the world further grief.

To an outsider, this would seem an almost pointless and mad activity, but Conner seemed to know what it was for, because as soon as he began tiring, he stopped. With sore hands, he walked slowly back into the main house and collapsed on to the couch.

He looked around him. This house was out in the country, with a study, living room and two bedrooms, along with his housekeeper's quarters. He liked to come here when he had to get away from the hustle and bustle of the city, and it helped him to be at ease, not that it was helping him much right now, though.

The landline cable was with his housekeeper and his phone was with her as well. His typewriter was ready. He knew how prone to distraction he was. He needed complete concentration for his writing.

Being an author was...a complex job. Everyone had different styles, different methods. There was really no set way of going about it, and that was great. The way the author wrote often reflected his personality, and that could mean writing in a dingy room with a typewriter, or writing in a notepad in a park in the bright sunshine. But the *real* beauty of it was that no matter where you wrote, whatever edition it was, the basic story remained the same. The *story* shines right through, using the words as sunlight, burning the images on to the readers' minds.

Conner had dabbled in writing in his youth, but he never really thought he could make a career out of it, or even needed to, for that matter. (Later he realized he *did* need to, though not for the money). He remembered the first real story he had written. At the memory, he sighed and wearily sat leaning forward with his head in his hands. He stayed like that for a minute, and then went out the front gate.

He breathed in the fresh air and surveyed the surroundings. It was mainly countryside. Though he knew there was a town around somewhere, he had never been there.

Then he went back inside and sat down in front of the typewriter again. The blank page seemed to be taunting him; he could almost imagine swirling words on the paper, which formed into a sentence that read, "You can't write, Conner White!"

He shook his head and they disappeared; however, a voice seemed to be whispering the same line into his ear, but he knew whose voice that was - his own.

Conner slumped back in his chair. He hated this... this feeling of... inadequacy that he carried around with him. It was a feeling that everyone felt at some point or the other, but they generally buried it under mounds of work or frivolous activity just to pass the time, so that they never would have to face the emptiness inside them. It's not that nobody wanted to stop and stare at the forest; it's not that they couldn't make the time. It's just that they didn't, because they were scared of what they might see; of the monsters that might see them looking, and attack them.

Conner always felt that he carried around more of these repressed feelings than anybody else; ironically though, he stopped and stared at the forest the most, and as a result, he often ended up with the worst kind of scars, the mental kind; the ones that cannot be seen by anybody except those who were willing to look, and that often didn't include the person himself.

So how would Conner heal these mental scars? He had found the way, through his writing. Writing just to express emotions, to pour your heart and soul into the page was the purest form of writing, Conner believed. And so, he wrote, not because he wanted to, but because he *needed* to. There was this burning urge within him, similar to an alcoholic or a junkie who felt that if they didn't drink or do drugs, the world around them would close in on them and engulf them with its myriad problems and complications.

Whenever Conner wrote something, it was all his thoughts, all his emotions on that page. That was how it had always been. Almost always, at least. In the beginning, he had written a few stories in school which he had quickly forgotten about; those were very different from the style and nature of the stories he wrote now. But, thinking back, he regarded those stories as rubbish, simple stepping stones to a better writing future.

However, the thing about Conner was that he suppressed most of his thoughts and feelings. While he often thought about them, he never let it get to the point of losing control and so it all stayed within him, often touching but never really reaching that breaking point.

But when he *did* reach that breaking point, however, he turned to writing for respite. For his first novella, he had reached the breaking point rather unexpectedly. He closed his eyes and transported himself back into that time, when the last possibilities of a better life were slowly melting away from him. He opened his eyes and he felt like he was back at his old home...

It was an early, sunny morning. A young man, still not fully attuned to the cruelty of the world, stared at his phone, waiting for his girlfriend to call. She usually called by that time. 'She should be awake...but maybe she overslept.' It was the first summer after college ended. She was allowed to do that. He shrugged and waited patiently. Then the phone rang. He picked it up happily. The voice that crackled over the line was morose, and it was not the voice of his girlfriend, but of her father. Slowly he delivered the news. She was dead. Suicide, it seemed. There was no note...but apparently she had been depressed lately, spending more time in her room and such. She had had too many sleeping pills. Quick, painless death in her sleep. There had been more said but the young man wasn't listening. The phone dropped from his hand and he started crying.

There had been no signs, or maybe he just hadn't understood the signs. The time before the incident always seemed hazy, but that day and the ones after, never left his mind.

He was depressed for days, blaming himself, wondering what had gone wrong, what he could have done differently. The guilt and pain was a lot for him. One day, he just snapped. He started yelling at everyone, pushing things around; he even locked himself in his room for the entire day. But by the end of it, he was so exhausted, he just lay down. The thoughts came easily to him, and on a sudden impulse, he grabbed a notebook and started writing down all his thoughts, all the feelings he was feeling and all the things he felt about those feelings. He had fallen asleep writing, pen in his hand, book on his chest.

When he woke up the next morning and looked at what he had written, he realized that there was some good stuff in there, and it could be the start of a great story. So once he got the beginning, the remaining was relatively easy; the words flowed quickly filling the paper. Everything he had written was what he really believed in the world to be, and what he believed the people living in it should realize. When he looked it over, he realized how many people would regard it as negative writing, but he didn't care. He believed in it. But he wasn't sure if anyone else would consider it good. So he hid it away and it got lost in the recesses of his cupboard and eventually, his mind, for a long time.

Conner shook his head and got up. Why couldn't he write? His breaking point had been reached; his mind should have blocked all extraneous information and focused only on one thought: the story at hand. It had worked before. However, his mind was unable to conjure up a new story; instead, it was thinking about the old ones.

Conner stared at a picture of his late wife in the photo frame. She had died about two weeks ago. It was a heart attack; she was so young...He picked up the frame and sat down, looking at her deep blue eyes, her thick blonde hair and her rich smile. After finding out the cause of death, the first irrational thought that came into his head was, "At least it wasn't suicide." But upon thinking that, he had gotten even more upset, thinking about the loss in his life.

Now it brought tears to his eyes. He lovingly caressed the picture. He had put his wedding band back on his finger. That reminded him of last night. That had been a stupid move, but after Sophie's death, he had been holed up in his house the whole of two weeks, as if paralysed by an inability to comprehend his beloved wife's passing.

Last night he had decided to try doing something different, but he regretted it. It had done nothing but magnify his longing for

Sophie. That was not how he was - egoistic or vain. With other people he was painfully aware about his negativity, and he could never be sure if they recognized it as that, or as something else - like egotism. Now his negativity had once more driven him into such a depressed spiral in his life that he had decided it was time to write a new story to let out his emotions.

But it wasn't being written, and suddenly Samantha's words echoed through his mind, "...A great writer, but he could write much better stories with his talent..." He shook his head and dismissed her talks as idle ravings of a headstrong youth (which is what most adults think of *all* the views of those they consider "too young").

He looked again at Sophie's picture. Many people wondered, some openly speculated, how someone like him could end up with a wife at all, much less a wife like her. He often wondered that himself.

Resigned to the fact that he was going to continue reminiscing, he settled back in his chair and closed his eyes.

He had got a useless degree from college and settled into doing a nominal job in his father's company. This made him wealthy. He was not good at business and found his job boring. His routine became foreign business trips in which he simply talked a load of reassuring nonsense. He was not a big spender, so the wealth he garnered didn't give him any pleasure. He suffered from bouts of restlessness in which he wondered what he was doing with his life.

Most people would be delighted to have money to spend and no work to do, which allowed them to indulge in whatever pleasures they desired. But Conner was all too aware of the gaping hole which urged him to do something other than allow himself idle pleasure, and so he searched...

When Sophie came into his life, she was the one who made him feel as if the hole could become smaller, if not completely vanish. In the initial days, he knew she hadn't felt the same and that pained him. Then he had written her a story, hoping she realized how much he loved her...

After reading that story, she had looked at him differently. It was as if she was seeing all his emotions, all his feelings...but the best thing she did was encourage him to write. She had been surprised when she read his novella; she said it was 'different from the story, but still written well'. So he got his novella published through one of his business contacts, and from there, his writing career had taken off. He gave up his position in his father's company and decided to make writing his full-time career.

Conner's eyes suddenly opened. There was something amiss...

Conner sat up straight, eyes wide open. *I can't remember the story I wrote her!* he thought. *There was something about darkness; about help...I can't remember! What is* wrong *with me?! Here I am, mourning my wife's death, and I can't remember one of the most important parts of our relationship!*

He started pacing with renewed energy, agitated. He just couldn't remember! Every time he thought he was close to it, it sprung away like a cat that doesn't want to get caught. He put the frame facing down on his desk. He couldn't bear to look at the picture for fear of seeing reproach or accusation in those beautiful eyes.

He sat down at his desk again and faced the blank white page. No words came to his mind. The only thing that did enter his mind was the beautiful girl who was pointing a finger at him and screaming, "You're a killer!"

What did Samantha mean by that? Did he really drive that boy to suicide?

Was he a killer?

There was only one way to find out. He had noticed Samantha's university card on her desk, along with her university books (she seemed to have a few psychology books, too; no surprise there). He would go to the source and find out.

****

Soon he was driving his car to the university. It was not far; just outside the nearest town there was, where he had met Samantha. He didn't know where in the university Samantha would be so he hoped to find out from the bar the students frequented - a little distance away from the university. Other than knowing that he didn't want to attract too much attention, he had no idea what he was doing, no tangible plan in mind; he just felt that if he didn't get this cleared in his own mind, he wouldn't be able to write, and consequently, not be able to live.

He reached the bar, parked his car nearby and got out. He had dressed inconspicuously so as to blend in.

He went in and quickly scanned the place. It was all clear. He sat down in one of the booths. It was still early, and there weren't many people around. He ordered a drink and looked around to see who he might ask for some information. Suddenly the door of the bar opened revealing the very person he had come looking for!

On spotting her, Conner quickly ducked behind the booth he was occupying. She was with some of her friends. She didn't notice him; she was engaged in conversation. She and her friends slowly made their way to the booth behind Conner's. She was in mid-sentence.

"And then it turns out that this guy is Conner fucking White!"

"The author?!" exclaimed a very surprised voice. Conner winced. He knew that voice very well.

"Yes!"

There were murmurs. Conner couldn't understand the words. They sat down and ordered their drinks. Then their conversation continued when one of them asked a little loudly in a teasing kind of voice, "So was he good?"

Samantha seemed to take a breath before answering, "Yes, he was great! Right up till the point I found out who he is, though."

The others giggled. Conner didn't hear the familiar voice joining in. "And then what happened?" the fourth girl in the booth asked.

"Well, he asked me why I was so surprised he was an author. I was just surprised because he didn't seem the type to be writing that kind of stuff, not because he was such a good lay, as he suggested!" The two girls again squealed with laughter while the third remained silent. Conner winced. Samantha asked, "Hey, Megan, why you so quiet? Something wrong?"

Megan said in a slightly bitter voice, "Nothing wrong." And changing her tone, she diverted the topic. "So...this guy, what did he say then? His wife died recently, right? What is he doing picking up women in a bar?"

Conner closed his eyes. Samantha said, "Why do you sound so angry, Megan?"

Megan's voice returned to its normal level and she said, "It's just that...it's wrong." Samantha's voice was sceptical, but she continued, "Okay...he said he was trying a rebound, but it wasn't working; he was just missing his wife more. He also picked up my copy of his book and asked me what I thought of it! I told him that the writing style was good though the subject material was pretty much crap. I'm pretty sure only the first part of my opinion went into his inflated head."

Her voice was laced with disgust while spitting out the last few lines. There were no laughs now, only silence. Then Samantha continued, her voice slightly lowered because of which Conner had to strain to hear, "And I also told him about...Roger. But of course, he didn't believe it." She seemed to sigh. There were more murmurs, and Conner's heart sank. So then it was true! Someone named Roger had committed suicide because of him. His mind was unable to comprehend that fact.

The girls gradually moved on to other topics, and Conner switched off. He just wanted to get out of there without being spotted, to deal with the swirl of madness and thoughts that was his mind.

Suddenly Samantha said she was going to the restroom. Another girl got up to accompany her (because, after all, a girl can never go to the bathroom alone). Conner ducked under the table as if he was searching for something. As soon as she passed by, he got up, paid and rushed out as fast as possible, keeping his head down and away from the girls at the table.

He got into his car and started it up. He started driving, and just as he was turning the corner, he saw the bar door open.

After ten minutes, he looked in the rear view mirror and saw he was being followed. He pulled over. He knew who it was.

The car behind him also pulled over. The car door opened and a girl got out. She started walking (actually stomping) towards his car. Conner got out slowly. He was dreading this moment.

"Hi, Dad," the girl said in an icy voice.

"Hi, Megan," he said weakly.

His daughter Megan was of average height, with black, wavy hair. She had just one feeling for her father – hatred. While Sophie was alive, for her sake, they had been on talking terms, but after her death, their relationship had become strained; they had not spoken to each other after the funeral. Conner did not think this would be a very happy reunion.

Megan had been treated differently throughout her school life. Parents were not willing to let their children associate with her because they always wondered what kind of upbringing and home environment the daughter of Conner White would have. No parent wanted their children to be exposed to that kind of influence, so Megan was practically an outcast. After graduating, Megan started using her mother's maiden surname in order to keep secret the fact that she was the daughter of Conner White. Conner was not surprised when Samantha had talked about being with him, because she didn't know that Megan was his daughter.

"What the hell do you think you're doing, Dad?" she screamed angrily, looking directly into his eyes with the deep blue ones she had inherited from her mother. "Sleeping with one of my classmates, that too less than a month after Mom dies?!"

Conner put his palms up in a gesture of peace, backed off and leaned against his car, folding his arms. He looked at the ground. "It was exactly what I said it was. It was a rebound. I was really upset about it and I needed to get out of the house..."

"So, seriously, Dad you-" Megan started but then she stopped talking. She clenched her eyes shut, as if restraining herself. Then she opened them and said in a voice brimming with anger, "You're pathetic, Dad." When he didn't reply, she asked scathingly, "So why didn't you go home and write one of your depressing *books*?"

Conner looked up. "I tried, Megan," he said softly, "But something your friend said the other day really hit me. That's why I came here...to find out if it was true."

Megan raised an eyebrow, "What thing?"

Conner's voice dropped even lower. "The," he paused, as if gathering up courage to say the word, "suicide."

Megan's expression grew pained. She walked over and leaned against the car next to him.

"Yes, it's true."

Conner's expression was blank. "What happened, exactly?" he asked softly.

Megan spoke in a low voice, "Well...there was this boy named Roger. He seemed troubled, but he never spoke of it. He needed some encouragement, some belief. But he found your books instead, which gave him pages and pages that said life was only made of sadness and despair; and that the people who needed help would never get it. He probably couldn't live with that so he just gave it all up. You're lucky the papers didn't get hold of it."

Conner didn't say anything. He just stared out into space. "I can't believe it," he finally said softly.

Megan looked at him, a bit of her anger returning. "You better believe it. My friend is dead because you couldn't face up to your own problem!" And then she seemed to say more to herself, "And he was not the only victim."

Conner looked at her. "What's that supposed to mean?"

Megan stared stonily at the ground. "Nothing," she said.

"Tell me, Megan!" said Conner, his voice growing louder.

"You really want to know?" she said, turning on him. "You killed my mother, and what's worse, you did it while she was still alive!"

Conner blinked and took a step away. "What?" he said, bewildered.

"Don't look so confused," she said, "Your writing killed her. Don't be so surprised! She hated the kind of things you wrote! Every time she read it, it pained her! She thought you could do much better than that. She wanted you to realize your potential, and move on to better writing. But every time she tried to broach the topic with you, you just deflected, like you do to every single problem in your life!"

When Conner didn't respond, she continued, "She showed me the story you wrote her. It was beautiful. She always wished that you could write more like that." She went over to her car, opened her bag and got out an envelope. "Here, Dad. I took it from home when Mom died. Hopefully it'll remind you of who you can be." She handed the letter to a dumbstruck Conner and paused. Then she continued,

"She believed in you for some reason known only to her, Dad. She thought that lives could be improved, even your life. Maybe you should write a book about that. Honour her memory, if you couldn't honour her life."

She spun around and walked back to her car, tears streaming down her face. She got into her car, turned it around and sped away before Conner blinked. He looked down at the envelope in his hands. For a few minutes, he didn't know what to do. Then he slowly got into his car, put the envelope on the passenger seat, and drove off.

Conner didn't know what to think. There was too much to think about.

He was passing through a wooded section of the countryside. He slowed his car down to a stop. The running engine rumbled as if wondering what they were doing in the desolate countryside. Conner looked at the dark trees and the beauty of it all.

Conner looked out into the woods and saw the monsters of his mind creeping along the edges of the darkened woods. He wasn't scared. He wanted them to embrace him, to make him either so strong that he would be able to fend them off, or finish him off once and for all.

Running from yourself will just tire you out.

Chapter 3

The Small Town That Wasn't

The green grass shivered in the light breeze shaking the small, almost delicate drops of dew off. The breeze was able to do this under the cover of darkness, so it was disappointed, as it was every morning when the golden rays of sunlight started spreading over the grassy field, revealing to the world the glistening drops of dew and the mortal injustice that the wind was committing.

On the hill which marked the west end of the barren green field, stood an old man watching the sun rise slowly. He closed his eyes and let the warm sunlight wash over him. As he did, he murmured under his breath softly. After a while, he opened his eyes and took a look around him at the now-lit world. Not because he wanted to know what was there, but because he liked looking at it. He had a bird's-eye view of his surroundings and he made use of it like a hawk would. Everything seemed to be in order, but it was still early. He was mournful, because he had predicted great tragedy for the day. Be he had to pray, hoping that he would find the solution.

He turned his attention back to the green field. For miles around there was farmland, except for this patch. It had historical significance, but that was not what the man was thinking of now. Religious history was the only kind that interested him. He turned around and looked up at the *Sinome*, or *The Home of The Sun*. It was a beautiful place of worship for the people of the beautiful town of Levion. He had admired the intricacies of the Sinome's construction many times. He instead looked up at the tall towers that dominated the structure. There was a tall bell tower and another, more prominent tower. This tower rose slightly higher than the other. But the really stunning feature was the symbol that was engraved into more than half the length of the tower. It gave outsiders a sense of foreboding, but the townspeople felt safe looking at their symbol.

The priest looked up at this symbol, prayed to Natis, the one and only God, according to him. He noticed the mayor was watching him from his window. Father Godfrey didn't give any indication that he noticed; he simply walked into the Sinome.

The mayor of Levion had gotten up a few minutes ago and was staring out of his window at the Sinome, praying. This ritual he performed almost every morning. And like almost every morning, he saw Father Godfrey. He regarded Father Godfrey with the same amount of respect as every other Leviite. But everyone also feared him, mainly because he was the connection between Natis and the people, and his anger could result in Natis' anger raining down on the offender. Mayor Frank Dobbs knew the power and influence the priest held over the people and it made him feel insecure about his own position.

Suddenly a pair of arms snaked up from behind and wrapped themselves around his neck. Frank turned to see his beautiful wife, Rosaline, standing there, smiling.

"Stop worrying, honey," she said softly. "You'll be most influential in Levion one day."

Mayor Frank smiled. His wife was useless at politics. Then she whispered something in his ear and he remembered what she *was* good at. He decided his mayoral duties could wait for an hour. As he hurriedly drew the blinds, he noticed Dr. Clark walking by below with his medical bag.

Dr. Clark was on his way to a patient's house. It was quite possible that this patient was going to exhibit symptoms that would confirm that he was going to die in a few days. Yet Dr. Clark didn't hurry to deliver this news quickly and get it over with; neither did he walk slowly out of dread for what he might have to pronounce. He simply walked with a measured pace and a calm demeanour. Nobody could remember Dr. Clark anxious or panicky. Maybe that's what happens to a man who faces death on almost a regular basis.

He reached the house of Jon Peck. He raised his hand to knock on the door when it opened. It was a very worried looking Lori Peck, wife of Jon. Dr. Clark assumed that she was watching from the windows, waiting for his arrival.

"He seems to have gotten worse, doctor," said Mrs. Peck worriedly.

Dr. Clark nodded with barely a smile, which didn't exactly provide comfort. "Where is he?" he asked.

She led him to the bedroom where Jon was lying on the bed, uttering soft moans of pain. His daughter, Lindsey was standing over him with a worried look on her face. When she saw the doctor, she whispered to her father, "Dad, Dr. Clark is here."

Jon opened his eyes and tried to sit up, but collapsed, clutching his stomach. Dr. Clark told him to relax. Then Dr. Clark's face transformed from an expressionless one, to one with life, interest and involvement. He took out a notepad and a pen from his pocket, and started his examination. He noted reactions to pressure on different parts of the body, asked questions of the family and finally started jotting down notes in his notepad. After he was done, he took out a syringe filled with liquid from his bag and administered it to Jon. Then his face was again a blank mask, giving the family no indication of what the diagnosis was.

He shook his head.

"A week, at most."

Both mother and daughter started crying. Dr. Clark stood there watching them for a few minutes. He did not offer any condolence or sympathy. It wouldn't cure the ill man. And at this point, Dr. Clark knew they weren't really even listening. He also knew that if

Natis believed that they would survive without Jon, he believed it too, so they didn't really need sympathy, just faith. He let himself out quietly.

After exiting the Peck household, he started climbing up King's Hill, the hill on top of which the Sinome was situated. He prayed for a few seconds to the symbol on the west tower and then proceeded to the west wall, where there was a board that had been built into the Sinome. It was a whiteboard that had a glass covering which could only be unlocked by a special key, possessed by only the doctor and the priest. Dr. Clark now removed his key, inserted it in the lock and turned the key. The glass swung out easily. On the top of the board written in bold letters was "Death Watch" and below it two columns, namely, "Name" and "Estimated Time".

In the first column, he wrote, 'Jon Peck' and in the second, he wrote, 'One week'. Then he pressed a section in the bottom right of the board, a button, the location of which, again, only two people knew. He locked the glass in place, and started walking towards the entrance of the Sinome as a loud chiming emerged from the bell tower.

As he walked into the Sinome, a girl came out, her face pale, and started rushing towards the board. Everyone in Levion knew what that bell meant.

Not another one, was 20-year old Victoria's first thought when she reached the board and scanned it. Jon Peck had one week to live. She knew his daughter, Lindsey. Victoria turned away from the board and looked up at the sky. She would go offer her condolences later. She looked back down over her town. She stood there, frozen. She didn't know what to do. She could go in and pray for a while or she could go back to town and wander aimlessly, or maybe find something useful to do. Her feet were yearning to move, yet they couldn't move anywhere, stalled by indecision of the mind.

She closed her eyes, but they flew open after a few seconds, taking in her surroundings, reassuring herself that her recurring nightmare, which had forced her awake today as well, wasn't real. She shook her head as if to shake off the lingering strands of the nightmare loose, and then she started walking into town after casting a last glance at the Sinome. As Victoria walked, she ran her hand through her hair and wondered yet again what she was doing with her life. Every time her parents, an adult or even her younger brother asked her what she was going to do now, it terrified her, because the truth was she didn't know. She had a macabre smile on her face. Yes, there was one profession she believed she would be good at, but for that she would have to leave town, which had a tumultuous effect on her mind. She stopped in front of *Barker's Emporium*. She thought, like she had so many times, that it was an anomaly, a huge megastore in the middle of this small town. Maybe that's why she liked spending time here; she felt the same about herself. She understood the purpose of the *Emporium*, though, like every other Leviite, whereas she was still lost as to her own purpose. She entered, greeted politely whoever was polite enough to greet her first which meant practically everybody who walked past her, and some who didn't. Victoria had heard in big cities people just left you alone and some avoided you even if they knew you. She would have probably liked that.

After browsing around in the first building, she went to the next building. The second building had two restaurants on every floor, which totalled up to six restaurants. Well, two were fast-food joints, so she went to one of those and ordered. As she munched on a burger and some fries, she thought about this morning, which had been essentially the same as all the mornings for a long time.

She had woken up suddenly because of a bad dream, and had tried to go back to sleep but had been unable to. Instead she got out of bed and decided to have breakfast with her family, which was often more troublesome than trying to sleep. Her parents went on and on about how her friends had all gotten jobs, while she was undecided. It was not that hard to decide, they had said. Victoria had wanted to scream at them, like she had wanted to scream at everyone who had asked her with a polite but supposedly concerned expression, why she hadn't got a job or gotten married yet. She wanted to scream at them that all the jobs they expected her to take were monotonous, that they were all a result of generations being stifled into following their parents' expectations. She wanted to yell at them to just leave her alone, to give her time to decide on her own. But, like always, she kept quiet, set her face devoid of expression, nodded her head and shrugged her shoulders. She stayed that way until they gave up or she finished breakfast, whichever came later. Then she walked out without a word.

She then went to the Sinome for some quiet time, where, she had decided a long time ago, she would not tell anyone her problems, but simply sit there. If He was ready to show her the way, she was ready, waiting to read the signs. But she hadn't found any, and so she waited.

Suddenly she jumped when someone pulled up a chair in front of her. Literally jumped. The chair was overturned and everyone around was staring at her, including the boy now sitting opposite her. "Hi to you too," he said in a pleasant voice.

Victoria indicated to everyone that it was okay; she picked up her chair and sat on it, though she didn't push it all the way in. She had a feeling one of them would be leaving soon.

"Hi Harold," she said in an icy voice.

"I see you retain your pleasant attitude towards me," he said with a smile. He held out a packet of mints he had in his hand. "You want?"

Victoria seemed repulsed by the mint and pushed it away before she said, "You just startled me. When did you come to town? And more importantly, when are you going back?" Harold smiled again. "I came here because I was craving a burger. And hoped to run into you because I wanted to tell you myself before you heard it through the grapevine. I finished early and am coming back to work with my father." He paused. "Maybe we can start our friendship again."

"We were never friends!" Victoria said vehemently.

Harold's smile was gone. He said in an imploring voice, "But I loved you, Victoria. And you never loved me back."

"I didn't because you were crazy and I bet you still are!" Saying so, Victoria got up and stormed out, not bothering to turn back to see Harold's expression.

Well, she had been asking for a sign; she got one.

****

She was in deep thought when she exited the Emporium. It had been decided that she had to get out of town, for a little while at least, to decide "what she wants to do with her life" as her parents put it. But she didn't have enough money saved up for such a trip and her parents wouldn't fund it. Even if she made up some bogus excuse about friends or work opportunities, they would easily be able to check it up. So she needed money. Unaware of where she was heading, she was walking away from the centre of town. Eventually when she looked up, she saw the inn.

Something in her brain clicked. It was perfect! They needed someone to do odd jobs and bartending. She immediately set off for the inn.

There she met the cheerful innkeeper, Mrs. Stewart, who gladly gave her the job. Victoria walked out feeling a little satisfied about the fact that she had made progress.

The feeling didn't last long, though. She walked out and went to the green field at the foot of King's Hill. There she stood and watched the sunset, the sun rays scattering till the sun finally disappeared under the horizon. She felt a profound sadness every time the sun's rays dissipated. She finally turned around and started walking back home, crushing moist blades of grass under her feet as she walked.

Chapter 4

The Real Breaking Point

Have you ever felt happy?

Yes, of course you have.

Have you ever felt that special kind of happiness that comes when you're doing something that makes you feel like you're truly in touch with your inner self?

Yes, almost everyone experiences that at some point or the other, even though some just lose touch with it after a time.

I want you to imagine yourself doing that something special that makes you feel fulfilled, feel like you're doing what you were born to do.

Imagine yourself in that peaceful, happy state.

Now imagine yourself torn from there; imagine that everything you've ever done is claimed to be the cause of misery for every person you love; imagine that the work you are doing might *not* be the work you were born to do.

Put yourself in that place and experience it for a minute.

Now you know a little of how Conner White felt.

****

The speedometer was edging forward. Trees, fields, all flew by as Conner pressed the accelerator further. Conner swung the steering wheel wildly at the corners, and though the turns were not too hard to manoeuvre, it was a miracle he didn't crash into anything.

Conner didn't care if he crashed. In fact, he was more than half-hoping he would crash into a tractor or some other speeding author hurtling wildly down the road.

Thoughts were racing through Conner's mind as fast as his car was speeding down the road. They were just random flashes; one thought was replaced by the other in a manner of seconds, but they were enough to make Conner even angrier at himself. How could he do all that?! How could he miss it?

He suddenly glanced over at the passenger seat. The envelope must have fallen. He couldn't lose it! He slowed the car down to a stop, removed his seatbelt and bent down and started searching for it. He found it under the seat. Just as he straightened up, a pair of headlights turned the corner of the road and sped right past him. He looked behind and realized that if he had kept speeding, he would have crashed and most probably died. He looked at the plain white envelope that had saved him.

Then he remembered what was in it and all it represented. All the thoughts came rushing back again; he slammed his hands on the steering wheel and screamed, "Damn it!"

He lost his grip on the envelope and it fell to the floor again.

****

Considering his state of mind, it was a miracle that Conner reached home with only a minor injury on his head. He had lost control of his car and crashed into a tree. The car refused to start. He was nearly home so he simply abandoned his car and walked the remaining way home.

His housekeeper was waiting for him; she was terribly worried when she saw his bruises. Conner tried to convince her that he was fine. She finally calmed down but insisted on dressing his minor wound. Conner complied, mainly so that he would be left in peace later.

Conner lay down on the living room sofa, staring at the ceiling, envelope clutched in hand. He was calmer now, which simply meant he was not able to block out the pain by being angry; he let the pain engulf him.

He was responsible for someone dying. He thought of his dead girlfriend, how he suffered, how her family had suffered. He knew how much it hurt, and now *he* was responsible for inflicting that same hurt on another family. Maybe Roger had a girlfriend or a boyfriend; they would be hurting now too. A logical part of his brain said it was not his fault; that that boy had made his own decision and he shouldn't blame himself, yet Conner had been the one who had pushed him further into the brink of that pit of despair.

And were his ideas wrong? Apparently his own wife, the person he had trusted the most, had seemed to think that way.

He looked at the envelope in his hand. He was all the more disgusted with himself by the fact that he couldn't remember the story inside it. It was supposed to be his best piece of work and he couldn't even remember it! It was no wonder that he had started writing different stuff; he couldn't remember the story that had started him out!

He didn't delay further; it was time to find out.

He opened the envelope and took out the sheets of paper inside.

It was a story, written in his handwriting. It was entitled, "The Dark Alley".

He took a deep breath and started reading.

A man was walking down a road. He walked down that road every day. Some parts of the road were so dark that he couldn't see a few feet ahead of him; sometimes it was so bright that the light blinded his eyes. He often wondered why it was built this way, but he just cursed both parts and continued walking.

However, there was one thing the man always noticed. It was in the moderately lit sections, a particular alleyway at the mouth of which someone was always sitting. Sometimes it was the same person as the day before; often the same for days together, till someone else came in. The person could be either man or woman, but they were always in rags and looking completely lost. They seemed to be staring at the alley like it was a bottomless pit that was ready to engulf them.

The alleyway was pitch dark and the man couldn't see beyond the mouth. He had always wondered what was at the end of the alley and where all the people disappeared. But he believed that they belonged to a different world, and he didn't know what he could possibly offer them. So he let it go.

Then came the day when he lost everything he had been working for, and his life was ripped apart. He found that he had no home to go to, no work to do, and nothing save the clothes on his back. Then he wandered around and eventually came to the alleyway he had always looked at. For the first time, he saw that it was empty and he sat down before anyone else came to the spot.

As he sat down, he felt an immense weight on himself. It was like he didn't want to get up; he didn't want to leave this spot. At first, he didn't fight the feeling, letting all kinds of thoughts come into his head. He relished those thoughts; they were the kind that helped him get release from all his misery, if only for a time.

Then after a while, he didn't want to sit there any longer. He started fighting the thoughts; he wanted to get up and fix his life. But there was too much burden on him. He looked towards the alleyway, and then he saw a small point of light through the darkness. He struggled hard, and finally managed to get up and walk a little through the alley.

But then he found that he didn't know the way through the darkness. At times, the point seemed lost; at other times it was stronger. He didn't know where to go; he was utterly lost. All the thoughts of fixing his life were crumbling; he slumped down and closed his eyes. When he opened them, he was back sitting on the corner where he started.

The bad thoughts took control over him again. After a while, he again decided that it was time to get rid of them. He tried hard to get up again, in *vain. He saw people passing by on the street. He looked up at each of them. He wanted desperately to reach out to them, to say something or ask for help. But every time they looked at him, he just looked away and pretended not to be interested in them. He was afraid that they wouldn't understand what he wanted to say, which would leave him worse off, so he just didn't say anything.*

Maybe he would be crushed under this immense weight, all alone, with no one to rescue him. Suddenly he heard footsteps and looked up, though without much hope.

He found a woman walking down the street. There was something different about this woman. She walked right up to him and smiled down at him. Then she sat down on the corner next to him.

They started talking, and the immense weight started lifting off the man's shoulders. He told her about his problem. She understood, helped him and together they went hand in hand through the alley. It was still hard, but it was easier for him now.

When he asked her how she knew her way through, she replied, "I don't know. I'm taking your help."

The other side of that alley seemed to be a whole new world. He felt stronger, healthier and ready to take on any challenge. He found that his old life had been restored, but it had become better because the woman was now with him, now a part of his life. And he felt happier for it.

That street was the street all of us walk on every day, living our lives. We see people in need, but we often don't try to help, until one day we're in that same position wishing someone else would help us. Then we get desolate and are sucked into finding ways to escape our problems. We lose sight of what we truly want, and then comes a point where we try to fix our lives, but manoeuvring that dark alley alone is almost impossible.

And that's why you need someone there to help you go through it. That person may be a friend, a lover, family, but you need to let that person be there for you to lead you out of the dark alley.

For me, that person is you, Sophie, and I want you to help me through my
dark alley. I want you to be there for me, and I want to be there for you.

Conner read the story. Then he read it again. He touched the
slightly crumpled paper again and again to make sure that it was
real. He looked at the letter again. Yes, that was his handwriting,
but the content of the letter being his, was unbelievable. That
story had been...hopeful. And poetic. And beautiful. And all the
other things his usual stories weren't. Then he remembered the
night. He had written it, rolled it up and put it in a rose. Then he
had put that rose in her bag and waited for her to find it. He had
written this story, knowing no ordinary story would be good
enough for her. He had wanted her badly, and he was ready to
do anything for her; and this was certainly the most romantic
thing he had ever done.

Reading this made Conner want to take another look at his life. If
he could write something like this, then why did he have to write
stories that drove people to suicide? He realized that after he got
Sophie, he had seen no need to write more beautiful stories like
that, and so he had stopped. Sophie had always protected him,
trying to criticize him gently, but he had not seen that. Or rather, he
had not tried to see that.

He got up and went to the kitchen. He poured himself a glass of
water. While there, he saw knives casually placed on the kitchen
counter. He stared at the sharpest of them. He could so easily pick
one up and drive it through himself. It seemed so simple.

But it was never that simple. Many people would wonder how a man
with his attitude and thinking had not already killed himself. Truth
be told, he often thought about it, and in his depressed states of the
past, he had often come close to doing it. But then he remembered
his dead girlfriend, about how much pain it had inflicted, and felt
that he couldn't do the same thing to others. Of course, there were
times when he believed no one would care, but he still couldn't do
it. Because when you came right down to it, killing a human being,

even yourself, is not easy. You need a certain amount of willpower and courage to end a life. And Conner lacked that. So instead he died inside every day, and his living death affected many other lives.

Conner picked up the knife. He looked at it. Then he thought of the story he had just read and knew that this was not the way. He put the knife down. Enough of taking the easy way out, he decided.

He went back to his desk and looked at Sophie's picture. He was at the entrance of the alley sitting down, he realized. The woman smiling at him was the one who had tried to take him through the dark alley several times, but he kept returning to the entrance and sitting down, believing it was not possible to go all the way through.

Finally she had disappeared from that street forever, and he was left sitting there yet again. But he looked into her eyes and it was as if she was imploring him to get up. Conner set her picture down and looked at his typewriter, the same typewriter on which he written all his books. He picked it up and went to the garden. Then he tried to throw it so that it smashed against the wall in a move to symbolically destroy his writing past, but he misjudged its weight and it just fell from his hands, almost not-so-symbolically, destroying his foot. Luckily, he wasn't badly hurt, so he jumped around for a few seconds before continuing his journey of self-realization.

He remembered Megan's words. *Write a book to honour her memory.*

He went to his room and starting searching. He finally found it. Then he went to his study and sat down at his desk again.

The story had been written on several sheets of paper on both sides; the reverse side of the last sheet was blank. He put down the journal he had retrieved from his room. This book would be the best thing he had ever written and he would not use the typewriter – he would write it by hand. And the first page would be written on the back of his best story to date.

He got up and walked to the garden, avoiding the broken typewriter. He looked in the distance and could barely make out the town in the horizon.

He made a few phone calls, but could not find anything about Roger - where he came from, who his parents were - nothing. Where would he go from here? Then he focused on what little he could see of the town. He needed some great ideas.

Getting through this dark alley would be hard, but he felt a presence beside him. He didn't look, because he knew who it was and knew that she would help him through.

Chapter 5

Interrogating Victoria

That night, Victoria didn't sleep.

Now that she had started down a path, she was scared of what lay at the end of it. What was she hoping to achieve? A temporary respite or an escape? How was she eventually going to support herself? Would her plan for an eventual long term job actually work? She couldn't stay under her parents' roof forever, nor did she wish to. She sat up straight in bed and vowed to herself that she would start working in order to have enough money to be able to leave her parents' house. She didn't want to stay in Levion. The hardest loss would be the loss of her religion. She would miss going to the Sinome every Sunday, listening to the priest talk about life, but she knew if she ever took such a permanent step as running away, she wouldn't be able to return.

The idea had been growing in her mind for quite some time, but now she was determined. She lay down and closed her eyes. Her body lay still, but her mind was active.

****

Victoria's eyes opened automatically at the crack of dawn. She got out of bed without any trace of weariness, machine-like. She went about her room quietly, trying not to alert anyone to the fact that she was awake. She did her business in the bathroom, brushed her teeth and showered quietly. Then she changed into a green top and a denim skirt and checked the time. Her dad and brother must have left for work and school respectively, and her mother was probably out gossiping with her friends. Perfect time to slip out.

Or so she thought, anyway. As soon as she entered the dining room, she was shocked to see both her parents sitting there, in deep discussion. They looked up when she came in. They looked grim. It looked like they had been waiting for her. *Uh-oh.*

"Sit down, Victoria," her father said, indicating a vacant seat at the table.

Victoria walked hesitantly to the seat, as if it was booby-trapped. As soon as her bottom touched the seat, her mother asked, "Would you like some breakfast?"

Victoria felt like she was in an interrogation room, with her interrogators offering her something to drink so that they could lift her prints off the glass. She shook her head, not wanting to delay the inevitable.

Her father started, "We heard that you're not a bartender. That's exactly what I envisioned my daughter to be."

Victoria knew this would happen. This was why she had wanted to get out of the house without anyone knowing. Now her parents would start with their lecture and, this time, she had a feeling she would have to answer.

Victoria nodded, deciding to face it head-on. "Yes, I took the job at the inn. But-"

"But what?!" her father exploded. "We've been treating you with patience and trying to let you find your own way, but you can't reciprocate! Without consulting us, you run off and go and become a bartender?! Is this a temporary thing?" Victoria opened her mouth to answer, but her father wasn't done. "And if it isn't, then what? You're giving up hopes of any real career at all? If so, say it! Tell us that all you want to be is a housewife!" He banged his fist on the table. "But *don't* ruin our reputation by going off and doing things without even giving us prior warning! What are we supposed to say when the neighbours come in and tell us that our daughter is going be serving drinks while their sons and daughters are out, following in their footsteps!"

"That's it!" Victoria screamed. "I've had enough!" She got up. "I don't want to follow in anyone's footsteps! I don't want any of the goddamned careers here, if they can even be called that!" she snarled. "You say you treat me with patience. But really all you do is badger me incessantly to become someone like you. I don't care about what the neighbours think! I don't want to be like them. And yes, the bartender job is just temporary, don't worry. I just took it so that soon enough I'm out of your hair!"

She was about to stomp off as usual when her mother, who hadn't said anything during the argument, spoke, "You used to be so different," she said softly. Victoria stopped. "You used to be so kind, smart, driven and respectful before the accident. It really changed you." Victoria could hear the sorrow. She couldn't bear to look back and see the tears she knew were there. Instead she simply said, "I'm sorry." And walked out.

****

Victoria walked. She was upset, but she was used to being upset. So she just walked away from her house and her problems with her parents. She kept walking until she reached the inn. She decided that the sooner she got started, the better. She entered the inn. The innkeeper Mrs. Stewart was a hefty, cheerful, homely looking woman, the picture of what all innkeepers are supposed to be. She was surprised to see Victoria there so early. Victoria explained to her with false eagerness that she wanted to learn the ropes. Mrs. Stewart didn't look too convinced but she started showing her around.

Victoria already knew the ins and outs of the inn, having come here many times when she was younger, to look at the foreigners. She knew that there were no visitors right now since it wasn't peak season so her primary duty would be bartending, serving drinks to the townsfolk who came here to unwind after a hard day's work and some who came after a not-so-hard day's work. Gossip flowed as much as alcohol, and she knew a lot of it would be directed at her. What joy.

Mrs. Stewart smiled at her and said, "Well, it's not your work hours yet. Why don't you go out and enjoy yourself? We have a guest scheduled for arrival later today, but till then you're free! You're young; you don't need to spend time here."

Victoria forced a small smile and nodded. As she was turning to leave, Mrs. Stewart said, "Oh, and Victoria?"

Victoria turned to see a concerned look on the woman's face. "I hear the gossip too, you know." She paused. "You can keep this job for as long as you need to figure things out, no pressure from my side."

Victoria smiled genuinely this time. "Thank you, Mrs. Stewart. Thanks a lot."

Mrs. Stewart just smiled and waved her off. Victoria turned and exited the inn.

****

Victoria looked around her at the beautiful countryside which she knew so well. The inn was located a little distance away from the town proper, so that visitors could avoid the hustle-bustle, however little it may be compared to big cities. Also, the inn had a nice view of the rest of the town as well as of the countryside with farmland all around.

She decided she needed to take a walk out of town, primarily because she didn't want to run into anyone she knew, which meant everybody in town.

She walked quite a distance down the path, admiring the simple beauty around her. She had been exploring nature paths ever since she was a little kid, and knew them like the back of her hand. She felt safe here, as if nature was protecting her from the evil words and deeds of "civilised" humans.

When she was quite deep in, she stopped and closed her brown eyes. She could feel the rush of the breeze against her fair skin, picking up strands of her raven-black hair, and her nose picked up the delicate scent of the flowers. If she opened her mouth a bit more, she could probably catch a taste of the honey made by the bees. All her senses were fully attuned to the radiance of nature.

Suddenly her eyes snapped open. Something was trying to come towards her quietly. She kept her panic under control and tried not to make any sudden movements, reminding herself that it could be a wild animal who could be easily startled. There were not too many dangerous wild animals around here but one could never be sure. Her hand moved into her pocket and gripped the object there as she turned around slowly. There was a man standing there looking sheepish.

"You idiot!" she said angrily. "I was scared to death, thinking that there was a wild animal behind me ready to pounce on me!"

"I'm sorry." He looked embarrassed. "I tried to move quietly to avoid disturbing you. It looked as if..." He stopped mid-sentence looking embarrassed, and then continued, "It looked as if you were having a moment there."

Victoria didn't know whether to get angrier or to laugh. "A moment? What is that supposed to mean?" she asked.

"Well...you know. A moment of peace, tranquillity, harmony with nature," the man said in a weak voice.

Victoria burst out laughing while the man stared awkwardly. "So, how were you going to get past me without being noticed?" she asked between laughs. "Were you going to use your extremely well-developed stealth skills?"

The man looked down at his feet and muttered, "Umm... I'm not sure; I haven't thought this conversation through."

"Yes, it was painfully apparent!" said Victoria, laughing a little more. Then she straightened up and said with a smile, "I needed that. So, what made you cross my path, o traveller?"

The man straightened up as well and said, "Well, o fair maiden, I am trying to get to the town of Levion."

Victoria's eyebrows crinkled and her face took on an expression of fury. "Fair maiden? What, I laugh a little and you think two minutes after meeting me that you can hit on me?"

God! The first meeting with someone new and I'm screwing it up. The man's mouth opened and he managed to stutter, "N-no, I didn't mean it that-" but stopped when Victoria started laughing again.

Victoria gave him the once-over; he was quite attractive. He was a clean shaven man of average height and build, but with blue eyes and dark hair. He was carrying a rucksack. "You're in luck. I live there. Let me lead on. And don't worry, I'll try not to have any more 'moments'." Chuckling, she started walking. He blinked, and walked faster and caught up with her. Victoria asked him his name.

"Conner Wh-...Fry."

"Is the hesitation part of the name?" asked Victoria with a straight face. Then she chuckled and extended her hand. "I'm Victoria Parks."

"Are you always in such a good mood?" asked Conner a bit ruefully.

Victoria's good humour seemed to dissipate and a dark shadow passed across her face as she said, "No." Then she clammed up. They walked in silence for a few minutes before Victoria asked, "So what are you going to town for? You don't look like a labourer and it's too early for tourists."

Conner seemed reluctant to share. "Well..." he started slowly.

Victoria seemed to sense his reluctance and said, "I might not pry too much, but people in Levion will certainly want to know and will definitely try to get it out of you, so you better feel comfortable talking about it. Some will already know via gossip but will ask you anyway to see if you give them some more details. My suggestion: give everyone a standard answer so they stop probing for more."

Conner considered this for a second before he took a deep breath and said, "Well, recently my wife died. I loved her a lot and her death has kind of thrown me. I couldn't concentrate on normal life and so here I am, trying to get away from it all and to clear my head."

Victoria was about to ask if that was a cover story, but then she saw the look of anguish on his face which convinced her that his story was true, if not the whole truth. "I'm sorry," she said instead.

Conner nodded, his face expressionless. They passed a moment in silence during which time they passed a few stone blocks that seemed to be purposefully kept there. Conner was about to ask about them when Victoria, probably thinking it best to change the subject, said, "So, do you have any kids?"

Conner seemed startled as Victoria's question had jolted him back to reality. He shook his head.

"And your job?"

Conner shrugged. "I do things here and there. Nothing special."

Victoria didn't look convinced by anything Conner had said, but she continued anyway, "So why did you choose Levion? I'm sure there are tons of other towns you could have visited instead."

Conner shrugged again. "I don't know. This town...called to me."

Victoria snorted. "I pity the things you hear, then."

Conner gave Victoria a curious look and said, "You don't like your own town very much. That's strange. I thought it was all brotherhood, community and love."

Victoria looked away angrily. Even this stranger was judging her. Before she could retort, he said quickly, "Hey, I was just asking. But I guess I forgot that there is criticism for everything, even what looks great from the outside. And sometimes that criticism is right."

Victoria's anger faded as she looked at Conner. He seemed to mean that. She said, "Life in Levion is very... let's say, different. It has a lot of good things to it, but sometimes I wish I could just-" Then she stopped. She had been about to tell this stranger what she hadn't told anyone else. Maybe it was just because she really couldn't, considering how the townspeople reacted to such talk. Conner waited for her to continue, but when she didn't, he let it slide.

Victoria was quiet for a moment, and Conner used the opportunity to make an inquiry or two of his own. "So," he asked, "How far from the town are we?"

"Quite a bit more of walking, actually."

"Mind telling me a bit more about the town? The history and all that?"

Victoria said ruefully, "I'll try to be as unbiased as possible." And before Conner could say anything she continued, "The town of Levion was once the capital of a great kingdom. The kingdom encompassed most of this state and two others. Then there was a great war and we lost...that's when most of the capital was burnt down. The inhabitants were still determined to survive, and through the hard work and determination of our ancestors, we've become such...a great town."

Conner chose to ignore the hesitation and instead asked, "I've been wondering..." He paused. "If you don't mind me asking... why aren't you hanging out with your friends? Why are you here wandering the woods alone, beautiful though they may be?"

Victoria debated in her mind whether to reveal her woes to this apparently in-mourning lover, and decided that this man would probably leave in a few days, and no one would be any wiser. She also got this strange vibe from him that made her want to push on, which she rarely ever did.

A bitter smile came to Victoria's face as she said, "That's because I'm not one for friends. I used to be, but then..." She hesitated again, and a faraway look came into her eyes. She shook her head and said, "Something changed. I missed a year of school; my friends went a year ahead of me, and I found that I preferred the solitude." Victoria became quiet.

Conner looked uncertain about what to say next. He wanted to ask her what had changed, but he realized it wasn't his place. Something was wrong with this girl, and he got the strange desire to know what was wrong, and help her. "Sometimes you want to be alone. I can certainly relate to that feeling."

Victoria didn't hear him, or acted like she didn't hear him. Conner then asked, "So what are the main occupations of the people here?"

"Well, some people become farmers. We have crops that are unique to the area, and that really helps the income. Then some go to the town nearby where they can obtain employment, mostly for their intricate knowledge of the area. A few become teachers at our school. During the off season, some pose as guides for tourists and archaeologists who frequently visit the area because of its historical significance."

Conner nodded. "So, do you have a lot of people moving out of the town, for bigger and better opportunities?"

Victoria laughed, though again Conner thought it was bitter. "Well, here people have a very conservative attitude, to put it lightly. The school here also teaches courses that prepare residents for future jobs within the town. Parents encourage their children to stay here, and generally discourage too much outside contact. Very few are determined enough to go out for higher studies, but they..." She shook her head and continued, "So basically this is the only world we know. I'm sorry to say, but no outsider manages to stay here for too long, unless you're marrying someone in town."

"So if the same occupations persist and no new people come in, that must make things pretty quiet and somewhat monotonous, right?"

Victoria suppressed a small shudder and said, "Things have a way of getting interesting enough around here, even if you don't want them to."

When she didn't say anything more, Conner prodded, "And how is that?"

Victoria's face conveyed that she felt that she shouldn't have said that. She shrugged noncommittally and said in a forced casual voice, "Oh, you know, this and that." Conner got the feeling that of all the things she didn't want to talk about, this was at the top of her list.

Conner added it to his list of things he needed to find out. He asked, "So do you have a job? Have you decided on what you're going to do?"

One more person asking her this question! Victoria had to control her rush of anger. She snapped, "I haven't decided what to do yet. Nothing here interests me."

Conner didn't seem to get even mildly fazed by her snappy retort, which oddly irritated Victoria. He said pleasantly, "That's all right. It's better to stay and find out what you're good at and choose something you'll be happy with; otherwise what's the point?"

Victoria looked at him strangely. Who *was* this guy? Then she noticed they were nearing the end of the path and said, "We're here."

They emerged from a clearing and the sunlight hit Conner full on the face. When his eyes got adjusted to the sunlight, Conner could see the entire town.

There seemed to be a large number of houses, and miles and miles of farmland all around. There were two four-storied buildings that towered over the rest of the town, but that was not the first thing that caught Conner's eye. Not by a long shot. The first thing that Conner saw and couldn't take his eyes off from was the building on top of the hill. It was obviously a place of worship, but on one of the towers was a symbol, which was intricately designed. After he stared at it for a while, he said, "Is that an eye?"

Victoria smiled cheekily and said, "Welcome to Levion."

Chapter 6

Another Town, Another Bar

Conner tore his eyes away from the building on the hill long enough to turn to ask her the obvious question, but she was already answering.

"That is our Sinome," she said. "It is where we worship Natis - 'He Who Watches Over Us All'."

Conner noted that even though she had been speaking about Levion with a strange sadness and resentment, when she spoke of her religion, it was with deep reverence.

"The hill on which it is built is called King's Hill," she continued. "There was a castle built on top of the hill. The king was the first to rise every day. After it was destroyed in the Great Fire that destroyed most of the town, a Sinome was built in its place."

Conner wanted to go and examine it closely, but there would be time for that later. Victoria interrupted his daydreaming and told him that they should get to the inn. Conner followed her, taking in the area all around. They finally reached the inn.

The inn seemed to blend in perfectly with its surroundings, with construction that was fairly modern, yet reminiscent of an age where there were no fancy hotels, just simple inns for weary travellers on the road.

Mrs. Stewart was surprised to see Victoria with this strange man. "Yes, who is this?" she asked, her voice still pleasant but confused.

Conner walked up to her and extended his hand. "Hello, my name is Conner Fry. I've made a reservation in my name for today." He gave her a smile. "And you must be Mrs. Stewart."

Mrs. Stewart gave an *ahh* of recollection and then, "Why yes, Mr. Fry, welcome! We've been expecting you. I see you've met Victoria." She turned to Victoria and gave a hearty laugh. "First day and you come back with a guest? You'll be good for business!" Still laughing she opened the book to the appropriate date and then gave him a pen and indicated where he should sign.

"So, how many days will you be staying, Mr. Fry?" she asked before he signed.

Conner hesitated before saying, "I'm not sure. It could be quite some time. I can pay in advance. How much is the room for?"

Mrs. Stewart quoted the price. Conner took out his wallet, smiled and handed over money for a month. Mrs. Stewart seemed startled by the amount, but took it nonetheless. "May I ask what the purpose of your visit is, Mr. Fry? I'll be able to direct you better once I know."

Conner paused, and a pained look came over his face before he said, "The thing is...my wife died recently. I need some time on my own to reacquaint myself..." He saw Mrs. Stewart's face flicker before she regained her composure and offered her condolences. Conner interjected in a polite voice, "It's okay. If I'm done here, I would like to go to my room to unpack."

Mrs. Stewart nodded. She asked Victoria to guide him there after handing him the key. He smilingly accepted it and said, "And you can call me Conner."

Victoria took Conner up two flights of stairs, and then to the last room on the left. It was a spacious room, more of a suite. It had a small kitchenette, a large bed, a nice bathroom, a desk and a couch.

"The only room better than this is the honeymoon suite. Mrs. Stewart must have been happy with such a large advance during such a slow time," Victoria said.

Conner nodded. "Is she always that nice?"

Victoria's subsequent smile was tinged with sadness. "Most of the time. She can be a real tough cookie when she has to be. After all, her husband died quite some time ago and she's been running the inn all by herself."

Conner nodded slowly, probably empathising with Mrs. Stewart's pain. He went to the window and looked out. He was greeted with a breathtaking view of the countryside around him. He could also see most of the town, including the Sinome on King's Hill. "Wow!" he said, retreating from the window and looking at Victoria.

Victoria smiled and then gestured towards his rucksack, which he had sent down. "Does that have enough clothes for a month?" she asked.

"I'll have to buy some more soon." He sat down. "Look, Victoria, I'll need a guide. Not only will I need to see the important places, but I want you to also tell me about the people, the culture, what is happening in the town; that kind of stuff. I really like to know where I'm staying, and I love making myself familiar with new cultures."

Victoria hesitated. Did she really want to escort this man who she barely knew? Conner seemed to sense the hesitation and said, "Look, I can pay you, if that's the problem."

Victoria considered it, and then nodded. He fished in his pocket and brought out a cell phone. This was a cell phone he had purchased with a new number, effectively cutting off all contact with everyone he used to know, for now at the very least. If there was an emergency, his housekeeper had his number.

"You have one of these, I presume? We can use it, if necessary. Just give me your number."

Victoria hesitated for a second. At worst, she could block him. She gave him her number. He nodded and thanked her.

"Do you need anything else?" she asked.

Conner shook his head. "I think I'll go around town tomorrow. Thanks for everything. I'll see you later."

Victoria paused before she said, "The bar opens at six. You really should come. You'll see some of the townsfolk there, and I'm sure they would like to see the big spender who lost his wife and is with us for a month. And besides, I'm the bartender." With a small smile, she left the room. *And I assume you tip well*, she finished the sentence in her head.

Conner waited till the door shut firmly before he slumped onto the couch and put his head in his hands. He wrestled with his thoughts, trying not to let the negativity dominate. He stayed like that for a few seconds before he straightened himself and let out a deep breath. He had been used to pretending to be normal and happy-go-lucky (as much as they expected him to be) around people, but this time, he was really trying to be normal and not morose with depressing thoughts and statements. It had been quite an effort, but he thought Victoria was largely convinced. She seemed like a nice enough girl; though bitter with her situation.

Conner got up and looked out of the window. He had lied about the details, like his job and daughter simply to avoid further questions, but he was honest about one thing: he *was* here to get over his wife and he was going to turn his life around. He thought it would be a good idea to see the lives of normal people, their joys and sorrows. He felt that he had been disconnected from the rest of the world for a long time, and he had just become aware of that fact. He wanted to regain that connection. He believed that only if an author is able to connect with his readers can he portray them in such a manner that they believe they are *in* the story. And not revealing his real identity would help him to better make that connection, because if they knew who he truly was, he would feel once again like he had been feeling all his life, as if he were in a cage and the world at large was staring at him.

But would it really work? Conner shook his head to dispel these thoughts. The time for negative thinking was over. It was time to actually *believe* that his expectations would fructify, and not crumble away. More than that, he needed to believe in hope and the possibility of a happier future.

Conner stretched. He decided to go for a shower and change before he went downstairs to the bar. A drink would do him good.

****

As Victoria looked around the empty bar, she realized that she would probably prefer this to the crowd that would pour in later, once people got off work. Conner hadn't come down, but she suspected he would.

Then she reflected. Why was she helping him? She told herself it was obviously for the money, because he seemed loaded, but somehow Victoria felt it was more than that. There was...something about Conner Fry she really couldn't put her finger on. Maybe she sensed a kindred spirit in him. Then another thought struck Victoria. He was *nice* to her, and not in a secretly condescending adult kind of way; he was simply being nice. And on top of that, he seemed to understand her; he wasn't judging her or her detraction from the "normal" way of life in Levion.

But the greatest thing, Victoria realized, was that he was a stranger. She didn't have to pretend to be normal, or conform to the standards set by the townspeople, or worry about every word she said being morphed into some huge town rumour. No, she could do as she pleased, and that was something she had not had the opportunity to do for a long time.

So Victoria decided that she would help this man, who seemed to understand her, until he did something that completely ruined the good image she had of him, which, in her experience, happened quite soon with most people.

Victoria checked the time. It was 6:00 p.m. And right on time, some customers came in. Victoria sighed and started her first day of work.

At half past six, Conner walked in. He had changed into casual clothing. Victoria smiled at him as he sat down at the bar. "Yes, what can I get you, sir?" she asked.

Conner smiled back and ordered his beer. Victoria nodded.

As Victoria gave him his beer, she said, "People must have already seen us walking together into town, so it's no good pretending that we don't know each other. Still, I need an excuse to keep coming back here and telling you about the main players in town, and I can't seem too overeager." Victoria didn't care what people said or thought, but she knew that if certain types of rumours reached her parents' ears, she would probably be forbidden to meet Conner.

Conner nodded. He drank half his beer in one gulp.

Conner noticed that from the moment he had walked through, people were sizing him up, seeing what he was like. They were contemplating whether the rich man who had come to their town would stay for long and spend lavishly. They were already aware that he would certainly be there for at least a month. They were discussing about him being in mourning over the loss of his wife. Conner caught all these snatches of conversation about himself. He was sitting far enough to not mix in with the regular crowd, yet close enough to see and hear everyone clearly.

A man walked into the bar. He was formally dressed. He greeted everyone. Conner heard some people call out, "Hey Mayor," or "Greetings Mayor," after which the Mayor responded in kind. The Mayor stopped for a second near Conner, but then proceeded on as if he hadn't noticed him.

He sat down and ordered a drink.

Conner finished the rest of his drink and gestured for a refill. Victoria walked over nonchalantly. As she was pouring him a refill, she said quietly, "The man is Mayor Frank Dobbs. Likes to come down here to be with the townsfolk, although he doesn't need to. Comes from a long line of town mayors; the position might as well be hereditary."

Conner looked at the man again. He was tall, well-built with red hair and a charming smile. He looked the way he was supposed to - a politician.

At that moment, another man walked in. Everyone he passed looked up and nodded at him with deference. He clearly scored over the mayor. Conner caught the word "doctor". The doctor sat down next to the mayor, whom he greeted shortly. He ordered a drink. Conner closely observed him. He was a middle aged man with dark hair and pitch-black eyes that seemed to scrutinize everyone in the place. He was not strongly built, but he exuded an aura of control, which was seemingly accentuated by the respect that people were showing him. He initiated a conversation with the mayor who assumed a serious expression and listened to the doctor attentively. People came up to him and started talking to him. He nodded his head patiently, and then told them each something, which Conner couldn't catch.

When he finished his drink, Victoria came to give him a refill. She updated him, "That illustrious man is Dr. Clark. He's very well-respected, as you can see. He has a very hard job." Saying this, Victoria turned away quickly. *Why am I giving away so much? We're not supposed to be friends with the outsiders.*

Then a woman walked in. She was an attractive woman, with curly blonde hair and light green eyes. She was of average height but she carried herself well. She was casually dressed in a light blue top with a denim skirt. As she walked, most of the men subtly gave her a look, including Conner. Conner then realized that besides Victoria and this woman, there were very few women in the bar.

The woman went up to the mayor and kissed him. Then she greeted the doctor and sat down next to the mayor. She ordered her drink. The bar was getting increasingly crowded and Victoria was completely occupied. It was some time before she could approach Conner on the pretext of refilling his beer mug. When she did get there, she whispered, "That, as you've probably guessed, is the mayor's wife, Rosaline. She comes to the bar occasionally. Everyone is of the opinion that she's all beauty and no brains, though most argue that for her, beauty is rather enough." Conner didn't seem to notice that Victoria's voice was tinged with amusement, as if she knew a joke no one else did. Instead he whispered back, "At least you didn't say she comes from a long line of mayoral wives."

Victoria stifled a laugh and went back to serving drinks.

Conner was sipping his drink, looking at everyone around (a few of whom were looking back at him) when he saw the mayor walking over. He sat down next to Conner and introduced himself. Conner shook his hand and smiled politely.

"I've heard that you're going to stay in our town for quite some time. I have also heard the unfortunate circumstances due to which you have made this decision. I offer my condolences. I'm married myself as you might have noticed," he said gesturing towards his wife, as if Conner could have *not* noticed, "and I would be absolutely devastated if something happened to her. I welcome you here and if you need anything, we are available." The mayor gave him what Conner assumed was a crowd-winning smile.

Conner nodded and thanked him. After the mayor made the appropriate but always dull small talk, he got up to leave. Then a plump man with dark hair came up and slapped him on the back. "Hello Frank," the newcomer said. "How's it going?"

The mayor smiled and introduced the man to Conner. "This is Arthur Barker, our resident shopkeeper, if we could call him something as tame as that."

"No, you can't!" roared the man with good-natured amusement. "I own both those large buildings in the centre of town, which contains more than you can even think of getting in meagre shops."

When Conner merely smiled politely without responding, the man said with a toothy salesman's smile, "Why don't you drop by? I'm sure there are a dozen things that will catch your fancy." And then both retreated after customary goodbyes. Conner noted that Arthur didn't offer him condolences. Maybe he was too busy with his sales pitch. Suddenly the doctor got up and went outside the bar, passing Conner along the way.

****

Father Godfrey picked up the telephone at the first ring.

"I was expecting your call, Clark," he said as soon as he heard the voice on the other line. "What has happened?" Father waited while Clark spoke. Then he waited for a few seconds before he said, "Yes, I knew something was coming. I have gotten very strange signs from Natis about him, and I shall have to meditate on them before I know for sure. But for now, thank you, son."

After the Father hung up, he plunged deep into thought. And he remained so for the rest of the night.

****

The doctor returned to the bar. Conner noticed the doctor giving him a brief glance that felt a little strange.

Conner had had enough for one evening. He had keenly observed the people around and the atmosphere. He called for his bill. He gave Victoria a very hefty tip. "Thank you, kind Madame," he said, trying to be suave as he exited.

One person watched him more intently than the others.

Chapter 7

The White Blank Page is Defeated!

The town was dark. The wind was so loud that it seemed as if there was a monster that was howling at the top of its lungs, threatening to blow away the entire town. The town seemed to be holding strong, though.

Conner sat at the window of his room, looking down on the darkened town. He wished he could be as strong against the perilous winds that he had himself created, that were threatening to blow him down. He was struggling not to give up on this mad transformation he was planning for himself and his life with the thought that it was too difficult. He had to stop from slipping back into the black abyss which he had barely crawled out of. He had to get over the thought that he was worthless and that everything he did was worthless which had destroyed lives, including his.

He looked at his phone. His perpetual insomnia, which he constantly battled with, had gained strength of late. Lately, he spent more nights thinking and less nights sleeping. It was 5:00 a.m. when he finally gave up on trying to fall asleep and crawled out of bed.

Now, half an hour later, he sat looking at the town from his window. A day or two ago, his housekeeper had come into town to do an impromptu reconnaissance for him, and Conner could see now why she hadn't gotten very good results.

She had, however, managed to gauge that the townspeople were quite religious, and Conner could believe this even though he didn't really know what the religion *was*. He looked at the Sinome on top of the hill. Even in the dead of night, he could make out that twisted *eye* or whatever it was. He wondered what kind of religion was followed, what kind of prayers were offered in that imposing and oddly captivating structure up on that hill.

Then he turned his attention to the biggest structure in town. He presumed it was the one Arthur had talked about. He was certainly curious to see what it would hold, but it wasn't successful in retaining Conner's attention.

While surveying the town, Conner went into deep thought.

This town is a strange place, he thought, *but it somehow seems to have kept pace with the rest of the world. If Victoria is right, then there are hardly any immigrants, no emigrants, and yet it seems to be flourishing.* Conner decided that he would find out what secret this small town seemed to be holding.

Conner got up and looked at his watch. Half an hour had passed. He was feeling restless.

He looked at his phone. Conner wanted to text Victoria and ask her all his questions right now, or just talk to her simply for a distraction, though Conner wasn't sure what Victoria thought about him, and it disconcerted him. The girl was strange, but not necessarily in a bad way. She just seemed very bitter, angry and resentful. *Something must have happened to her that made her this way.* Conner once again had that strange desire to find out what had happened. He wanted to help the girl who was standing in the middle of the forest with her eyes closed but her senses open. He had been in misery all his life, or at least thought he had been. But he had never really bothered to think about the misery of others, always assuming his was the worst and ignoring the rest.

Something in him snapped. He decided it was time to write.

****

He sat down at his desk and got out the story he had written for Sophie. He read the story again for strength and finally came to the last page. Conner usually wrote when he had reached his breaking point, the point where he could not hold his emotions in any longer. But this time, he didn't need that. This time he wouldn't be motivated by an outburst, but by Sophie's love.

And so he faced the white blank page. Again.

This time, though, he was ready to fight it. He didn't know if he was going to write a compilation of short stories, a novel, or a novella; he just knew he was going to let it flow. He was going to write. He took a deep breath, pulled out his pen, and put it to the paper. All the story ideas that had been developing in his mind came together.

He started writing.

It was dark. He was trying to think about why it was dark, but he couldn't figure it out. Then he realized his eyes were closed. He tried opening them but all he saw was more darkness so he pressed them shut. Slowly he felt as if he was regaining feeling in the rest of his body. Both of his arms were outstretched; the left hand was against something hard, and his right was against something wet. His legs were spread, and he could feel socks but not shoes. He now realized that he was lying on the ground. He lifted his head and opened his eyes.

He was lying on a patch of damp grass. He got up into a sitting position slowly, and blinked his eyes. He looked around him. It seemed like a small clearing. There was a small opening through which he could see a road. A tiny amount of light filtered in through the openings in the leaves. He stood up shakily. He blinked his eyes and tried to think. Where was he? Then he blinked again. Who was he? He couldn't remember who he was or what he was doing there.

He looked at the spot where his head had rested a while ago. There was a small rock there. He felt his head. There was a bump there.

He went through the opening in the trees. It was the early morning sun. There was a dirt road which led in both directions. He looked at himself more carefully. He was wearing a coat and a plain shirt, and simple trousers. He didn't know what year this was, so he had to assume this was what everyone wore. His pockets were empty and appeared to have been turned out. He looked in both directions. What was he supposed to do?

He sat down, resting against the tree; trying to regain some part of his memory. He figured that somebody might come down this road and he could get some help. But neither of those things happened. After a while, he got up. He decided it was better to move somewhere. Once again, he pondered on which direction to go. Suddenly something caught his eye. It was a mark on the other side of the road. It seemed to be tracks of a wheel going east. He started to follow the tracks. The tracks were not consistent and it seemed that the vehicle, whatever it was, was on the verge of toppling.

And so it was. Some way down the road, the man found ruins of what seemed to be a horse drawn carriage. It seemed to have crashed. He wondered if it was his and whether he had lost control and been thrown out of it. He searched the debris but could find no clues, other than some confused horse tracks, which meant that the horse had probably escaped. There were no bodies either, which probably meant he was travelling alone, or there were survivors nearby. He yelled out, "Hello!"

There was no response. Nobody was nearby. He shrugged and started walking. In all probability it was going to be a very long walk.

Conner stopped. This seemed good for now. He seemed in touch with this story, and it was surprisingly easy to write it. He didn't know what came after this, but he supposed that it would develop as he developed his new found...way of living, for lack of a better name.

Conner got up. He looked at how much he had written. It was fraught with cancellations and it had easily passed the remaining page of his proposal and extended to a few pages of his journal. He now thought about where he was going to keep it. He couldn't carry it around, it was kind of bulky and he didn't need it.

But for now, where to keep the journal? Keeping it in open view was not advisable; in a curious town like this, he had no doubt that the people who came to clean the room would be tempted. So he opened his rucksack, and hid it at the bottom among the folds of his clothes. He carefully noticed how it was kept. Now if anyone moved it he would be able to see. Was he being paranoid? Maybe. But rather test his defences now when it was just a small thing rather than later when there was more to be found.

He checked his watch. It was six a.m. He decided to go for a shower and relax for however long he could. Then he would order breakfast. He glanced at his phone and wondered again when he could text Victoria.

****

Victoria glanced at her phone. She wondered if Conner was awake. She had the strange urge to text him, but she didn't want to seem too forward, so she waited. It was six a.m. She had woken up early again. She hadn't been able to sleep after her late night. She didn't know what to do so early, and she was definitely not going to go to the inn early again. Mrs. Stewart would perhaps start taking her early attendance for granted.

She thought about Conner again. He seemed to be genuinely distraught about his wife, and Victoria wondered what that must be like. To be so in love that the death of one impacts the other greatly. To have your whole life turned around by the death of just one person.

When Victoria was really young, she dreamt of true love and marriage like every other person. Then later she had realized that she wasn't meant for love; it was simply not possible for her. So she had hardened herself to the fact that she would live life alone, and she had changed her interactions to suit that thought. It was better not to trust anyone, for fear of what they might do later.

But now those old feelings were trying to come to the surface, as if Victoria's mind was once again yearning for love. Victoria shook her head, angry at herself for even believing for a second that it was possible. She threw off her covers and got out of bed. Yet even as she went to the bathroom, she knew she would ask Conner about his wife soon enough.

She took a long bath and once she got dressed, she checked her phone. There was a message. It was Conner asking if she was awake, and if not, he was sorry for disturbing her and asked if she could call him once she woke up.

Victoria waited for a minute or two, not wanting to look eager and then called him. He picked up on the second ring, as if he was expecting (or hoping for) a call. He seemed pleasantly surprised that she was awake and asked when she could get ready and come over for a tour of the town. She said that she was ready and would be there in half an hour. She tried to sneak out again, but in vain; her parents were waiting for her - again.

"Hello Victoria," her father said, sipping his coffee, not looking too surprised to see her. "You're getting out of bed earlier nowadays. Any special reason for that? Excited to be anywhere?"

Victoria shook her head. Before she could say anything, her father continued, "Want to sit down and join us for breakfast? After all, this is the only time we seem to be able to talk to you nowadays. You're out Natis knows where during the day. You eat lunch and dinner elsewhere. Sometimes I feel if you didn't have to sleep at home, you wouldn't."

Victoria wanted to say that he felt that way because it was true, but she held her tongue. She decided it would be better to have a quick breakfast and leave. She started to make some toast, when her mother got up and told her to sit down, despite Victoria's protests.

So Victoria sat at the table, looking down at it, not saying anything. "So, we didn't really get to complete our conversation yesterday." He said this casually, as if commenting on the weather.

Victoria looked up to find him intensely gazing at her. She looked him straight in the eye and said firmly, "Dad, I know what I'm doing. I am *not* a little kid anymore. This job is just a way to start earning and get on my own feet before I finally start something I really want to pursue, and no, I haven't decided what that is yet. But I will, in time, so can you please let it go for now?"

Her mother served her toast. She started eating quickly, but it seemed her father wasn't done yet. "I've heard that you're getting close to that new man who's come to town, that Conner Fly."

"Conner Fry," Victoria corrected, her mouth full of toast. "And no, I'm not getting 'close' to him. I'm just acting as his guide for the day. He pays well." She finished her toast and got up. "Thanks for the breakfast, mum. See ya dad." Nodding at both her parents, she left.

"It's as if she isn't here," said her mother sadly.

"I don't think she's really been here for a long time," replied her father.

****

Conner stood at his window, staring out at the town below, the hustle and bustle of the townsfolk heading to school and work. He wondered how they coped with life, how they progressed through routine without descending into a pit of loathing and hatred for their life. They were just normal people in that respect, he supposed.

His thoughts were interrupted by a knocking on his door. He opened it to see Victoria standing there. They smiled at each other and he invited her in.

"So do you want to go see the town today?" Victoria asked him.

Conner nodded. "When will it be okay to head out?"

"In a while," said Victoria. "You don't want to attract too much attention right now, going out and showing yourself to everyone when they're on their way to school or work."

Conner nodded. He sat on the sofa and invited her to do so, which she did. "What happened to Mrs. Stewart's husband?" he asked.

"He died of a sudden illness." Victoria abruptly stopped talking and seemed reluctant to volunteer more information. This frustrated Conner, though he didn't show it. He paused and then said, "Thanks for helping me, Victoria. It's good to know you have someone there to help you." Victoria looked away, confused. What was his game? Was he trying to make it look like he cared? Then another, much scarier thought came into her head. Was he being genuine? Was that even possible?

"Victoria?" Conner asked softly. "Did I say something wrong?"

Victoria looked towards Conner, who seemed to have an honest face, but that had fooled her before. She shook her head and told Conner, "No, I was just wondering...what was your wife like?"

Conner looked at her to see if there was something more to it, but then decided to let it go. He sat back and said, "Her name was Sophie. She was beautiful."

Victoria said quietly, "You never mentioned how she died."

"Heart attack," Conner replied just as quietly, "Much too young."

In the silence that followed, Victoria noticed Conner's eyes, staring out into space, probably remembering the times he spent with Sophie. There was love in those eyes, but also...a deep sorrow. And regret. Lots of regret.

"I miss her," he said softly. "I miss her a lot. She really was a good woman, too good for me, in any case. There are things that I should have done when she was alive; I could have made her so much happier. I didn't see it though, and it shows I didn't deserve her." He paused before saying, "I guess it's true when they say that in times of great loss, you look at everything differently."

Victoria shuddered and drew her clothes closer around her, as if experiencing a sudden chill. She folded her arms and looked down at the floor.

"Did you lose someone, Victoria?" asked Conner.

Victoria was startled out of her reverie and said much too quickly, "No; why would you think so?"

"You seem disturbed by me talking about this," he said. "I can stop, if you prefer."

"I haven't lost anyone, don't worry," said Victoria, *Except myself,* she finished inwardly. She forced a smile. Then she touched her neck, or so Conner thought at first. When he looked closely, he saw that it was a silver chain.

"Is that a pendant you have there?" asked Conner, "I've never seen it before."

"Well, I'm glad you weren't admiring my neck too much," Victoria said. She tried to pass it off as a joke, but there seemed to be an underlying seriousness. Before Conner could respond, she removed the pendant from under her top and showed it to Conner. Conner took it gingerly in his fingers and examined it. It was not a simple pendant design. There was a small circle around which there was a larger circle. There were two curly lines that almost touched each other at the tips, and almost touched the circle at its centre.

"This is an image of that symbol you have on your Sin- your place of worship."

"Very observant. Yes, this is a representation of the Eye of Natis."

"Kind of hard not to recognize," said Conner dryly.

Victoria smiled and said, "Yes. Every Leviite carries a symbol of Natis with him wherever possible."

Conner let go of the pendant and nodded. They sat in silence for a few moments before Victoria asked, "So why are you here, Conner? Why this town? What do you think will happen here?"

Conner let out a sigh. He wanted to say, "I have no damned idea, I'm just a clueless guy searching for *something*, and the only reason I picked this town was because it was close to my country house." But instead he said, "I don't know. It just feels right. I have to just go along the path, see where it takes me and what I find along it. I have to believe that I will find something, or I will never find anything."

Victoria seemed taken aback by this frank statement. Most people tried to make up reasons and excuses to justify their actions; they generally never admitted that they didn't know something.

"I'll try to help you any way I can, Conner." The words came out of her mouth without her thinking. And the funny thing was that she meant it.

He smiled a small smile and thanked her.

Then she said softly, "And I really doubt you're that bad."

"Sophie said that too," said Conner sadly.

"Well, maybe you should learn to believe it then. Do you really want to make the same mistakes you made when she was alive?" Victoria didn't know what was happening to her. All these words were coming unbidden out of her mouth, but she realized that she had never loved as deeply as this man, and probably never would, yet both of them were suffering. He had known true love; he should be rejoicing, not sitting here, moping.

That statement seemed to rattle Conner. Then he realized that she was right; he was here to get *rid* of these thoughts, not bring them back. He nodded slowly and sat up straight. "That's right. I'm not that bad."

Victoria smiled, feeling a strange rush of joy. She checked the time and said, "Okay, it's okay to get out now. Let's go."

She got up and looked at him. He got up as well. As she proceeded towards the room door, she paused and said, "And besides, if we wait too long, Mrs. Stewart will wonder what we're doing up here."

****

As they exited the inn, Conner said to Victoria, "You said that this was a kingdom and that a lot of historians and the like come here.

But when I was looking at the town from the window, I didn't see any historical ruins as such."

Victoria explained, "Well, the truth is, a lot of them come to the *area*. You must realize that the kingdom occupied a large area, not just Levion. They don't think Levion is worth exploring. But we have the best accommodations and the best supplies. So they stay nights, and then go to wherever they have to."

As they passed houses, Conner noted that one section of houses seemed more modern while there was another section that seemed to be older, more decorative and elegant. He pointed this out to Victoria who said, "Good eye. That's right; some parts are older than the others. That's because a part of the town survived the Great Fire that destroyed most of the town. Newer houses were built as the town inevitably expanded."

Victoria abruptly changed course and took another direction. Before Conner could ask, she explained shortly, "I didn't want to pass by my house."

Conner asked cautiously, "Things bad at home?"

Victoria had a sour look on her face. "Let's just say they're not great."

There was silence for a few seconds before Conner asked, "How many members in your family?"

"Four, my parents, me and my brother. My father was born in this town along with his brother. My mom is one of the very rare people who came from out of town, and settled here after marrying my father." Victoria paused. "Because she was married to one of their own, the townspeople welcomed her and she got used to life here. But she used to tell me stories when I was younger about life outside this place, and I wished that one day, I too would have those kinds of stories to tell, stories that didn't involve the same characters in the same situations in the same places that you see every day, but I'm sure that it's impossible."

Conner seemed surprised, but he looked at her and smiled kindly, "I'm sure you can achieve that dream one day."

Victoria didn't comment. Conner waited till he was sure she had nothing to say before he pointed to the tall pair of buildings and said, "Is that the 'shop'?"

Victoria smiled mischievously. "Right you are. You'll enjoy that. Let's go there."

They walked up to the building. Conner's eyes went wide. There was a huge sign saying, "Barker's Emporium!" Wares were displayed in the store windows, and they all looked tempting. They entered.

Conner was amazed at what he was seeing. There were rows and rows of items; they were stocked with every possible item. It was divided into sections, including liquor, luxury items, etc. There were things that Conner had only seen in popular stores in big cities, and others that he had never seen before. He turned to Victoria. "Wow," he said simply.

Victoria smiled at his awestruck face.

"Is a big store like this really necessary? I mean, how much can people buy?"

Victoria smiled wider. "Well, everyone in town shops here. And a lot of the local products, made by housewives are sold to the store and then exported."

Conner looked around. "But you seem to have *everything*. Even branded products!" Something caught his eye. He picked up a packet of cookies. "You even have *Rosaline Chocolate Cookies*!"

Victoria laughed. "You know, those cookies were first *made* in this town."

Conner's eyes grew wide again. "You're kidding. I love these. How?!"

"Well, there's a baking competition held here. The winner gets made into a product. If it's really good, a lot of big companies often pick it up."

Conner seemed even more amazed. Victoria said, "Come on, the other building has restaurants. Let's get something to eat."

After a delicious lunch, they continued, bellies full. Conner decided he was going to get back there soon. He suspected there were even more undiscovered delights in there.

"That shop was a result of many generations and the many ideas that all of them contributed to it, with every new one adding a few more features."

They then reached what Victoria said was the town square. It was a large beautifully constructed, well… square. The buildings surrounding the square were the best in town, and the square itself was bare except for a curious object in the middle of the square.

It was a pedestal on which there was a pair of golden legs, but the entire statue from the shin up seemed to have been destroyed.

Victoria said, "That's said to be the statue of one of the great heroes of the town. They say that when the kingdom was at its most vulnerable, this man came and saved the entire kingdom. How he did it is not known. His name was lost but he was either a young man or an old boy. When the invasion came and ravaged our town, the statue was damaged this way."

"How come no one has tried to repair it, if he was so important?" interrupted Conner.

"I was coming to that. Well, the king had his main history records a little way off, and he used to record historical events here and then send them there after a certain period. Well, before he sent the latest batch, the capital was attacked. As a result, most of those records were destroyed, and during reparations, I suppose the legend got lost. So nobody's repaired the statue because nobody knows what he looked like. She paused, "He did a great thing, but the sad truth is that he only delayed what was coming; and I guess nobody bothers about the small victories when everything is destroyed anyway."

Victoria paused. "The other records were unharmed, thankfully, and they've been compiled into books that have been kept in the library in school."

She glanced subtly from side to side to ensure nobody was close enough to listen; then she whispered, "I'm definitely not supposed to be telling you this, but I've heard that there are books on Levion in the library at the university nearby as well, but nobody seems to have access to it and I'm pretty sure nobody here even knows about them."

Conner was intrigued. "Why all the secrecy?" he asked.

Victoria shrugged. She became quiet momentarily and soon seemed to forget about his question eagerly pointing to the big building adjoining the town square. "That's the town hall, along with the mayor's quarters." As they walked, a pair of eyes from the town hall was on Conner, watching him.

They passed an old building, which could only have been the school, considering the noise coming from within its walls.

"That's our fine institution of learning. It must be recess time. You probably won't be allowed in now. C'mon, let's go to the Home."

Victoria started walking towards the hill.

"But isn't that the opposite direction from your house? And didn't you say we weren't going there?" Conner asked perplexed.

Victoria smiled slightly. She stopped and pointed to the top of the hill. "I was talking about the Home of Natis, the Supreme One. Sinome means 'Home of the Sun' and is sometimes shortened simply to 'Home'." She paused.

"Let me explain the history of our religion to you," she continued, "Back before the Great Fire, there was another religion, and the people were displeased with it. There was unhappiness in the kingdom, and that was said to be one of the reasons the invaders felt confident that they were going to meet little resistance. At any rate, a new religion called Natism was formed revolving around the true God, Natis. Natis is all around us, in every pore of our body, in every tiny particle of earth. He is the creator, the provider, the destroyer! He guides our life and our Destiny." She paused. Conner once again noted the reverence with which she viewed her religion. "He expects us to follow some simple principles, have love for our community, and believe only in Him with all our hearts."

"Natism spread to some other parts of the then fragmented kingdom, but it didn't last too long. Maybe people in the other parts were too uncultured to appreciate it. This is the only Sinome left." She paused, as if in sadness. "At any rate, the great religion started in this town, in that Sinome." She pointed, "And that's another reason we call this Sinome the Home of Natis." She paused again. "If I ever leave this town, going there every Saturday and Sunday is one of the few things I'll sorely miss."

Conner stopped and turned to Victoria. He said, "Okay, there is one thing that has been bugging me, and I would really like a straight answer. I know something is not right here, but I sense that it's a grave problem in the town. Here are some of the things I've gathered: Nobody moves away, very few people immigrate here, you told me that I shouldn't appear *too* interested in the town and Mr. Stewart apparently died of some illness that you didn't want to talk about. There is something that you're trying to hide."

Victoria stopped and looked at Conner. She sighed. She knew this question was coming, but she felt that lying to Conner wouldn't be of any use. He seemed to be able to figure it out eventually; she had given away too much. She tried anyway, though. "Conner, I can't really tell you. You might just want to leave, and if it spreads, it'll scare off other tourists. You shouldn't even know this much."

Conner stared at her. "Victoria, what can be so bad that you have to hide it like this? You can trust me, Victoria. I'm not going to tell anyone. Maybe I can help."

Victoria considered this. She had never told an outsider before. But there was something different about this one, and she felt that she could tell him, that she could trust him, even a little. That was a feeling that she had not had since a long time, so she was going to use it. She took a deep breath and started, "Conner, I seriously doubt you can help." She paused again. "The reason why people don't leave Levion is because we're all under the threat of death."

Conner was stunned. "What?!" he exclaimed. "Who's threatening you?"

"Nature is," she said sadly. "All Leviites are under the threat of a disease called Levitis." She paused and shuddered, as if remembering all the victims of the disease. Then she continued, "After the Great Fire, two things were born: Levitis and Natism. Levitis prevents us from leaving town, and Natism helps to keep us in town so as not to endanger others."

"I don't understand that," said Conner, confused.

"Well, the main problem with Levitis is its unpredictability. It affects people apparently randomly. It can strike anyone at any age, though most of the time it afflicts people above the age of 40. Another terrible thing is that it has different symptoms - some go quietly, some go very painfully - and it's almost always fatal.

"There is no known trigger for it. There is a genetic component to it, though most people agree that the unique crops grown in the area also have some bearing on it, maybe through their pollen. At any rate, that's why we're self-contained. We go out of town only for work; that's why we have such a huge mall containing every possible supply and that's why we can't mingle too much with outsiders. They might want to join us, and then their kids will also have to suffer the whole cycle." Her pause was slightly longer this time.

"Natism helps to keep us sane, to keep us faithful." She continued, her voice stronger, "We know that Natis will provide for us. But over time, Levitis has become stronger..." She stopped mid-sentence.

Conner took this opportunity to interject by saying, "And that's why you don't want people to stay here for extended periods of time, because you're not sure how it will spread."

Victoria nodded. "But nowadays people are becoming disgruntled. They want alternative medicine, consultations. We think that a breakthrough is possible. However, Dr. Clark says we can't really risk it. One of the most disgruntled is Mrs. Stewart." She took a deep breath. "Remember when I said that her husband died suddenly? He died of Levitis. Mrs. Stewart had been talking to a patron who told her about these alternative medicines, and she wanted to take her husband to Baronsville to try them out or get a second opinion. Dr. Clark didn't allow it, and Mr. Stewart died. She always blamed him after that, even refused to go for her checkups. People called her many names, behind her back though, since she controls too much of the town's revenue for people to openly oppose her."

Conner nodded, taking all this in. Victoria gestured with her hand to speed up and said, "Come on, let me show you something."

They continued climbing, and in spite of the horrible things Conner had heard, he couldn't help but admire the Sinome. They finally reached; he was breathless. The Sinome was imposing, yet beautifully breathtaking and elegant at the same time. It was made of cut stone. Conner could see the symbol on the tower more clearly now. It was the same design as on Victoria's pendant, but it seemed to carry a certain amount of power and fear, etched into the stone. He looked at Victoria, who had not entered the Sinome, but instead had gone to the side.

There she showed him *Death watch*. "The names of the people who are afflicted currently with Levitis are listed here. Every time a name is added here, the bell in the bell tower is rung. This board was placed after a particularly nasty outbreak a long time ago, and it has been updated ever since. We usually tell tourists that it's from olden times, and that we preserve it as remembrance. If there's a name, like there is now, we tell them it's there to remind people who is sick and needs to be visited."

Conner tried to take in the sheer enormity of it all: A town where every person knows he might die the next day, and everyone seems to...accept it; in fact, they try and work around it, make do with what they have. It showed the resilience of the human spirit and the faith that the people had.

Before they went inside, Victoria pointed to the barren field on the other side of the hill. "That's where the final battle was fought. This land is purposefully left barren in honour of those men. You see those blocks?" She pointed at the clumps of blocks far away, "You'll see them around the perimeter of our town; they symbolically represent the town's walls which were destroyed."

The inside of the Sinome took Conner's breath away. He had been to places of worship before, but he had not been to one as large and grand as this one. There was a stained glass window on both sides of the room, with the east side having the image of the sun amongst clouds with sun rays shooting downwards at different angles. The west one had sun rays falling from the sky to the ground, where men and women knelt on the ground reverently, their hands joint in prayer. The glass was very delicately and intricately placed, and the rays of the east window to be coming down from the sky at the same angle as the rays in the west window fell to the ground.

There were two aisles and on either side of them, long pews led down to the aisle. In the middle, there were supports, some wooden and some stone ones. They were painted in such a way that they didn't create a distraction from the beauty of the place.

Conner turned to the end of the aisle, his mouth open. An intricately carved altar sat on a slightly raised platform. But it was what was behind the platform that really caught Conner's attention. On the wall behind the platform, the same eye that Conner had seen on the tower was painted in such a way that the head of an average-sized person standing on the platform would be right in the centre of the eye. Suddenly a door at the far end opened.

An old man emerged and started walking purposefully towards

them. He stopped to talk to one of the women praying in the pews (Conner hadn't noticed her) and then walked up to Conner and Victoria.

Conner studied this man. He was of average height, but held himself straighter than any man for his age, or even a younger age. His eyes were deep green, with a deep sense of knowledge in them. He was nearly bald; the little hair that remained on his head was white and he was wearing simple robes. He nodded at Victoria and said in a voice that was soft but seemed to command authority, "Always a pleasure, Victoria dear."

Then he turned to Conner. "And I assume this is the Conner Fry everyone is talking about. You're showing him around?" Without looking at Victoria's nod, he continued, "Well it's good that you brought him here. It's always nice for others to see what a great religion we have."

Conner nodded. "I've heard a little about it, and it seems really good...umm," Conner hesitated. "How am I supposed to address you?"

The old man laughed. "I'm surprised that Victoria hasn't told you." Victoria started apologizing, but he waved it off. "It's all right. I'm Father Godfrey." He looked Conner over with a shrewd, calculating eye. "What religion do you follow, Conner?"

Conner looked down at his feet, then looked up and said, "I don't follow any religion."

The Father looked at him for a second, nodded and suddenly turned around, and started walking towards the altar. Conner, unsure of what to do, waited for Victoria to follow before he did. Was this because he was religion-less?

"I've heard why you're here," said Father. "Loss is a terrible thing, but it helps us learn. I certainly hope our town will help you learn those lessons that have already begun evolving in you because of that loss."

Conner's mouth almost dropped open. This man spoke with such conviction about what Conner was only beginning to understand, that Conner felt that he might be able to help him. They had reached the end of the aisle. Father went behind the altar and suddenly raised his hand for them to stop. Then he spoke in a calm, forceful voice. "Conner, approach the altar." He had a no-nonsense attitude, as if everything he said was expected to be obeyed.

Conner was startled and looked around him to see if there was any other Conner who had magically appeared in the Sinome. Then he slowly approached the altar. The woman who had been praying looked up to see what was going on. Slowly she reached into her bag and started typing.

Conner went and stood in front of the altar on the platform. Father looked deep into Conner's eyes, as if he was stripping off all his defences, and his soul was being laid bare. Conner wanted to look away, but he didn't think he could escape those green eyes.

Father Godfrey stared into his eyes for a minute. Conner had heard some people enter quietly, but his eyes didn't waver from Father's. Suddenly Godfrey blinked and took a step back. He was about to say something-

There was a flash of bright light! Everyone was blinded for a few seconds. Conner had taken a step back and fallen off the platform. The light disappeared as quickly as it came; everyone started looking around to find the source, and failed to find any. All of them seemed confused about it, all except Godfrey, that is. He hadn't moved from where he stood and was staring at the fallen Conner.

"That was a sign," he said in only a slightly shaken voice. He slowly raised his index finger, the other fingers not being bound in a fist, simply hanging loose. The finger was pointed at Conner.

Chapter 8

Conner Gets the Finger

Slowly he started walking towards Conner, who had cautiously risen to his feet. The finger had also lifted along with Conner. Every footstep of his echoed in the large space, and every onlooker watched in tense anticipation of what was going to happen next. Was this outsider going to be deemed unfavourable to Natis? Would he be declared a saint proclaiming a message of peace?

With every step, the tension seemed to build. The eye on the wall seemed to be staring accusingly at Conner. His nervousness was building. He glanced at the exit and considered making a run for it. But then he realized that the women would probably barricade his way if they had to.

So Conner stood, considering the outcome of every possible scenario. If he was not accepted in this Sinome, he doubted that he would be accepted anywhere in Levion, and a peaceful exit from town would be the best case situation then. If he was made out to have some special blessing or something (which was a preposterous idea), then he most probably wouldn't be able to deliver.

All these thoughts passed in the seconds Father took to come up to him and keep the finger a few inches from his chest.

Finally, he spoke. "There's a lot of potential in you, Conner." This was said in a slightly prophetic voice, which is probably the effect he was going for. "You can do either a lot of good, or a lot of bad. Natis is watching you closely!" he proclaimed loudly, still looking at him. The finger didn't go down. "So you better watch what you do," he said in a whisper.

The finger finally fell and he turned around abruptly, and walked through the door from where he had emerged, leaving a lot of shocked citizens staring at an even more shocked Conner White.

Conner looked at each of their perplexed faces, as if he was expected to give some sort of brilliant speech proclaiming his purpose, and then disappear in another flash of light or a blaze of fire. He needed to get out of here; at least he could barricade himself in his room. He took a deep breath and a tentative step. Nobody moved to stop him; they just stared. So he started walking down the aisle faster.

The aisle seemed to stretch on endlessly. Conner didn't want any other flashes of light to trip him again, so he walked with his head down and his eyes watching the ground in front of him. His steps echoed, just like the priest's, but, unlike the priest's, these weren't steps leading up to a big conclusion; these were steps running away from the big conclusion.

He finally reached the end of the aisle. Everyone was still staring. Conner hurried past them to prevent them from grabbing him. Grabbing him? Blaze of fire? He really had an overactive imagination. He finally walked out. Victoria wasn't following. So he started walking down the path Victoria and he had walked earlier that day. He walked fast with his head down, avoiding all the people in his path. If he had worn a hat and a coat with an upturned collar, he would have met the description of a 1960's PI. Everyone he passed turned to look at him; most whispered. News travels fast in a small town; at least Levion stuck to *that* rule.

Conner finally reached the inn, after a lot of wrong turns, and went up to his room without saying anything to Mrs. Stewart who also didn't have her normal sweet look on her face.

Conner quickly opened the room door, locked himself in, drew the blinds and then lay down on the bed in his now dark room. Then one thought came to the forefront of his mind.

What the hell *had happened?!*

An inexplicable flash of light? A sign from God? And for *him*?

Was he really meant for greatness? It didn't seem like it. *Natis is watching you closely.* Father's words ran through his ears. Was that why he had picked this very town to quest for redemption? Had Natis guided him here? Conner looked around as if expecting to see a wise-God like creature sitting a foot away from him, ready to offer him counsel on what to do next. But, of course, there was nothing.

Conner remembered his experiences with religion. He had often gone to places of worship in his youth, trying out different religions even, searching for answers. But he hadn't found any. There was no reason for the suicide of his girlfriend, for all the torment he got while he was younger. He had looked up to the sky, and expected some kind of reply in return. But he never got it and so had given up on religion. It was one of the things he wrote against in his books.

He was confused. Why should he, a non-believer, get struck by a miracle? Was it because he was a non-believer; so that he could restore faith in life and himself? That seemed plausible, if there really was a God, which Conner had never accepted. *Maybe now is the time to accept it,* he thought. But what exactly was he supposed to do? A town full of strangers was observing him to see whether he was branded a saint or a heretic, and Conner was worried. He looked up at the skies as he had done in the past and thought, "Natis, if you really are there, please hear me. As you must know, I have made mistakes, but now I'm going to change; all I wish is that you help me, and I promise I will try to believe in you."

He waited for a few seconds with his eyes closed, but there was no response, and he wasn't expecting any. He had a sudden thought of running away from the town, but he closed his eyes and steeled himself. This time there was no running away from problems. He was going to face them, no matter what the consequences.

Suddenly there was a knock on the main door. Conner got up. Maybe this would lead to the sign he needed.

****

His arm trembled, then his other arm; soon his whole body was going through a series of convulsions. He lay there, writhing on the cold floor. He vaguely remembered being on a comfortable surface, then he had gotten off and staggered some distance before collapsing. He would have probably figured out what was happening under normal circumstances, but now the pain was too much. It was coursing through his entire body.

Not too far, a sterilized syringe was quickly filled with a purple liquid. A finger tapped it and then squirted it a bit. An indication was made, strong pairs of arms held the writhing man still while the syringe's needle was inserted in the man's arm and the plunger was depressed. The liquid seemed to have failed because his body started convulsing even more and looked like he wanted to scream, but didn't have the strength to. The same process was repeated with a clear liquid, which seemed to have an immediate effect - the man stopped convulsing almost immediately.

Tentatively, the men holding him down moved away as if they expected him to start moving again any second. Which they probably did. But the man didn't move.

The doctor stared at the man. "Move him to the bed," he ordered in his soft authoritative voice. The man was picked up and put on the bed. The crowd of onlookers moved away to give him passage.

Now for a decision to be made.

The man's eyes remained closed as they lay him down on the bed.

****

This is the perfect time to search this place, he thought as he opened the door. He had searched many inn rooms before, and he had the duplicates close at hand. Now he was supposed to be searching for some kind of story, mostly a negative one. He wasn't supposed to disturb anything if he could help it, so he carefully sifted through anything that might give him a clue as to what this man was *actually* doing here.

He started looking through the drawers for a writing pad of any kind, but he couldn't find any. Then he looked under the bed and found Conner's rucksack. If he dumped everything out and then searched it, Conner might suspect. So instead, he carefully moved his hand around the rucksack, displacing as few things as possible before he felt a book and carefully extracted it. On pulling it out, a piece of loose paper from the journal fell to the floor. It was a letter.

He read the first part of the letter and was surprised. This was not a negative story, the one he had been told to expect. Then he read another story that was written for the most part in the journal within which the letter had been slipped in. It was in the same handwriting. He carefully replaced the journal and letter back at the bottom, trying to make sure everything was as he had found it. Then he put the rucksack under the bed, opened the main door and checked the corridor. Clear, just as he expected. He got out, locked the door and continued on his way.

****

Conner opened his eyes. There was still a crowd of people around him; they all still looked upset and disturbed. Luckily, he was standing at the back and he went relatively unnoticed. He had closed his eyes to get the image of the man writhing on the floor out of his head. Jon, they said his name was. Jon Peck.

Victoria was beside him. She looked sad. Conner realized how many times she must have witnessed such a scene. He thought how terrible it must be for her, and all the people of the town to see something like that over and over, especially since the person would be someone they had lived with and closely known. When Conner turned towards Victoria again, she was looking at him. While she appeared to be sad, there was also a hint of confusion in her eyes that he managed to discern before she turned her face away and started fingering her chain again.

Conner remembered the sorrow on Victoria's face when she had knocked on his door and told him that someone was succumbing to the disease suddenly and Father Godfrey had asked him to be there. Conner had almost not accepted, but figured that that would look even worse, so he had complied. It wasn't going well. The only good thing to come out of this was that it seemed to have made everyone stop talking about him. And although the Father hadn't spoken to him, he could see him consoling the family of the victim. Everyone in this room knew that they would mostly end up with this kind of death, and maybe it was this awareness of death that made them so religious and hardworking.

Conner noticed the doctor also conversing with the family; they seemed to be unable to reach a decision about something. The daughter, who looked like she was Victoria's age, was crying hysterically. She seemed to want to run to her father's bedside and cry over him, as if that would wash away his illness and allow him to wake up.

Conner turned to Victoria and whispered, "What's going on?"

Victoria seemed to have snapped out of her reverie and whispered back to him, "This is one of those situations where the family is given a very difficult choice. There's a very slim chance that the doctor's specially prepared medicine will help him get better, or it might have a bad reaction and extend his suffering. Or the doctor can give him something that'll....help him pass away in peace."

Conner winced. "Can't they just try to see if the medicine works, and if not...?" Conner let the sentence hang; explanation was unnecessary.

Victoria shook her head. "If it fails, the person dies a long-drawn and horribly painful death."

Conner shook his head. He wished he never had to make decisions like that. Suddenly the wife of the ill man, who had been trying to maintain her composure, now completely broke down and asked Father in a teary voice to make the decision. Now everyone looked at him. Conner suspected this wasn't the first time he had been made to decide. He closed his eyes, pointed his head skywards, and started praying.

After a few seconds, Conner got a bad feeling. Then Godfrey suddenly snapped his eyes open and looked at Conner. "Natis has spoken to me." He raised his finger, once again, and pointed at Conner. "He will decide."

As everyone turned to look at him, his first thought was, *Again with the pointing! Can't he just flip me off like a normal person and leave me be?!*

****

Everyone turned to stare at Conner. He continued looking down, afraid of what he would see in people's eyes. Then suddenly someone spoke in the silence. "Are you sure about this, Father?!"

Conner lifted his head up. It was the doctor who had spoken, judging from the direction the crowd was looking towards. Father ignored everyone and then the two men went to the corner and started speaking in low voices. Nobody seemed to be able to hear. After they were done, the doctor seemed convinced.

Father Godfrey then spoke to everyone gathered, "My children, Natis speaks through me. He wants Conner to do his will today. Have faith."

Immediately all eyes turned towards him. In the faces of the people he saw complete faith in their religion and their Father. They were all looking expectantly at Conner. Even Jon's wife and daughter had stopped crying a little and were looking at Conner with some hope in their eyes.

"You do know what choice you have to make, right, Conner?" Father asked quietly, taking Conner aside. Conner nodded. The Father seemed to know how, and didn't ask. Instead he said, "This man's life, even if for the next few minutes, rests in your hands. Choose wisely."

As if Conner didn't know. How was he supposed to choose? A few months ago, he had been at his home with his loving wife who didn't really tell him what he needed to hear; his daughter had moved far away from home because of him; and he had a writing career that had mostly been based on self-destructive thoughts and principles. Okay, maybe his life hadn't been that great to begin with, but that didn't mean he was even close to ready for something like this.

He shook his head. *Focus!* he thought to himself. Now if he gave Jon medicine, then he would encounter extreme pain and then die. Nobody wanted to see that kind of pain and suffering. Nobody should also have to suffer that much pain in their last moments of life. On the other hand, it might cure him. But if that had a high level of possibility, wouldn't they have risked it anyway?

If he told them to kill him right away, he would have a peaceful death, and his family wouldn't have to see him suffering anymore than they already had. That wouldn't be their last memory of him.

Conner closed his eyes, praying to Natis, if there was a God like that to be believed in, and asked for His guidance. He begged for the ability to make the right decision. He promised that if he did, he would...believe in God again.

He opened his eyes. He had made his decision. He somehow felt connected to that man who lay there, his life ebbing away slowly. If he was to truly give his own life a second chance, he had to give that man a chance. Slim chance or not, it might pain a bit but if he was going to die anyway, he might as well fight for his life first. Conner looked at the doctor and said, "Give him the medicine. Try and save him."

This time, Conner had his eyes only on the doctor. His expression didn't change, but he looked at Godfrey, who nodded. Then he started moving quickly.

He opened his doctor's bag, extracted some green fluid in a syringe, cleared it of air bubbles as he had done earlier and moved towards the bed. He looked at Conner as if to ask, *Last try. Want to change your mind?*

Conner recalled the look on the family's face. There was still hope. It was time Conner hoped and had faith in God or a higher power. It was time he *believed*. Yet when Dr. Clark looked at him questioningly, he put his hand up and said, "In case it goes wrong...shouldn't these people leave the room so as to avoid seeing him suffer?"

Conner heard Father Godfrey say, "If anyone has any problems, they may leave."

Conner kept his eyes on the doctor. As far as he could make out, nobody moved.

"Well, then," said the doctor. He unceremoniously inserted the needle into Jon's arm once again and depressed the plunger.

The next few seconds were some of the longest that Conner had ever experienced. Jon barely moved and everyone looked on anxiously. Conner suddenly started noticing tiny details, like every wrinkle on Jon's face, every crease on his clothes. The way his hand was slowly trembling...Suddenly Conner noticed that the trembling was moving up his arm, and slowly to his whole body. Then his eyes flew open and he screamed.

It was an ear piercing, lung shattering scream that made everyone cringe and look away. He paused for a few seconds, and then screamed again for half a minute before he stopped and closed his eyes.

Everyone then apprehensively looked towards him again. His daughter and wife had already gone to his side and were screaming his name as if he were only in a deep slumber from which they had to wake him.

Conner was horrified. He had caused this. He had made the wrong decision. Jon wasn't going to survive anyway, and it seemed that he had made him go through extra pain. Was he never going to do anything right? Was-

Conner's self-criticism was interrupted when he saw Jon's eyes flutter. Jon slowly opened them and said something in a hoarse voice to his wife and daughter.

Dr. Clark told them to move aside and quickly checked his pulse and vitals. Then he looked up and announced, "That scream was a result of the medicine reacting. He's dehydrated and weak right now, but he'll be fine. I need to make the necessary arrangements, but he'll live...for quite a while." He walked halfway across the room, but stopped at where Conner stood and nodded wordlessly at him. Then he walked out before Conner could reply.

Everyone was stunned for a few seconds, and then their faces broke out into a mixture of relief and delight. The family was already crying tears of joy.

Conner felt like a weight had lifted from him. He had made the right decision; he had saved the man's life. He closed his eyes and offered a silent prayer to Natis, who suddenly seemed much more real.

After the initial few minutes of joy, they turned to the man who was responsible for this - Conner.

Father Godfrey spoke quietly. "It was just as I suspected. This man has the blessing of Natis."

This time he didn't point. There was no need; everyone knew who he was talking about. Jon's daughter came up and hugged him thanking him through her tears. Her mother offered the same thanks.

Conner nodded. He really didn't know what to do. He didn't know what to expect from here. But mostly he didn't believe that he was worthy of being someone who was "blessed". To him, it seemed that a weight had been lifted to make place for an even bigger weight.

Suddenly the rest of the world turned dark to Conner. It was just him, on an empty stage. Suddenly the same light that he had seen in the Sinome was illuminating him, like a spotlight guided by the hand of God.

Conner wasn't used to being in the spotlight. And he had a feeling he wouldn't like it very much.

Chapter 9

How the Lowly Have Risen

Conner lay down on bed, looking at the ceiling. This had been...a crazy day, and he should know; he had been having too many of those lately. But this was the unlikeliest of all. How was he, the person who was responsible for at least one person taking his own life, blessed or chosen by God in any way?

The worst part was that he didn't know what was going to come next. Victoria had not known how to act towards him. The other townspeople had started treating him with respect because of the miracle, as they called it, he had performed. He felt that he had not earned that respect. They were all beginning to ask for miracles or blessings, before the Father stopped them and said that Conner needed to rest. Conner had gratefully taken this opportunity and escaped to the inn, as quickly as possible. He had switched on his lights and lay down on bed. He was not hungry after his big lunch and confusing day.

How *had* he performed that miracle? Was there really a God named Natis watching over him? Even though Conner felt his faith returning in the moment when he had performed the "miracle", Conner's doubt was resurfacing. He couldn't believe that there was someone guiding him, someone he could *believe* in. Or maybe that was because he didn't believe in himself. The only other alternative to believing in Natis, however, was to believe that random flashes of light and miraculous life choices were a normal part of his life.

Conner sighed. He closed his eyes. Within minutes, he was asleep, or at least, dreaming.

His dream was more of a memory. It was about a month before Sophie died; she was very sick on the night that Conner was recalling. Sophie just wasn't getting sleep, and Conner had tried to comfort her.

He had been sitting next to her on the bed, his arm around her, stroking her hair. Looking at her pitiable state he said, "Why are you so sick when you're the sweetest thing? I do so many bad things and I'm perfectly fine..."

Sophie had playfully punched him in spite of her discomfort and said, "You shut up; you don't do anything bad. The worst thing you do is think you're bad. You're destined for greatness, Conner, but it'll only happen if you believe in yourself."

Conner had looked at her tenderly and said, "You really think I can be great?"

Sophie had said softly, "Only if you believe you can."

Conner continued stroking her hair for a few seconds before he whispered, "Okay. I believe that I can make you feel better."

Sophie had smiled a little. Conner had kissed her on the forehead and made her lie down. She had her back to him. He had an arm under her, and another encircling her from the top. He had gently kissed her neck for a few seconds, and then had moved onto the cheek. She turned her face a little towards him and he had given her a small kiss on the lips. Then he nestled his face in her hair and pulled her close to him. He gently kissed her on the back of her head and neck for a while; he continued this even after he could hear her soft breathing when she fell asleep.

The feeling that Conner had, holding her sleeping form in his arms, gently breathing, was the closest his heart had ever felt to Heaven. He was lying awake for a long time, cherishing that feeling before he fell asleep.

The next morning, he found her lying next to him, awake and staring at him. "You look better," he had whispered.

"I'm fine now. See? I told you if you believe in yourself, you can do so much." She kissed him softly on the lips. "Even if you think you've done something bad, do something right in the future. And you can't always do wrong, can you?"

Conner shook his head and smiled at her. He had felt good that day, but eventually he had gone back to his normal negative life. A month later, Sophie had died.

Conner may not have heeded to those words, but even now, as he slept, when he thought back to that memory, he experienced that same heavenly feeling. And he smiled in his sleep.

****

Conner woke up later than usual, which just meant that he woke up at the crack of dawn, and not before it. He stretched. The warmth of last night's memory still washed over him. He sighed. He missed Sophie, but she was right. He had not recognized his potential, and he had made countless people lose hope in themselves. He could have made Sophie's and Megan's life so much better; instead he had made them suffer by seeing him suffer. He had to have faith in himself and live his life more positively in future. So he would. For Sophie. For Megan. For himself.

He looked at the town through his room window once again. He noticed a small figure on King's Hill, and although it was too far to see, he had an eerie feeling that the Father was looking at the inn. Conner shuddered and moved away from the window. He decided it was time to write again. He felt under the bed for his rucksack; it was in a different place from where he had kept it. He examined it and then took a closer look at the items inside the bag. As he had feared, someone had broken in and read his letter and journal.

He needed a better hiding place. Someone could have done this while he was with Jon. But as far as he could see, everyone who wasn't working was there, so it might have been while he was taking a tour of the town, since his room was vacant then, and he hadn't checked the journal in the brief time after he had returned.

But what did it mean? Was it someone who was just curious and wanted to find out more about him? But now that the person had read this, would he realize that Conner was an author? Then something worse struck Conner: Did the intruder *know* that Conner was an author? Conner dispelled that thought. If someone knew, surely they would have said something?

He took out his journal and turned to where he had last stopped. Time to continue.

It had been a long walk, but suddenly a town was visible in the distance. His pace picked up; he was very sweaty and tired, but now he experienced a burst of energy. He sped up. Soon he saw three men. He hailed them. They looked surprised to see a man so far away from town.

"Yes?" one of them asked, "What is it you desire?"

"I am lost," he said, "I don't know where I am, and I seem to have suffered an injury which has made me forget how I got here."

They looked at each other. Then the second one asked, "So, do you have a name, injured stranger?"

A pause. It was better to decide a name so he wasn't deemed completely crazy. "Of course. My name is Marvin."

They looked at him with stunned gazes. The man, who we shall now refer to as Marvin, eyed them curiously. "Something wrong?" he asked.

They muttered to each other and then the first man, apparently the leader, stepped forward and extended his hand. "It's nothing. I'm Tyson and these are my friends, Pierce and Daniel," he said, pointing to the second and third man respectively. "Come on, maybe we can get you some help in our town."

Marvin nodded gratefully and they started walking.

"So aren't you hungry?" asked Daniel, speaking for the first time since Marvin had met them.

Marvin shook his head. "Well...no. Somehow I know the name of the herbs that are edible, and I've eaten enough of them to satiate my hunger."

They looked sceptical but before they could say anything, they were able to hear a commotion up ahead. They sped up and reached a crowd of people that had gathered around a man who was on the floor, writhing and screaming. The crowd saw them approach. A man was standing over the writhing person; he was apparently the doctor. He looked at Tyson and said in a grave voice, "Poisoned, just like the others."

Tyson knelt down next to him, looking worried. "Is there nothing we can do?"

The doctor shook his head gravely. "I can try giving this, but I don't know if it will work."He held up a small green plant.

Something about the writhing man was familiar to Marvin. He pushed aside the people and knelt down next to the writhing man and examined him. He suddenly stood up, snatched the plant and announced, "That will only kill him faster. I know what this man is suffering from."

There were murmurs among the onlookers. He ignored them. The doctor and Tyson were whispering to each other. Instead of waiting for their response, he rushed to the forest and started searching frantically around for something. The people turned to stare at him. Suddenly Marvin seemed to have found what he was looking for. He grabbed a few leaves and started crushing them together as he walked towards the writhing man. The doctor blocked his path. "What experience do you have?"

Marvin pushed him aside, knelt down and put the crushed leaves in the man's mouth, tilting his head so that he managed to swallow it. Everyone waited to see what would happen. After a few seconds, the writhing man screamed. A few strong men came and took hold of Marvin, while the doctor said, "He has given him poison which has made him suffer even more!"

Marvin ignored all of this, watching the man on the ground. After a few seconds, he indicated with his head, "Look."

The man had stopped writhing, and everyone was stunned. Marvin broke free from the now-loosened grips, and propped the man's head up against the nearby well.

He seemed to be regaining colour in his face. Everyone gathered around to see if he was really feeling better. The doctor checked him and said, "Yes, he's much better."

There was a murmur among the crowd. "I understand you can't remember anything about your past..." asked the doctor. "And yet you can remember sicknesses and their remedies?"

Marvin nodded. "I'm not sure how it happened. I hit my head after a violent crash, I think."

The doctor thought for a while and then said, "I think only your personal memories, like your friends or places you've been to, have been forgotten. Maybe some trigger will make you recall them. Do you know what you call yourself?"

A hesitation. "Marvin."

There was a flurry around the crowd. The name "Marvin" seemed to have some kind of meaning to these people. Suddenly the poisoned man groaned. Everyone's attention turned to him once more and the doctor hurriedly exclaimed, "Give him some water!"

As Tyson stepped forward to draw the water, Marvin exclaimed, "Stop!"

Tyson stopped and looked at him. "You said there were others poisoned?" Marvin asked.

Tyson nodded. Marvin stepped forward and drew water from the well. He sniffed it and sipped a bit of it. Then he spat that out and threw all the water on the ground. Everyone was, once again, surprised.

"This water is the source of your poison!" he exclaimed. "Does anyone know whether the poisoned victims had drunk this well water?"

Slowly people started giving affirmative responses. Suddenly one person said, "I've kept it home for later use."

Marvin's eyes widened and he shouted, "Go run ahead and tell them not to use it! If they are sick, take a few leaves of this herb, crush it up and feed it to them! Quick!"

Marvin brought several of those herbs and gave them to Tyson who rushed along with a few other people.

The rest started walking quickly towards the village. The poison victim, who was now cured, slowly rose, and supported by two men, left the place to go home. After a while, everyone was checked. They were a few others who were poisoned, but they were all saved. After everyone was confirmed safe, they stood around looking at Marvin reverently.

"You're a saint!" one of them screamed.

Marvin was taken aback. "I'm no saint."

One old man who was standing behind in the crowd, suddenly came forward and said, "Marvin was the name of our saint. You appear out of nowhere and save our town, bearing his name. You are his reincarnation."

And then they all hailed a very bewildered Saint Marvin.

****

Conner looked up, satisfied with his work. He looked at his watch. It was late enough to order breakfast. He called for breakfast requesting for it to be left outside his door. Mrs. Stewart had a strange tone to her voice, but she agreed.

Conner went for a shower and by the time he got out, the food had arrived. He took the tray in and ate. It was delicious. He felt refreshed. He looked at his phone. There had been no activity on it since the previous evening. Victoria had not tried to contact him in any way, and Conner wondered what she was thinking. He decided that he should wait till she texted him.

Suddenly there was a knock on the door. Conner was surprised. Had someone come to take the dishes? So soon?

He got up and looked through the peephole. It was a woman, a very attractive woman. He wasn't going to forget that...face (among other things) easily. What was the mayor's wife visiting him for?

There were only two ways to find out. The first one involved mind reading, and since he couldn't do that, he decided to just open the door and find out for himself.

When he opened the door, she smiled widely and extended her hand, like a politician...or a politician's wife. Conner shook it and smiled back.

"Hello Mr. Fry. We've never been formally introduced but you've met my husband, Frank, the mayor. I'm Rosaline."

Conner said, "Well, I'm sure that I need no introduction, since everyone probably knows who I am by now. Please, come in. And you can call me Conner."

Rosaline laughed and entered. As she passed Conner to enter the room, he could smell her intoxicating citrus perfume which lingered for a few seconds. He stood frozen at the spot. Soon he realized that he looked stupid standing there with the door open. In any case he could smell her better while sitting next to her on the couch. So he closed the door and sat down beside her. She was still smiling.

"So, what brings you here?" asked Conner. "Is it for divine blessing? I'm not really sure how I'm supposed to give that, contrary to what everyone expects."

Rosaline laughed again. "No, Conner. I saw what you did yesterday; I *do* believe you're blessed, even if you don't yourself believe it, which seems to be the case." Conner didn't know what to say. He had probably been too engrossed in the dying man's predicament to notice even her. She continued smoothly, ignoring his reaction, or lack of it. "I just wanted to come in person and meet you."

Conner nodded, though he suspected there was more.

Rosaline looked around. "You know, this is the best room in the inn. Only rich guests stay here, usually businessmen. You must have been really good at your job if you could afford to spend as much money as you're rumoured to have without breaking into a sweat. What *do* you do for a living?" Before Conner could answer, she pointed to the papers on his desk, "And are those work papers? Aren't you supposed to be on vacation?" she asked in a slightly reprimanding tone.

Conner paled. Damn! He had left them out! He quickly rose to put them away. She smiled and waved him down. "I was just kidding. A bit of work is good to take your mind off things. Sit."

Conner slowly sat down. This woman didn't seem to miss a thing, and yet she seemed so nice. "My father was a very successful businessman. I'm the owner of the company, though I don't do much work, to be honest."

"I'm sure you contribute a lot," she said seriously.

"Thank you," said Conner with a small smile. "So, does the mayor of a town like this have a lot to do? Does that leave you with any duties?"

Rosaline shrugged and made a dismissive gesture. "Not too much. Sometimes I give him advice and help in meetings. Oh and of course, I'm responsible for the children." Her face seemed bitter for the first time since she had come in.

"I think taking care of children is a difficult and rewarding task," Conner said gently.

Rosaline seemed startled and hastily said, "Don't get me wrong, I love my children. But the thing is, sometimes that's all people expect me to be." She paused now, speaking slower. "Mother of my children. Once they're grown up, I could probably die and it wouldn't matter to any of them." She looked frustrated now. "Do you know this town has never had any female mayors? And if a mayor has only daughters, a male heir generally gets elected even if the daughter tries! I have a son and a daughter, and that means my son is predestined for leadership, even if he doesn't want to be!"

Suddenly Rosaline started crying. "I'm sorry," she said, her face buried in her hands. "I'm not usually this way."

Conner went closer to her and put his hand on her arm. "It's okay. Maybe you can still make a change in the system. And you seem like a very determined person. I'm sure you're doing great work right now and will continue to do it, even after your children have grown up. Nobody wants you dead, and the townspeople adore you. I'm sure your husband loves you as well and you have a lot to live for. Talking of death and negativity won't get you anywhere."

Conner White felt very strange saying these words, but he knew they were right.

Rosaline stopped crying and looked at him. "You really think so?"

Conner nodded. Rosaline smiled and gripped his hand. "Thank you," she said. "I could never talk to someone from town about this. I just *know* you won't tell anyone about this. Oh, wait, I have something for you."

She reached into her purse and took out a small box with cookies in them. They looked familiar and delicious. She handed them to Conner. "I bake a lot. Try one." Conner opened the box, took out a cookie and took a bite. A familiar rush of chocolaty goodness hit his taste buds. "You!" he said in surprise, "You're the Rosaline of *Rosaline Chocolate Cookies!*"

She seemed surprised as well. "You've had them before?"

"I *love* them! They just melt in your mouth." He took another bite. "The mayor is a lucky man. He has a smart, beautiful wife who can bake amazingly well."

She smiled for a few seconds before tearing up a bit and then stood up. "I need to go to the bathroom." She took her purse with her and walked to the bathroom. Conner put the cookies down. What had happened? Had he been too forward? Confused he walked to the bathroom door and knocked. "Are you okay in there, Rosaline?"

Suddenly he heard the crack of glass and a loud curse. Conner knocked on the door harder. "Hello? What was that noise?"

The door opened slowly. "Don't come in. There's glass on the floor," she said. Her arm was bleeding. "What happened?!" Conner asked.

"I tripped, dropped a lotion bottle and cut my hand on one of the bigger pieces," she said simply. She looked down and carefully manoeuvred around the glass as best as she could, clutching her bleeding arm. Conner helped her out and looked at the arm. It was luckily not a deep cut. They moved to the couch. Conner got some cotton and a band-aid out of his rucksack, cleaned the wound and put a band-aid on it. "You're fussing too much. It's just a small cut," she said.

Conner ignored her and continued till the wound looked better. "Thank you," she said, smiling at him. "You're a really sweet man."

Conner smiled at her. She got up. "I think I should clean up the glass in the bathroom. Someone might step on it and get hurt."

Conner got up as well and waved her down. "Stop. It's alright. I'll do it. Sit down and relax."

"You're sure?" she asked softly.

Conner nodded. She sat down and Conner went to the bathroom. There were a lot of pieces; Conner slowly brushed them up and then threw them into the waste bin. People who look so composed on the exterior seem to have such turbulent emotions within them, trying to get out, he thought. Once done, he returned to Rosaline, who was standing with a serious look on her face.

Before Conner could say anything, she said, Look, Conner, I've feeling guilty about this from the beginning, but now that I've seen you and I realize what a good person you are, I feel even worse. I didn't come here just to talk to you." She paused. "Frank sent me here to get information about you. He didn't believe you really performed that miracle; he doesn't believe that you are special. He said that if I had to, I should..." she shuddered and then whispered, "Seduce you."

Conner's eyes widened. He didn't know what to say, not for the first time today. He stepped forward and put his hand on her shoulder. "Hey, it's not your fault that your husband stoops so low. You're a wonderful woman and it shows. You didn't go through with it, did you? That shows that you're better than him."

Rosaline looked up at Conner, nodded and hugged him simultaneously taking Conner by surprise and overwhelming his nose with her perfume. She broke out after a few seconds and, standing close to him, looked him in the eyes. She stood like that for half a minute, then leaned very close, kissed him on the cheek and whispered, "Thank you," and pulled away.

She looked at Conner sadly and said, "I have to leave. But don't worry, I'll deal with Frank. Thank you for everything. Enjoy the cookies." She turned around, opened the door, gave Conner a small backward glance and walked out, closing the door behind her.

Conner stood rooted to the same spot, the citrus fruit smell floating around his head, messing up his thoughts. He wondered why the mayor distrusted him.

Rosaline passed the front desk and smiled at Mrs. Stewart on her way out. Mrs. Stewart watched her leave.

That woman is always so poised and charming, she thought. *I wonder if she ever breaks down.*

Shrugging, she went back to work.

Chapter 10

The Room Of Secrets

Conner sat across the table from Father Godfrey. Shortly after Rosaline had left, someone had come to take him to the Sinome where the Father wanted to meet him. He had hidden the story more carefully this time and had then left, less reluctantly than the previous day, mainly because he was a little more confident about what he was doing.

He had tried to avoid talking to any of the townspeople, especially after the variety of looks he was getting from them. Finally he had reached the Sinome and the Father had ushered him into a side room. There were two doors in the room; the south one led to the altar and pews, while the north one led to what he assumed was the inner sanctum of the Father.

Now they were seated on simple chairs across a small table. Conner was on the north chair, the Father on the south.

Father put his hands on the table and said, "Hello Conner."

"Hello Father," said Conner uncertainly.

Father smiled. "Relax, Conner. I've not called you here for a test. I know you were just chosen, as I was, to follow the Divine Path. There are no qualifications you have to fulfil."

Conner laughed and relaxed a little. At least the Father understood, even if Conner himself didn't. "Even if, as you said, there are no qualifications, I really don't know what kind of good I've done to

deserve it. There is also some-" He stopped. He was about to say
that there was probably some bad he was supposed to be punished
for, but he didn't want the priest to ask for the reasons, so he kept
quiet.

"Look, Conner," Father said, maintaining eye contact, "I have seen
a lot of humility, a lot of good in you. Everyone has done bad deeds
in their life, including me. I've done a lot of what others would
consider "wrong", and I will continue to do it, because I know what
I believe in. We all make choices, some we consider mistakes, but
it happens. So even if you have made mistakes, doing good will
go a long way towards redeeming yourself for that bad." Sophie's
words echoing the same thing rung in his ears.

"Let me tell you about what happens in this room. People can come
in here any day to talk to me about anything they want to. I guide
them, but sometimes all they need is someone to *listen*. And that is
what I mainly do; I listen to everything they say and put them in
the right direction when required. Every Saturday and Sunday, I
give sermons, and after those sermons, I generally call someone in
and talk to him. It makes me available to the townspeople and the
townspeople trust me. Everything that is said in this room is strictly
confidential. It's nicknamed 'The Room of Secrets.' An outside soul
will not hear a word of what you say here, I promise you. You can
speak freely."

Conner regarded the sincerity in the priest's voice, and nodded.
"Yes Father," he said. "Can I ask you something?"

"Of course."

"What's it like having a connection with Natis? Does he speak in
your ear, or move your hand or...?"

He laughed. "Well, I get signs. All of us get signs; we just have
to find them. What sets me apart is that I can feel my spiritual
connection stronger than others. Sometimes I feel that Natis is
standing right next to me, and with His guidance, I can perform
miracles. Sometimes I do talk to Him, but He replies in an indirect

way. We have to work to see what He wants to convey to us. I also sometimes get these surges of energy which make me feel...*alive* and ready for any task."

Conner nodded slowly. Then he said, "I have one more question, which may sound strange. Why aren't you sitting closer to your quarters? Wouldn't it be better if we switched positions? That way we won't have to cross the room to get out."

"That question isn't strange. It's quite logical, actually. The thing is that I want people to cross the room. A person's walk conveys a lot about him, and sometimes can even indicate his emotional state. Plus, if the person is unable to contain his emotions and wants to get out in the middle of our conversation, he'll have to get past me first."

The last statement was said in such a way that Conner believed that would be a difficult thing to do.

"But if the person really wants to get out, couldn't he just go into your chambers? In that emotional state, there's a tendency to take the nearest exit."

That same undercurrent of menace was present in the Father's voice when he said, "Every resident of Levion knows that going in there without invitation is a sin, and they are likely to be cursed."

Conner looked at the priest and wondered what he could possibly mean by that statement. Did he have the ability to curse people? What would that entail? He had a feeling it was better not to ask.

Father Godfrey resumed the conversation lightly, as if he had not noticed Conner's doubtful face. "Would you mind answering some of my questions now, Conner? I would like to know more about you."

Conner nodded, having a flashback of the conversation with Rosaline in the morning. He wondered if this was also a tactic to find out something about his background. At any rate, he had no reason for *not* answering.

"I know your wife recently passed away, which was the original reason for you coming here. How are you coping?"

Conner shrugged, trying to hide his pained look. "Going as well as it can."

An unconvinced nod. "How exactly did she die?"

"Heart problem."

"Any children?"

Conner hesitated, and then shook his head.

"Work?"

Conner gave him the same reply that he had given Rosaline. Father eyed him shrewdly, as if he didn't believe Conner. Conner decided it would be a good time for him to divert the topic. "So, Father, if I may ask, how did you become the priest of the town? I mean, what kind of selection process is there?"

"You may definitely ask, Conner. The presiding priest names a successor when he feels the time is right. He grooms this successor. That person has been chosen in some way by the Divine Natis. Natis came to Father Emmanuel in a dream and told him that I would be the reason our religion is changed forever. I was chosen the next day and I have taken to the Divine ever since."

"And what exactly is 'High Natish' you call me? Victoria told me Natish means all the followers of Natism."

"Ah, everyone is wondering if you are a High Natish. They are usually generalized as priests or missionaries; but a High Natish is someone who is in particular favour of Natis, destined to fulfil Natis' duty in some special way. You are one of those men. How you have to do it, you will discover in time."

Conner nodded.

"You said earlier that you don't follow any religion. Why is that?"

Conner took a deep breath and then exhaled slowly. "Well, let's just say I tried searching for God and never found Him."

Father raised an eyebrow. He waited expectantly.

Conner realized he had to continue. "Well, I had a very troubled childhood. I used to constantly pray to God to send me some help, but it never came. So eventually I gave up."

The Father looked like he wanted to say something, but stopped. After a few seconds, he asked, "You said you were born into a rich family, right?"

Conner sighed. He didn't like thinking about his childhood. "Yes, well, being rich doesn't mean being happy."

Father looked him in the eye and said, "I never said that. Go on. Tell me about your childhood," he prodded.

Conner sighed again. "Well...a lot of kids didn't like the fact that I was rich. For one, they naturally assumed I was spoilt and consequently bullied me, and there were others who envied me for my money." He looked down. "There were a lot of people who just used me for my money..."

"And how did that make you feel?"

Conner snorted. "How do you think that made me feel? I began to distrust everyone, and preferred to be alone rather than in the company of people. I became a loner, basically."

"Why did you not want to be with people? You felt that they would use you?"

Conner nodded. "And that they wouldn't understand me. I never let anyone in, because I learned that the people I let in eventually always ended up leaving me." He looked up at the ceiling, thinking of the relationships and friendships he had lost. "I now realize that sometimes I was the one who didn't want to keep contact; I felt like

I would do something wrong or I would mess up in some way, so I broke off contact before they did."

He looked at Father. "So basically, I've never had a close relationship with anyone for a long time. Somehow, I mentally sabotage it. I've never really been able to maintain a relationship over the long term, because in some way or the other, some part of me has already killed it off." He let out a hollow laugh. "Maybe I worried my wife so much that her heart gave way. She didn't stay either."

Suddenly Conner blinked and straightened himself. "I'm sorry, Father. I'm rambling. I'm not usually this way-"

"You're more closed off," completed Father.

Conner nodded slowly.

"Look, Conner. I think you're a smart man and you do a lot of thinking. A lot of people wouldn't be able to realize even this much about themselves without help from others. And since you don't seem to have taken any help from others, you haven't realized some things. Let me tell you what I think, from what I've heard. You generally distrust people, and because a few people did not understand you, you have generalized this feeling towards everybody. And so you used the excuse that nobody understood you as a way to keep people away, and not let them in.

"There was a point in your life after which you actually *believed* that nobody understood you. And that was the point where your downward spiral began and you stopped believing in yourself." He paused. "And from what I can see, your wife seemed to be the only person who really supported you through all that, the only person you *let* in and whose support you accepted through all that. And now that she's gone, you're even more lost."

Conner stared at Father. His face felt like it was being pulled in different directions as his emotions competed for expressions. There was shock, amazement and even fear. How could this man get so much from whatever Conner had told him and also what he knew of Conner over these few days?

He seemed to read Conner's many expressions because he said, "Like I said, I listen a lot. After listening to a lot of people talk, you make these observations much more easily."

Conner nodded. He was still a bit dazed with the information he had received over the past five minutes about his own life that he had never previously realized. "I think instead of a chair here, you should have had a long couch, and I should be lying down on it," he said, only half-joking.

The Father laughed. "I have a small one in my quarters; if you think that you would be more comfortable there, we can move there." Conner didn't know if he was serious or not, so he shook his head, at which Father laughed even more. Within moments he was serious again.

The Father then leaned closer and said, "Now listen, Conner. Even though you don't seem the type to let people in, you seem like the type who has listened to people, so I suspect you would be able to make these observations in others fairly accurately. Am I right?"

Conner nodded. Right, again.

"I want you to talk to some of the townspeople."

Conner's eyes widened. "Umm, I really don't know any of them. I'm practically a stranger. Why would they listen to me?"

"Did I say they have to listen to you?" Father settled back in his chair. "Like I've been saying all this while, you have to listen to *them*. And if they look like they're ready to listen to you, *then* you talk. You need to build a relationship with them. Only then will you be able to follow the path of Natis."

Conner's brow furrowed. "This thing you said I have to do...do you have any idea what it is?"

A hint of a smile played on the Father's lips. "All will be revealed to you in time, my child." He paused. "You haven't really asked about the religion surrounding the God that has chosen you for His great work, you know."

"Yes, I can't believe I haven't! I intended to, but I suppose I forgot in everything else going on." He had already gotten the basics from Victoria, but it wouldn't hurt hearing it again.

Father smiled. "No matter. I shall tell you. There is only one God, Natis; we have to desist from worshipping other Gods or even false idols. Natis is all around us, in every pore, every fibre of our beings; we just have to look for Him. One of the main beliefs is protection and love of the community, which is one of the reasons I want you to talk to the townspeople, let them trust you."

He leaned closer. "I have a feeling you weren't properly introduced to religion. When you say that your prayers were not answered, I don't think they weren't. I just think that you didn't see the signs. But that doesn't matter now. You can start your new religious life afresh here, by converting to Natism. Maybe the fact that you didn't follow any religion is a good thing, because now you can fully commit to this one."

Conner remembered the promise he had made before he made the decision that saved the dying man, Jon. It was time to believe again. He looked the Father in the eye, took a deep breath and nodded. "I will convert."

****

Conner sat alone. The Father had seemed pleased, though not surprised, by his decision. He had left the room to allow Conner a few minutes to compose himself before the first person came in. Conner waited with nervous anticipation. Then there was a knock on the door. He looked at it, not knowing what to do. He finally got up and opened it.

There was a young girl standing outside, looking up at Conner expectantly. She looked familiar. She had sandy hair, blue eyes, was of average height and weight, and appeared to have a cheerful disposition. He invited her inside. She smiled at him with what looked like...gratitude, and sat down on the north chair...the chair he had been sitting on. He hesitated, and then sat on the south chair, where the Father had earlier sat.

As soon as he sat down, the girl started speaking fast. "Hello, I don't know if you remember me, but I want to thank you deeply, from the bottom of my heart. Without you, my father might not have been alive today." Conner now remembered her. She was Jon Peck's daughter.

She shook her head. "Where are my manners? I haven't even introduced myself." She extended her hand. "I'm Lindsey Peck."

Conner nodded. "I remember who you are. I'm pretty sure at this point I don't need an introduction," he said with a small smile at the repeated joke.

Lindsey laughed and nodded.

Conner didn't know how to start. He asked slowly, "So, Lindsey... how's your father?"

She smiled and said, "He's much better now, thanks to you."

Then there was silence for a minute or two. Was he supposed to talk about specific topics? She was looking at him expectantly, as if she expected him to say anything. He looked at her face and realized that she would probably help him, seeing how grateful she was to him. So he decided to be direct with her. "Look, Lindsey, I'm going to be honest. I don't know what I'm supposed to do here. Father told me to talk, but I'm not really good at small talk. So can you tell me what exactly happens when you're here? It would be a great help. Please?" he said almost pleadingly.

She cheered up. "Don't worry. I'll help you. I probably owe you more than I can ever repay you." She looked emotional for a second, and then her expression turned thoughtful. There was silence for a minute or two before she said, "Look, you seem like a nice person, so you shouldn't have a hard time talking to people. You have to make them feel comfortable with you, because you're technically an outsider, but you need to show them you can be a part of their life. You need to let them connect with *you*, maybe by telling them some stories. Then encourage them to talk about their lives, first smaller things, and then bigger things. Ask them about their families, lives...understand them. Basically pay attention to what they're saying and try and *empathize* with them. Then show them that you understand."

Conner absorbed all of this, thought for a few seconds, then nodded. "You're a smart girl."

She smiled. "Nah, I just love psychology."

"At any rate, thanks for your help." He paused, unsure of whether to continue. Then he did so anyway. "And I'm not really sure that I helped your father by means of any divine blessing or anything, in spite of what it seems or what the Father says. I just did what I felt was right, and I'm glad that I did so because now he's okay."

She blinked. Then her face softened and she said, "I know it's difficult to accept, but you *are* blessed. I know what would have happened if you hadn't been there. My mother and I would have decided to give him a peaceful send off, if we really had to choose. The doctor's medicine almost never defeats that damned disease. It changes so rapidly, we can never seem to analyze it fast enough to develop a cure for it. But you decided to save him, and he was saved. And that made all the difference."

✱✱✱✱✱▲▲

The Father smiled. This was going exactly as he had expected. Conner had asked for help from a grateful Lindsey, who was willing to give it. Conner had said that he was not blessed, and he was clueless about what to do in the town, yet coming across as honest and humble while saying all this.

But how was the astute Father Godfrey able to listen to all of this? Well, the common wall between Godfrey's room and the room where Conner and Lindsay were seated had a section that allowed Father Godfrey to listen and see everything that was happening through strategically placed holes in the wall that could only be seen if someone was looking for it. They could also be covered up when they were not being used. Traditionally, they were used by the apprentice of the then-Father, who would use it to view the sessions, and see how delicate situations and personal problems were handled. Thus when they took the head position, they would be able to know the history of the person in question.

But, they were also used for other purposes. For example, when the priest wanted a dispute resolved, he would call the parties involved in and then have them talk it out in the room. Thus, he would know what their progress was. The Father's bedroom was simply furnished, with a bed, dresser and a few chairs. However, it was placed in such a way that it was easy to listen in on the conversations in the next room without getting too uncomfortable.

The "Room of Secrets" didn't keep too many secrets to itself after all.

Now he decided it was time to make a supposedly random appearance. He got up and opened the door leading into the small room. Conner looked startled to see him appear so suddenly; Lindsey didn't show surprise. "How is it going?" the Father asked cordially.

"It's Going well," said Conner with a small smile.

"If you're done with Lindsey, I think we can bring the next person in."

Conner looked at Lindsey expectantly. She shook her head, smiled, got up and extended her hand to Conner. Conner also stood, shook it and thanked her. She said, "No, thank *you!*" And then walked out.

"That seemed to have gone well," said Godfrey with a smile.

Conner nodded wordlessly. Godfrey went back to his quarters, still smiling. He was sure that Lindsey, being the social girl that she was, would tell everyone what a nice, humble, honest and trustworthy person Conner was, and people would believe her, making it easier for them to trust Conner. That would certainly help him, which had been the Father's intention all along.

And it did. Conner started gaining confidence with each person, talking to them more easily, sharing his life, laughing when a joke was made, serious when he had to be. The people also seemed to trust him more easily. None of them spoke about the intimate details of their life, but they were certainly taking to him. It helped that everyone in the town was a devout follower of Natism and they listened to what the priest told them, which, in this case, was that Conner was blessed and should be trusted. And he had proved that by saving Jon's life.

Finally the Father told Conner, "Last person, Conner. You're making progress. They really seem to like you."

Conner smiled and nodded. He was feeling much more confident himself. Every time he gave even a simple piece of advice to one of the townspeople, he believed that it would work. And Conner White believing in himself was itself a miracle, and it was slowly being achieved. Maybe he really was blessed.

Then the door opened and Conner turned to see Victoria walking in. She entered and took a seat and so did Conner. He looked at her and said, "I was wondering when I would see you again. Haven't spoken to you since..."

"Since you saved Mr. Peck's life?" completed Victoria. "Yes, I'm not likely to forget that." And although Victoria smiled, it seemed to Conner that it was an extremely forced and nervous smile. Although Conner didn't know it, Victoria *was* nervous. All the while that Conner was introspecting, she was having her own internal debate.

She looked across at the man sitting there. She knew there was something about Conner, and when that ray or light had shone on Conner, she had realized that it was a message from Natis, for *her*. He was showing her the way. Could it have been a coincidence that the first person she was really starting to have a connection with, however small, was somebody who was blessed?

She had been wondering if this day would ever come. Maybe this was just an excuse to unload on someone who had less chances of ruining her life with the information since he didn't know anybody around here. In any case, she was ready. Victoria's thoughts were interrupted by Conner's words. Her head snapped up to see him with a wary smile on his face.

"I'll repeat myself, since you obviously weren't listening. Is there any reason you've not spoken to me? Aren't people supposed to stay *more* around blessed men?"

Victoria said with a serious face, "Conner, I had a hard time processing the fact. I didn't know what to do, how to behave around you, or anything. I thought maybe I might be distracting you from what you were meant to do, or... I don't know..." She gave a frustrated shrug.

Conner smiled tenderly and said, "You're just being stupid. I'm still the same person, and you're not a distraction; you're an asset. I wouldn't have had the courage to go out and discover the town or its people by myself; you helped me do that, so thank you. Stop worrying." He paused while she nodded gratefully. "Now, is there anything you want to talk about?"

Victoria hesitated for a second, and then nodded. She lowered her voice and leaned closer, which helped Conner hear the tremble and sharp edge her voice had acquired. "Well, that was the real reason I didn't talk to you. I was deciding on whether to talk to you about a few things; but I don't feel comfortable discussing them here. I'll explain later. Is it okay if I come to your room and talk about it later?"

Conner seemed surprised, but nodded. "Of course you can."

She smiled that nervous, hesitant smile and stood up. "It was nice seeing you again, Conner. See you later."

"Same here. See you."

She quickly walked out. The priest walked in a few seconds later. "Well, that seemed short."

Conner nodded, making no comment.

"Well," said Godfrey, "I think it's confirmed. I shall convert you to Natism tomorrow in a special ceremony."

Conner stood up. For once, he felt like he was ready.

Chapter 11

Drunk and Damaged

Conner sat in his room, wondering how to pass the time. He wasn't really in the mood for writing, and he had three hours to kill before Victoria was expected to arrive. She had the day off and was going to tell her parents that she was going to be out with friends, so they could expect her to return late. Conner remembered the nervous, almost scared look on her face when she had been talking to him in the Room of Secrets. He assumed that she was going to tell him what had been bothering her, because it was pretty evident that there was some underlying turmoil. But what could she say here that she couldn't say in what was probably the safest room in the whole town?

The Father had said his ceremony was at about 7 the next morning, before the regularly scheduled Sunday sermon. It was to be pretty simple, and Conner was not as nervous as he would have been before. He was improving. Sophie would be happy. He looked up to Heaven and smiled. He also offered a silent prayer to Natis. Then his thoughts went to his present problem of what to do. Suddenly he remembered what Victoria had told him about the secret history books, which intrigued him. But they were at the university nearby which was...Megan and Samantha's university.

He wanted to research the history of the town, especially the history of this disease that had ruled the lives of the townspeople. And of the religion that seemed so simple and beautiful, yet had somehow not been able to spread to other places. He had a feeling that he would get more out of the hidden books rather than the ones easily available. He decided he would try to avoid the girls.

While on the way, he called Victoria and asked her to tell him the quickest way to the university. She informed him about the train that could get him there. He thanked her, confirmed that she was still coming over and headed towards the station. Her voice still sounded terrible. He managed to find the train and avoid inquisitive eyes and questions fairly easily. He also got into the library without much hassle. The librarian, however, was another case entirely.

She was a middle-aged woman whose spectacles seemed to only magnify the stern look that only the caretakers of books manage to muster. As soon as Conner mentioned the word "Levion" and asked about history books, she clammed up fast. She drew herself up straighter and told Conner that she had no idea what he was talking about. Conner pressed harder, and it took some time before she conceded that those books existed, but were specially protected, and Conner was not allowed access to them.

Conner realized that this was getting nowhere. He nodded and stepped back out of earshot. Then he made a call, got a number and then dialled it. When the dean of the university heard who was calling, he jumped. Conner explained that he needed some books for research purposes and told him that he was also considering a sizable donation to the university. Within minutes of hanging up, the library phone rang.

Conner couldn't hear most of the discussion that the librarian subsequently had, but he could see that it was pretty heated. The librarian slammed down the phone at the end of the conversation and walked off. Fifteen minutes later, she returned with two books that she handed to Conner. All she said was, "You better not damage these," though from her eyes it was clear that she wanted to say a lot more.

As Conner was walking away, she dialled another number.

****

As Conner put the books in his backpack, he wondered why these books were such a big secret. He resolved to find out. He decided that since he had time before he had to meet Victoria, he would get some supplies and then head back to town. When he was done, he returned to town and was in his room soon after.

He decided that he shouldn't keep these books out in the open. Just as he had finished putting them away, there was a knock on his door. He opened it; Victoria stood outside. She was wearing a red blouse and denim shorts. He invited her in. She smiled lopsidedly and walked in. Or more like staggered in.

Conner seemed surprised by this. "Are you drunk?"

She ignored this question, closed her eyes for a few seconds and seemed better, if only slightly. She had a strange look in her eyes. "Sit down," she said. "I'm going to show you what skills I have for the job I'm considering."

Conner thought this request was strange, but he complied. Then Victoria stared at him, as if pondering on her next move. Then she went up to him, and spread his legs slightly apart. He looked up at her in confusion and started to protest but she put a finger to his lips.

She then proceeded to turn around and bend. She waited there for a few seconds, before she sat down on his lap and said, "Mmm. You like this, don't you?"

Conner was stunned; he got up immediately, which resulted in Victoria getting pushed a little distance away and slamming into the table, where she fell to her knees. Instead of appearing to be hurt, she looked up and there was an almost...grateful look in her eyes. She said in a soft, almost pleading voice, "Yes, hurt me, please, I deserve it."

"Victoria!" Conner said forcefully. "What job is this? Why should I hurt you? What are you talking about?"

Victoria's eyes opened wide, as if she was immensely shocked. Conner hoped that it meant she was coming back to her senses when she said softly again, almost whispering, "You mean you don't see it? I always thought it was obvious."

Conner started edging closer to her. Something was going on in Victoria's head, and from the look in her eyes, it wasn't good. "See what?" he said, talking as softly as her.

She looked up at him and her eyes were wide. "Why, that I'm a slut," she said as if it was the most obvious thing in the world, but Conner could hear a slight hysterical edge to it.

Conner stopped moving for a second before he said, "No, you're not a slut, Victoria. Why do you think you're one?"

Victoria looked up at him again with those eyes that were open so wide, they were almost maniacal. Her voice had a matter-of-fact tone, but Conner could hear the hysterical edge sharpening, "Well, because he told me. And I can see it in people's eyes and when I look in the mirror - one big slut." She paused and said, "Hey, I just said big slut! But sluts can't be fat!" and then she burst into hysterical laughter.

Conner waited for a few seconds. She stopped laughing, and her eyes seemed to return to their wide-eyed, seemingly placid quality. "Who's he?" Conner asked slowly. He was almost next to her.

Victoria looked at him as if he wasn't there. She muttered, "He-he told me," before she started muttering something else which Conner couldn't quite catch.

"Okay Victoria, here's what we're going to do," said Conner in a calm, soothing voice. He reached out to put his hand on her arm and continued, "We're going to-"

But his words were cut off. As soon as he touched Victoria's arm, it was as if an electric current coursed through her. She yanked her arm away and took a step back. Her face was full of horror. She looked at Conner's face and the terror on her face deepened. She opened her mouth wide, as if to scream, but it was as if she had lost her voice. Then she clamped her mouth shut, and it was as if she was struggling to keep it closed. Then she squeezed her eyes shut, and her mouth opened again in a silent scream.

Then suddenly her eyes relaxed and her mouth closed. She crumpled to the floor before Conner could catch her.

****

The first thing Victoria was conscious of was the throbbing.

It took her a few moments to process where the throbbing was coming from. It was her head. As soon as she figured this, she also realized that there was something cold in that same area. She couldn't see what it was because it was completely dark. She wanted to move her arms to touch it, but her arms didn't seem to be moving. She tried to feel the rest of her body, and everything seemed to be in place.

She suddenly realized that it was dark because her eyes were shut. But she didn't want to open them. She wanted to first figure out where she was. Her memory was a haze. She remembered seeing Conner, and then, out of nowhere, another memory popped up.

Her eyes flew open and all her limbs suddenly seemed to be back in full functioning order. Her mind urged her to move, but Conner had anticipated this. He had set up a bright table lamp shining right onto her face, so as soon as Victoria had opened her eyes, she was temporarily blinded.

Conner had been watching her since she had blacked out. He hoped that when she opened her eyes and was blinded by the bright light, she would be distracted from whatever she was thinking of. But the panicked look on her face did not disappear. As soon as her eyes adjusted to the light, she lifted her head quickly, making the ice-pack he had applied there go flying.

Conner took hold of the bottle of water he had kept ready, and threw the water on Victoria's face.

It worked. One minute Victoria was about to run, the next she was standing shocked near Conner's bed with water dripping down her hair.

"Are you all right?" Conner asked unsurely. It was a stupid question, thought Victoria as she tried to comprehend everything that had happened. But she nodded dumbly, because she knew what he was trying to say.

Conner didn't seem to believe it, but for stupid questions you get stupid answers. Victoria collapsed onto the bed, which brought Conner to her side immediately. She raised a hand and said, "Just suddenly feeling tired. That's all," she said in short bursts, taking deep gulps of air in between. Suddenly she turned pale and started hyperventilating.

Conner immediately gave her the bottle of water and some snacks he had kept aside. She accepted the water but refused the food. Conner decided that he would try later. Victoria's breathing improved a little after she drank the water.

They looked at each other for a few seconds before Conner started, "Victoria..."

Victoria put a tired hand up again to stop him. She tried to sit up a bit straighter, but slumped back down. Frustrated, she tried to bang her hand down, but found she didn't have the strength for that. She gave up and said, "Conner, I know what you saw is bad, and I'm going to leave. Just let me get my stre-"

But Conner interrupted her, "Shut up, Victoria."

Victoria stared at him. He continued, "Shut up. I don't want you to leave. What I saw may have been bad, but that doesn't mean I'm going to just abandon you! You can stay here for as long as you want, and talk about whatever you want."

Victoria started to argue, albeit weakly, before Conner said firmly, "No, Victoria, you are not leaving until I think you're well enough."

Victoria seemed to reluctantly accept this and slumped back. Conner got up and gave her another pillow to prop herself against.

"Sit, please," she said to Conner who was standing over her like a watchful sentry. He shook his head stonily. "Please, it'll be easier for me," she pleaded.

Conner stood for a few more seconds before he reluctantly perched on the side table, keeping an eye on her.

Victoria studied him. He seemed genuinely concerned about her, even after seeing all that she did. Could it be that he actually cared?

Her thoughts were interrupted by Conner. "Did you know that you were going to react this way? Is that why you didn't do this at the Sinome?"

Victoria shuddered. She slowly said, "I didn't know what was going to happen. I... I lost control." She curled her legs up so that her knees touched her chin, her hands clenched around the legs, keeping them in place, and she assumed a faraway expression. "I started thinking, so I snuck out from home and started drinking. I managed to stop myself in time to come here, and trust me, it wasn't easy." She shuddered again. "I had planned in my head everything I was going to do, and the alcohol gave me the strength to do it."

Conner looked at this girl who was sitting in a foetal position with her eyes staring off into space and wondered if he had understood right. "So," he began slowly, "You wanted to do this all along?"

Victoria looked at him; there was a cold, defeated look in her eyes. "Of course I did," she said in a deadpan voice. "I told you, I'm a slut. You can't change who you are."

This delivery of words in calm tones was somehow much scarier to Conner than her wild proclamations could ever have been. Suddenly she repeated again, "I'm a slut," and she started trembling. Conner tensed, ready for her to lose it again when she put her head between her knees and breasts and started sobbing. Conner didn't do anything, remembering what had happened the last time he touched her. Her sobs intensified, and suddenly she started hyperventilating again. Conner grabbed another bottle and threw some more water on her. This time, it seemed to only stop her hyperventilation a little, and he gave her the water to drink.

Conner stared at her, trying to figure out what could have happened. Then he thought of everything she had done. Something inside him clicked and before he could stop himself he asked, his voice full of shock, "Victoria, were you raped?"

Chapter 12

Victoria's Secret

Victoria stared at Conner, her face blank. As soon as Conner said that, it was as if her mind went dark. She was paralyzed, her body and thoughts refused to cooperate. Out of the black haze came a single thought.

He figured it out.

And then, *He knows.*

The single thought seemed to multiply in her head, until it was like a thousand different voices whispering, *He knows,* over and over, louder and louder. She clenched her eyes shut, doing her hardest to drown out the voices. After about half a minute, she succeeded. But then something much, much worse came to the surface. She could hear footsteps, a face emerging in the dim light. *NO! Not that!* she screamed internally and started trying to block that image. Her mind seemed to accept her plea because the next minute everything went black.

****

After an indeterminable amount of time, her eyes suddenly opened after she felt some force on her cheek. She blinked and tried to recollect where she was. Her face felt wet and she was still on Conner's bed, fully clothed. Her head was lolling to the side; she straightened it. "Did I black out?" she mumbled. Her hands had unclasped and she was out of her foetal position.

Conner said worriedly, "Yes, you did. For about five minutes. Sprinkling water didn't wake you up, so I had to administer some light slaps. I'm sorry, but I didn't know what would happen if I let you stay unconscious."

Victoria nodded slowly. "It's alright," she said with a weak smile. She tried to straighten herself up, but failed yet again.

Goddamnit! I need to get out!

"Do you want something to eat? It'll make you feel better," Conner asked, pushing some fruit her way.

To his surprise, Victoria didn't object. *This will give me strength.* She had a few bites of the apple and felt a bit better.

Then she swung her legs off the bed and got up shakily.

Conner stood too, startled. "Where are you going? You can't go anywhere in this state!"

"I can't stay here," she mumbled. She started walking, taking support of the bed as she did. Conner went past her and stood in front of her. "You can't, Victoria," he said firmly.

"Why?" said Victoria. "You suddenly decided you want me too, because you know I'm an easy target?" She stepped back, and her face took the expression of a caged animal. She put her hand into her back pocket and took out a switchblade, which she then pointed in Conner's direction. "No, I don't want to be molested again."

But you're a slut. Drop the knife. You deserve it.

"Maybe I do." She lowered the knife. "Maybe I do deserve it."

Conner had taken a step back and raised his hands when Victoria brought out the knife; this reaction had gone unnoticed by her. Now he stepped forward and said slowly, "Victoria, listen to me. I'm not going to molest you. I'm not going to do anything to you. Please put the knife down. You don't deserve it. You're a great girl and-"

"Lies!" she said, bringing the knife up again. "I'm scum! You just found out I was molested! I'm dirty and disgusting! How are you even standing in the same space as me?"

This time, Conner didn't step back. He stood his ground and looked Victoria straight in the eye. He said, "Victoria, I'm not going to molest you." He paused to let the effect sink in and to let Victoria see that he was sincere. Then he said, "You're not disgusting. You're not scum. You're not dirty. You are beautiful. Since the moment I met you, that's all I've thought - you are beautiful. Definitely *not* a slut. And the fact that you were molested *does NOT* make you one."

Victoria looked at Conner. In his face, in his eyes, she didn't find deceit, ulterior motives, lust or hate. She found simple truth. As much as she tried to tell herself otherwise, Conner was being honest with her. He didn't want to molest her, nor was he disgusted by her. In a way, this was more draining than any pass or attempt he would have made. Did that mean that everything she had forced herself to accept was false?

No, it couldn't be. She looked at him and said, "Ar...Are you stupid?"

Conner gave her a small smile and said, "No, I'm not stupid."

"You...you must be," she muttered. However, something inside her, a voice long lost was telling her that he wasn't stupid at all. All the newfound energy seemed to drain once again out of Victoria. She slumped back onto the bed, her head in her hands. Conner sat down on the bed as well, a little distance away from her.

She looked up at him and there were tears rolling down her cheeks. "Then what am I, Conner? What do I believe?" The tears came faster now. "Why me, Conner? Why me?" She put her head back in her hands and sobbed harder. She didn't care if she was crying in front of a stranger, exposing her rawest emotions; in that moment, she didn't care much about anything at all.

Conner edged slowly towards her, waiting to see if there was any reaction from her. Soon he was close to her. He waited a few minutes to let her cry it out and then gingerly pulled her left hand away from her head. Then he took the right hand away. He lifted her chin from her chest and with the other hand gently wiped away the tears.

"Victoria, don't cry," he said tenderly. "You're safe here. Nothing can hurt you. Stop." He waited a few seconds while the crying decreased and she simply looked at him, a few tears still rolling down her cheeks.

"Victoria, have you ever told anyone what happened to you?"

She shook her head, never taking her eyes off him.

"Do you want to tell me? Nothing will happen to you here."

Victoria blinked. *That's never been an option before. Anyone would have been revolted and never spoken to me again, yet here is somebody, a man on top of that, who isn't. Shall I tell him?* She paused. *He's seen so much and yet he still wants to know. What is wrong with him? Is he getting off on this?* Victoria considered Conner again. *No, he still seems sincere.*

"Conner, if I start talking about it, I don't know what will happen, how I will react. I don't know if you'll be able to handle that, or if I will, for that matter. So are you sure you want to do this?"

Conner nodded without hesitation.

Victoria looked at him, getting a bit frustrated. *What is his damn motive?*

"Why are you doing this?" she asked bluntly. "What are you getting out of this? You could have just put me to sleep, kicked me out, called Mrs. Stewart, anything." She shuddered and then muttered, "Or worse."

"Because I care, Victoria, no matter how foreign that idea seems to you. I don't want to see you this way; I want to help you."

Victoria sighed. *He doesn't look like he's lying. Does he ever?* she wondered. Then she closed her eyes and made a decision. Conner knew enough already; there was no sense in hiding the whole thing. And in spite of all this rationalisation, Victoria knew that she was just aching to get this terrible burden off her chest.

She nodded. She took a deep breath. Conner could see she was still uncertain, so he took both her hands in his and squeezed gently. He said, "If you feel agitated or upset, squeeze my hands. And don't worry, squeeze as hard and as long as you want. I won't get hurt, don't worry."

Victoria looked uncertainly down at her hands. She squeezed Conner's hands hard for a few seconds before she stopped. He hadn't flinched and she felt better, albeit a little. She took another deep breath, collected her thoughts and started.

****

The sky was blue and calm; there was not a single cloud that day. There is this event that is held in Baronsville every year. It's kind of fun, and since we're not allowed out of town, I snuck out there, claiming I was going for a walk. I was wearing a black top and shorts. I was enjoying myself. The breeze was nice; I could see the beauty in so much. I wish that trait had not soon disappeared after.

It was getting dark, and I needed to get home. It was the last event of the day; a local band was playing on stage. There was cheering and I was having a good time. Suddenly I felt someone smack my ass. I turned but there were a lot of people moving around, and no one seemed to be paying particular attention to me, so I let it go, assuming that it was someone who had done it by mistake while passing.

Still, my good mood evaporated after that and I decided I didn't want to stay any longer. I started moving out. I needed to get to the train station. If I didn't get home in time, my parents would have been furious, so I started walking down the shortcut there, an alleyway.

The sun had set, so it was dark. The moon was not bright, and there was a little bit of ambient light. The smell was musty and dank. I could hear my feet crunching when I stepped on an old can or plastic. I was walking fast when I heard a noise behind me. I stopped. I turned; I figured it was a cat or a rat. I didn't see anything, but it did turn out to be a rodent, a rat of the worst kind.

As I started walking again, I suddenly heard a noise again. Before I could turn I felt pressure on my left buttock; someone was squeezing it.

I turned quickly, but it seemed like I was helped in that. The pressure shifted to the right buttock and there came a pressure on my back, pushing me forward.

And then I saw something *that was trying to look human, wearing a grey T-shirt and jeans. But it was his face - the face of a demon, grinning maniacally at me. There was a short break in the tip of his nose and a small scar beneath his left eye. His skin was pale. His eyebrows were pencil-thin. But it was his eyes. They were dark, very dark, the colour of coal. It was what was in them that terrified me. It was a lustful, hungry look. His light pink lips opened and he spoke two words, "Hello slut."*

I tried pushing him away, tried moving away but he was strong and I couldn't get out of his grip. I opened my mouth to scream and that was when he leaned in and put his lips to mine.

His breath was not rancid; it smelled of mint, as if he had just popped a mouth freshener. I tried to move my head back, but his left hand moved from my back to my hair and pulled it. He continued to try to kiss me fiercely and his right hand squeezed harder. I bit his lip as hard as I could and tasted blood. He jerked his head back but his face was not angry. It was more aroused, in fact. His grip had loosened on me and I used the opportunity to lift my right foot and stamp his foot as hard as I could. This surprised him and he let go off me. I turned to run. But he wasn't done yet.

I had taken a few hasty steps before he came behind me and his hand grabbed hold of the bottom of my top and pulled. The top ripped, and I stumbled, which gave him time to catch up. He gave me a final smack on the ass before I could start running again. As I ran, he yelled, "You can run but you can't escape who you are, slut!"

The whole thing had taken all of five minutes.

I ran and ran. I must have run all the way back to the station and I don't know how long it took or how I managed it without getting run over; time was a blur. I got into whatever train was pulling into the station and went into the bathroom. I locked the door. That was when I crumpled to the floor and finally started crying.

****

When she finished, Victoria had a far-off look in her eyes. Unbidden, small tears started falling again. This time, though, she didn't cover her eyes, or move her head or faint; she didn't even seem to be aware of them. But Conner felt as if, in that moment, she was once more in that train bathroom, overwhelmed by emotion.

Victoria had recounted the story with much more composure than Conner thought she would have. She had come close to fainting twice, trembled and shook and slurred her words; but, all things considered, Conner still thought she had done better than he would have if he was in her position telling such a traumatic story. Maybe finally getting it off her chest had encouraged her. And maybe, just maybe, almost crushing Conner's hand had helped her through it.

He waited a few minutes, before he softly said, "Victoria."

She didn't seem to have heard him. He said her name louder but when she still didn't reply, he shook her hands and she seemed startled. She shook her head and let go off Conner's hands and started wiping her cheeks. Conner stretched his fingers, trying to avoid showing the pain he was in. She looked down and saw his red hands and started. "I'm sorry!" she exclaimed. She picked up the now-melting ice-pack and applied it to his hands. "You must be in pain."

He took the ice pack from her and said, "Not as much as you."

Victoria didn't say anything, absently touching the ice-pack.

"I'm sorry, Victoria."

"Why? Did you molest anyone?" Victoria looked at him and asked him in a hollow, almost accusing tone.

Conner shook his head quickly. "No, no! Of course not! I'm just-"

"Then don't be sorry. You are the nicest person I've met. Th-" She looked up and her throat caught. This time, Conner knew it was out of happiness and not torment. "Thank you, Conner. For listening, for not treating me like an outcast, like trash."

Conner smiled and said, "Even if they knew, Victoria, I'm sure none of them would treat you like an outcast."

The pained expression returned to Victoria's face. "Please, Conner. You don't know what it's like to be in my position, what I've gone through. So please don't try to act like you know."

Conner didn't say anything. There was a minute of silence before Victoria said, "I told you something about myself that I've never told anyone before. Tell me something about yourself, at least."

Conner nodded, deciding that Victoria deserved to know the truth. He started slowly, "Well, Victoria, my real name is Conner White and I have a daughter, about your age. Her name is Megan and she's beautiful. The only reason I picked this town is because I have a country house close by." He paused and then started slowly, "And the truth is that I'm not only here to get over my wife's death. I...I'm an author. I've made some mistakes in my life and I don't know how, but I need to correct them. I'm hoping to find an answer here."

Victoria's face was expressionless. "What exactly did you do?"

Conner hesitated, unsure whether to tell her this. "Because of me, people have died."

Victoria continued to look blank. Then she slowly got up. "Where are you going?" Conner asked her, getting up too.

"So even you aren't who you said you were, in the end," she said softly.

Conner's eyes widened. "No, Victoria, it isn't that way!"

Victoria interrupted him. "Conner, I can't process anything more." She started walking towards the door. Conner followed her. "I don't know if I can talk about the rest right now."

Conner froze. "The rest?" he asked, almost wishing that she didn't answer.

She stopped and turned to him with a small smile that had no mirth in it. "You really thought that was all? Don't worry, there's more. There's a lot more."

Conner didn't know what to say. She turned to leave and he said, "Will you be able to get home safely in this state?"

"I've been in this state for a long time, Conner. One more night won't make a difference," she said without turning around while she walked out.

Conner stared at the closed door for a few seconds. *What more could there be?* He threw the ice-pack on the floor, finally tearing it and letting the ice cubes skitter across the floor, and then slammed his hand against the wall in frustration, forgetting that he probably had a broken bone or two in it. He cried out in pain and cursing, set off to bed though he knew he wouldn't sleep. But he had to try. After all, he had a big day tomorrow.

Victoria might have had a lot left to tell Conner, but neither of them had any idea that a lot more was going to happen to Conner soon enough.

****

Conner surveyed himself for the umpteenth time that morning. He had worn his best clothes even though Father had said there was no need for any special clothes. He was in the Room of Secrets, waiting. The ceremony was about to start in a few minutes. Memories of last night still swirled in his head, and he tried to push them aside, but that was impossible, of course. Victoria had texted him saying she had reached home, but he didn't reply. What was there to say?

Now Father poked his head in the room and told him it was time to come out. Conner took a deep breath and stepped out.

He was greeted with a torrent of noise that seemed to stop as soon people saw him. Then a few started cheering and soon all of them did. Conner was surprised at this reaction, but he smiled and continued onto the platform. The cheering stopped after a minute or two and Conner started scanning the filled pews. He spotted Rosaline and Mayor Frank, along with what looked like their kids. He saw Dr. Clark, who seemed to be as impassive as ever. He spotted Victoria with her family. She saw him looking at her, and she looked at her feet. He looked away as well. The whole town seemed to be here.

He also spotted one woman who seemed to be the only one not happy to be here. She looked like she was glaring at Conner. Conner had never seen her before in his life, and had no idea why she looked so angry. He shrugged and moved on.

Soon the Father raised his hand and everyone quietened down. He started, "Here we are today to convert Conner Fry to Natism and recognize him in his role as High Natish!" Everyone started clapping. Almost everyone, that is. Conner noticed that the angry woman wasn't clapping. She was still staring at him. Something wasn't right. The Father continued, but Conner wasn't listening.

Suddenly the woman got up. The Father stopped in surprise and everyone turned to her. The Father said something to her, but Conner wasn't listening to him. She didn't seem to be listening either.

She pointed a finger dead straight at Conner and said, "That man can never be a Natish, much less a High Natish!" she proclaimed in a stony voice.

Everyone started murmuring. Conner had a sinking feeling in the pit of his stomach. Something was going to go wrong. He could feel it. His newfound confidence was slipping away.

Again the Father said something that Conner didn't hear. The woman continued, "That man is a fraud! He is not who he claims to be! He is Conner White, the author!"

The mumbling grew louder. Conner couldn't take his eyes off the woman. The sinking feeling kept growing. This was not good. He wanted to ponder how this woman knew, what reply to give, but he couldn't. His brain was shutting down. Everything else around him disappeared apart from that woman and her angry, angry glare that seemed to be burning a hole in his head.

The woman was speaking again. "He is also a murderer. Because of him, my only son is dead."

The whole room went silent of which Conner was unaware. All he heard was this strange buzzing. His legs felt like paper, but he was still standing. He wished he had sunk into the ground, though, because it would certainly be better than standing here, staring at the mother whose life he had utterly destroyed.

Chapter 13

Secrets Discovered

Half a minute had passed. The room was still quiet. People were staring at Conner, trying to figure out if this claim was true. Conner couldn't bear to look up, though he knew they were staring. It felt as if their stares had glued him to his place, not allowing him to move. The sinking feeling had stopped somewhat, but now he just felt frozen and he could feel a sudden wave of hatred coming his way, as if he had dropped his pants and started urinating on the altar.

Suddenly whispering and murmuring broke out. Conner's mind said, "Run!" but his body refused to accept. Finally the soft chatter was broken by the sobs of a woman. Conner finally looked up to find the mother crying. Everyone was looking towards her. "One of the women went to comfort her and asked, "What are you talking about, Nancy? How did this man murder Roger?"

At the mention of her son's name, Nancy sobbed harder. Then she looked as if she was controlling herself. She wiped away her tears and said, "I never told anyone. My son didn't die in a car accident. He committed suicide! He hung himself!" She started sobbing again. She pointed at Conner and said, "This man was the one responsible! My son was reading the books that he wrote! And my son believed what he had to say. He believed that life was worthless, and so he threw it away! He THREW IT AWAY!" She stepped forward, her voice thick with venom rolling around on her tongue. "Because of him. Conner White."

Everybody turned to look at him again. This time Conner looked back.

Rosaline was standing there, expressionless. Her husband had a look that said, "I knew it!"

Father Godfrey had a mixture of shock, regret and horror on his face. Maybe he hadn't read Natis' signs right after all. Dr. Clark's face was stony, and he was looking at the Father. Lindsey looked as if she couldn't believe what she was hearing, or that she didn't want to believe.

But the worst was Victoria. She was standing open-mouthed with shock, horror and terror in her eyes. *She must be feeling so betrayed after putting so much trust in me*, thought Conner. *I did tell her, but finding out that it was someone she knew, maybe even was a friend of hers, is taking it to a different level.* He looked at her; he wanted to yell out something to her, anything. But his mouth didn't move. He just prayed that his look would convey his sorrow and regret.

A voice finally spoke out loud. It was the Father.

"Is all this true, Conner? Are you really an author? Do you really spread that much evil through your books that it caused a young man to commit suicide?"

There was silence, except for the quiet sobs of Nancy. She was the only one not looking up and expecting an answer because she already knew the answer. Conner didn't know what to say. Lying wouldn't help anymore. All it would do was make Nancy accuse him more fervently and the town would obviously believe her over him. He closed his eyes so as not to have to look at anyone as he whispered, "Yes."

There was stunned silence during which Conner opened his eyes and continued desperately, "I'm really trying to leave that part of my life behind, to change! Nothing like this will ever happen again."

The townspeople did not look as if they had really registered the last part. The murmurs and the whispers started again. A lot of people looked very angry, though most were shocked and confused. The man they had been about to proclaim a messenger of God had just turned into a murderer of one of their own.

In all the confusion, Nancy had stopped crying. She had started walking up to Conner and before anyone could do anything, she had brandished a knife.

Conner's survival instinct kicked into action as soon as he saw the knife. He jumped off the platform just as she climbed a step and came into stabbing range. In frustration, she threw the knife at him; she missed. By this time the townspeople had come forward and subdued Nancy, though they didn't look like they were doing it with too much enthusiasm.

Conner's limbs seemed fine now, having sprung into action so suddenly. Many people looked like they wished that the knife hadn't missed him; he decided to take advantage of his working body again and escape before they had a chance to go home and collect their pitchforks. He started scrambling through the crowd, aiming for gaps. He met no resistance, just stares. People seemed too confused to respond, for now, at least.

As soon as he was out of the Sinome, he started running. He ran fast and hard. This was not how it was supposed to be. He had changed, and his past was supposed to have been left behind. But Conner's past had caught up with him and in the form of a flying knife, no less.

He finally reached the inn. Mrs. Stewart was not at her front desk. There was a sign that said, "Gone to pray. Will be back at 9 or so. Thank you."

Conner rushed up the stairs to his room, taking two at a time. He opened his room door hastily, got inside and locked it behind him. He considered barricading the door, but he didn't know what to move against it. He decided he would just pack his bag quickly and leave. He started gathering up his stuff when there was a knock on the door.

They're here so quickly?

Conner didn't answer and instead started "packing": dumping his stuff into his bag as fast as possible. There was a knock on the door again and a voice said, "It's Mrs. Stewart. I have a key to this room, so you better open up. I've come alone, and I'm not going to hurt you."

Conner paused. She could open it anyway, so he grudgingly went to the door and opened it. Mrs. Stewart was panting slightly and looked a little red in the face, as if she had run or (more likely in her case) walked fast all the way here. She entered without invitation and locked the door behind her. She then strode to the centre of the room and fixed Conner with a hard gaze.

"Okay, so let's establish some things first. Your name is really Conner White?"

Conner nodded slowly, unsure of where this conversation was going.

"Were you really responsible for Roger's death?"

Conner put his head in his hands and said, "That's what I heard, that he had committed suicide because of what I had written. I wanted to make amends but couldn't find out where he was from; imagine coming to that very same place!" He looked up at her, "I'm as devastated over Roger's death as anyone here, maybe more because I was the one responsible for it. And I was a different person then. I believed in different things. I believed that life was bad, and I made others believe that it was. I hate myself for all that, but I'm really trying to fix it. I am." He looked at her imploringly, begging her with his eyes to believe him, to be the only person in town not to hate him.

"What made you want to change?" she asked, her face expressionless.

"My wife's death. She actually did die. And it was very painful and shook me up badly. Mrs. Stewart, I really want to change. I can't erase the mistakes of my past, but Sophie's passing has made me want to make my future better."

She looked at him for a few minutes, sizing him up, and then her gaze softened. She said, "You remind me of my husband a little. He wasn't the best husband in the world and made his fair share of mistakes. But I loved him, and I believe that if he was here today and I wasn't, he would be like you, struggling to change, finally doing the things that his loved ones told him all his life but which he never listened to. At least, I hope he would be." She nodded to herself. "Okay, you don't need to leave. You will be protected from anyone as long as you are in my inn, I promise you that. No one will dare say anything against me." She had a steely look in her eyes. "You have paid rent in advance, and you can stay for that full period of time if you wish to. Maybe you can find a way to prove to the town that you're a changed man." She paused, looked at him with a small smile and said, "Best of luck, Conner." With that, she walked out, leaving Conner staring after her.

****

Two hours passed. Conner had been tensed, his bag packed and ready to go. The blinds were drawn over the windows, but Conner glanced out at the town from time to time to see if there were signs of unusual activity. And though several times people had come into the inn, they had left looking even angrier than when they had come in. It seemed that Mrs. Stewart was living up to her word. Now that he was assured of his safety, for now, he sat down and let out a deep breath. *What am I going to do?* he thought. He couldn't stay at the inn forever. His phone was discarded to one side, switched off. If anything were to happen to him, he had no one to call. Was he being paranoid? After all, even in a town of close-knit folk, surely the maximum penalty they could give him would be to kick him out and ban him forever.

Then he remembered the way Nancy had attacked him with the knife, and feared that there would be fierce loyalty amongst the townspeople which might lead to similar attacks. So, the big question was: Should he risk it? And for what?

And what of being a High Natish? Was he actually one, or had Godfrey made a mistake? Why had Natis given him a chance to be part of their faith just to have it destroyed?

But the worst part was Victoria. What effect must this new revelation have on her? Her mental state was already fragile; what would this do to her, after pouring her heart out to him?

Conner realized that he needed to stay. If not for anybody else, if not for even himself, but for her. His newfound self-confidence was already evaporating, and the dark pit was opening its mouth hungrily, as if it knew this day would come and Conner would return to its clutches. Conner shuddered and composed himself. Now was not the time to break down. Now was the time to make decisions. He realized that if he had to redeem himself at any point in his life, this time and place was the best for it. He had to get rid of his past. If he could prove that he had changed to even that one grieving mother and to that one damaged girl, he would prove to be worthy to himself, if not to everyone else.

Now that Conner had decided to stay, he had to figure out what he was going to *do*. Mrs. Stewart would probably keep him safe, but how long would that last? Even if she protected him in his room for the whole month, that would be counter-productive. He had to get out of his room at some point. He needed a plan.

He couldn't hold it in any longer. He sat down on the couch, put his head in his hands and started to cry softly.

****

Conner wallowed in his misery for an hour before he finally regained control and stood up. He decided to try writing. That could possibly make him feel better. Then he remembered the two books he had gotten. In all the drama, he had forgotten about them. He decided he would read them after he wrote.

He extracted his journal from his hiding place. He had taken a blank sheet of paper and folded it around the written pages in such a way that it represented a bookmark, and only after it was completely unfolded and extracted could anyone see the written pages. He had shoved it into one of the books he had gotten and prayed that it wouldn't be found.

He read *The Dark Alley* again and the current untitled story he was writing. He didn't need to; he knew them by heart. He just did it for the comfort. Once he was done, he took a deep breath, picked up the pen and started writing, the ideas flowing into him already.

"Saint" Marvin was very confused. He had just saved a man's life even though it felt very unusual to him. Wasn't he supposed to have felt the sense of familiarity with saving people if he knew all about cures?

At any rate, people were praising him wherever he went. He had no money; nevertheless they gave him food and a place to stay. One of the people he had saved from dying had been the local innkeeper, and so he got a room at the inn. It was not impressive, but Marvin had a feeling that he had stayed in worse places. Anything more than vague feelings eluded him, though.

Suddenly there was a lot of noise coming from the square. Somebody yelled, "That's Saint Marvin!"

Marvin was curious to see what was going on. He set off towards the square. Everyone seemed to be gathered around a man who was holding a poster. Marvin went closer and saw that it was an artist's drawing of what seemed to be a picture of...him.

The man holding the poster suddenly saw Marvin and shouted, "That's him!" before producing a pistol and pointing it at Marvin.

"His name is not Marvin," sneered the man holding the pistol, who seemed to be a sheriff. "His name is Oscar Gibson. He's a mass murderer. Poisons people. Knows every kind of poison there is."

Marvin, or Oscar, suddenly had flashes of memory. People dying while he stood over them, watching his poison take effect. Tortured souls giving up all sorts of information, begging for an antidote.

"He was finally caught and was in the process of being transferred to a faraway prison when he found a way to disrupt the carriage's path. The

carriage driver and two guards were found gravely injured. He seemed to have been thrown somewhere, but we couldn't find him. And now we have."

Everybody turned to look at Marvin. All these images were slowly coming back to his mind. Someone said, "So that's how he knew how to cure us and is so well-versed with poisons."

At the sheriff's prompting, a pair of strong arms grabbed Marvin's arms. "When you didn't know who I was, you accepted me. Now that you've seen the bad I've done in the past, you forget all the good?" asked Marvin in a pleading voice.

Nobody seemed to be listening. Suddenly-

Conner paused. Now how was he supposed to get Marvin out of this situation? Conner thought. He couldn't have a mysterious poison on his person. There was no way the townspeople would release him. So he decided it was time for some divine intervention. He continued:

Suddenly there was a deep rumbling sound. The ground started trembling slowly. The trembling seemed to be coming closer to them. Someone shouted, "Earthquake!" and they all scattered, including Marvin, who took this opportunity to run.

Conner paused. This would be enough for today. He wasn't really satisfied with the last part. He wanted to write something that wouldn't involve a *deus ex machina*. A *deus ex machina* was a plot device in which a seemingly inextricable problem was suddenly abruptly solved by the unexpected intervention of a new character, event, ability or object i.e. Marvin suddenly getting a chance to escape by the unexpected yet fortuitous earthquake.

Conner decided he would think about it later. He decided to read the history of the town. Maybe if he understood their history, he would be able to better empathize with them. He was always a fast reader, and he settled down with the first book, which was entitled: *Levion, a History*.

Conner started reading. It was just a basic summary from the first surviving records of Levion to present day. The part before the

Great Fire was interesting in its own way, but it was the part *after* the raiders and the reconstruction that really interested him. That was when Natism had begun, when Levitis had started infecting people. As Victoria had said, Natism had started to spread, and Conner noticed how it was dwindling as time passed.

As Conner was reading, there was something troubling him at the back of his mind. It had to do with Levion's history, but he couldn't figure it out. He read the second book, and the feeling grew stronger. Conner finally figured out what it was. Something wasn't right.

He got a sheet of paper and started writing notes of whatever he could remember and what he had to check.

For most of the next two nights and days, Conner was hard at work. Writing down notes, re-reading parts of the book, piecing together whatever he could get.

He realized, however, that there were some gaps that he had to fill as much as he possibly could He gathered everything he didn't want found and left town quietly, promising Mrs. Stewart that he would be back, and called in his newspaper contacts in different towns, acquiring information, and searching through age-old obscure archives for clues. After four days of intensive research in which he called in several others to do the research with him, ensuring that nobody had all the pieces, he returned to his room in Levion and started piecing together the puzzle.

After he was done, Conner sat back. When he had started research and it was just a hunch in his head, he was scared.

Now that he had confirmed his suspicions, he was terrified.

Chapter 14

Deus Ex Machina

Conner looked down at the final summary that rested in his hands. After research, reading and logical completion of the gaps in information he felt were purposely there, it was done. He had reached a horrible conclusion that he desperately wished wasn't true.

He lay down and looked at the ceiling, feeling giddy. He calmed himself. He needed to be sure. It was evening by now. He looked at his phone. No calls, not even a text or voicemail. He took a deep breath and dialled Victoria's number. There was no answer. He decided to leave a voicemail. He closed his eyes and started, "Victoria, I want to start by saying that I had no idea that the... victim was from here. I tried to find him but I couldn't. I told you that night that I had made mistakes, and I was trying to correct those mistakes. That is still true. I want to do it, now more than ever. I am still the same person who wanted to listen to you, who cared about you and still cares about you. I'm trying really hard to change. I'll explain everything to you if you just come here. Victoria, when the time came and you asked me honestly, I gave you an honest answer with the whole truth. That's what you should expect from a person, not deceit and suspicion. I'm not trying to hurt you."

He paused. "And there is something else. Something much more important that you need to know. This is not about you, this is not about me. This is about the whole town. I've found out something and I need you to help me confirm it. It's important, and lives are at stake. Lives of the people you may not like very much, but lives of the people you grew up with. Please, Victoria."

He clicked off. There was nothing more he could say. He would just have to wait.

Victoria called him after about half an hour. She spoke with a slight edge. "I'll sneak in there after a while. This better not be a trick, because if it is, I will not take lightly to it. And don't think I haven't been practicing my knife skills." She clicked off.

Conner stared at the cell phone and involuntarily shuddered at the ominous statement. He called Mrs. Stewart at the front desk and asked her to let Victoria up secretly. Mrs. Stewart acknowledged his request without comment. He thanked her and then went about preparing a list of questions he needed to ask Victoria, and what exactly he was going to tell Victoria. The rest of the time alternated between pacing nervously and rapidly, and double and then triple checking all his research. Unfortunately, it was all accurate.

Finally, there was a knock on his door. He rushed to it. He looked through the peephole and saw Victoria standing there, alone. He opened it to allow her entry. She walked in without looking at him and stood in the centre of the room with her hands crossed, clearly not expecting to stay long. He closed the door but did not sit down. Her clothes were comparatively toned down, which reflected her mood, it seemed.

She looked at him with weary eyes which seemed to have shed numerous tears recently. "All right, Conner. Say what you have to say before I leave."

Conner took a deep breath and looked her in the eye. To her surprise, however, he didn't look sad or apologetic. Instead he looked determined. "Victoria, I'm sorry that things turned out this way. I know you feel betrayed and I really had no idea that you knew the...victim. That must be affecting you badly. However," and here he drew himself up straighter. "I am *not* sorry about lying or betraying you, or not being who you thought I was; because I haven't done any of those things. That night was the first real opportunity we got to talk, and that night was the night I told you everything, *including* my biggest mistake. I did *not* lie to you about that, Victoria, even though it was terrible."

Conner waited for a few seconds while Victoria's face remained blank. Then he continued, "I've spent my life apologizing for things I haven't done; often these so-called 'misdeeds' only existed in my head. But not now. These past few days I've come to the realization that I shouldn't have to apologize for things I didn't do, things I'm not responsible for. I've realized that if I keep doing that, I'm burdening myself with things I'm better off without."

He paused. "There is, however, a flipside to that statement. Our... talk the other night as well as what I've been working on since yesterday has taught me something else: That if we *do* have a responsibility and we ignore it, then it is even worse." Another pause. "What you told me deeply affected me, and I am making it my responsibility to make sure that you get whatever you need to get better. And all I ask you now is for you to give me that chance, because I'm determined to help you, but..." A longer pause. "You can't help the man who thinks he doesn't need help or needs it but doesn't want it."

Victoria stared at Conner long and hard, as if she was looking for a zipper that she could pull to prove that this was a disguise, or some loophole in Conner's story to prove he wasn't serious. But nothing like that was forthcoming or present. "Who said I need help?" she said defiantly, "I'm fine the way I am. I don't need help from the likes of a murderer like you."

Conner winced as if wounded, which he was, albeit mentally. "Victoria, there's nothing I can do to change that. But there are things I can do for you. And it's pretty obvious you need someone, Victoria." His voice became almost imploring now. "Look at yourself. This is not easy for you; it wouldn't be easy on anyone. You can't handle it by yourself and you've been carrying it around for way too long. Let me be that someone, please."

Victoria looked at him with those eyes that wanted to believe, but which were wary of believing. "And if I agree, what is it you intend to do?"

Conner said, "I would listen to you, for one. Wouldn't it be nice to have someone to just...talk to? Someone that you didn't have to hide from?"

Victoria looked away for a few seconds before she looked back at him and then said quietly, "Roger was my friend, you know." Conner could see that in spite of the quick topic change, he had made some headway. She looked back up at him. "Before everything happened, of course. Then I had my accident and I lost a year of school. He seemed determined to go to university, in spite of the risks, and he was the only one who succeeded. I wanted to go with him too, but then my life was focused on everything but my career." There was a long pause as Victoria seemed to remember those unpleasant times. "And then when he died, most people took it as a clear omen: It's not safe to get out of here.

"Roger was a very determined person, you know. Your books must have been really convincing and terrible to make him...do that to himself." Victoria shuddered. Conner started slowly, "I tried to find out about him...but I couldn't trace him back here." Then he abruptly stopped. This was not something he wanted to talk about. Despite his big speech, he was, in fact, still hurting.

Victoria didn't seem to want to talk about it either because she changed the topic. "What is the big life-threatening situation you called me here for? Or was that just a lie, because if it is, I think it's best if I go."

At the mention of the mysterious reason, Conner shook his head vehemently. "I almost wish it was." And on seeing her look, added quickly, "You'll understand when I tell you. Can you please sit down?" Victoria looked at him suspiciously, but complied. "As you can see," he continued with a wave of the hand towards the table. "I've been doing a bit of research."

Victoria looked at the books and turned towards Conner with a questioning look on her face. She was confused for a second before she exclaimed, "Are these what I think they are?" And when Conner nodded, she asked, "How did you get them?"

Conner grimaced. "It wasn't easy, trust me. And they had good reason to be hidden. But that's a story for another time." Conner paused and then asked her, "Can you promise me one thing, though? Please listen to me from beginning to end, no matter how absurd it may sound, or how terrible or crazy."

Victoria gave him a strange look before she said, "I make no promises, but I'll try."

Conner nodded and said, "All right. Let's begin."

****

Conner felt like he was at the centre of a stage, ready to dazzle the audience with his range of illusions and tricks. "Do you like history, Victoria?"

Victoria, who had sat down, seemed thrown by the question. "Yes, I like history. Why?"

Conner ignored the question and continued. "You may think you know history, Victoria, but the history you've learnt is the kind of history that has been carefully cooked up and then fed to you. I can guarantee that because there is no way they would have wanted you to catch this."

"Catch what. What-?" Conner had raised a hand.

"Please listen patiently," he said. He went over what he was going to say in his mind, nodded unconsciously and then he continued, "I love history, Victoria. You know why I love history? Because it's essentially a really big story. Of course, it's not so fun when you have to memorize it, but that's the gist of it. A story, in which events of the past are depicted. Events which actually happened with real people and real emotions, motives, desires, dreams, ambitions;

people like you and I, just born in a different time. Some are more unbelievable than storybook characters."

He paused. He was in his element, telling a story, weighing each word, trying to figure what to say and how to say it so that it was best conveyed.

"You know what I've realized? There is a God. I don't know if His name is Natis, if He has only one name or many names and has many forms, but I do know this. Whatever name He goes by, He is an author. The greatest author of them all. Because He is the one who writes the story of life, and He does so with amazing skill. We often don't understand why things happen, but any good author will tell you that events in the past, no matter how small, are often precursors for events in the future."

Victoria looked like she was about to interrupt again but Conner stopped her and continued, "I'm getting to it, Victoria. I assume you're not familiar with the term, '*Deus Ex Machina*'?" Without waiting for Victoria to respond, he continued, "It means 'God out of the machine.'" He explained the term to her. She nodded, wondering where he could *possibly* be going with this. "Now," he continued, "Writers prefer not to use this too much, because it makes it rather sloppy. For example, if your protagonist is a cop and every time he is facing a man with a gun, there is an earthquake or clap of thunder or something that distracts the man and the cop is able to overpower him; that would bore the readers. Who would believe that much luck? Agreed?"

Victoria said exasperatedly, "Yes, Conner! Now can you get to it?"

Conner's face adapted a troubled expression and he said, "Victoria, the Sun rises and sets every day, right? People are born and they die. Nature has a set of rules and patterns. Well, in case of the town of Levion, Nature and God are utterly random."

Victoria stood up, angry. "Conner, if you don't stop all the extra talk and get to the damn point, I'm walking out!"

Conner breathed in. This was the hard part. Victoria saw the look on his face and all the anger seemed to drain out of her. "What is it, Conner?"

Conner took another deep breath before starting, "Do you really think that Nature would kill off so many people over such an extended period of time with no apparent reason or basis?"

Victoria had an uncomprehending look on her face. "What are you trying to say, Conner?"

"What I'm saying is..." Conner paused before he went on, "...Is that Levitis is not a real disease; all those people over the years died by human hands."

****

Victoria stayed silent for a few minutes, with her mouth open and her eyes blinking, trying to absorb this information. Then she slowly turned to Conner and said blankly, "You know, Conner, I really thought you could have come up with a better story than that. If you had lied to get me up here, just do it and stop wasting time with this nonsense."

Conner raised his palms in the air and said, "Victoria, Victoria. Listen to me. I wouldn't make something up like this, not even in a story. I'm not spinning a wild theory out of thin air. I have evidence, though it's circumstantial. The gaps in my information you can help me fill."

"But what evidence? What gaps?" Victoria exclaimed.

"Victoria, I want you to close your eyes." Victoria eyed him. He continued, "Victoria, please just close your eyes. If you hear anything untoward, open them." She reluctantly closed them after giving him a dirty look. "Now, I want you to forget everything everyone has ever told you about Levitis." He paused for a second and then continued, "I want you to think of this rationally. It has a purely random nature, affecting people of any age? It rarely spreads outside of town; heck, even *inside* the town it doesn't spread virally!

There's no confirmed basis for it, the symptoms keep changing and so does the intensity. Name one other natural force that's so powerful yet so haphazard. There isn't any! This can only be the work of human beings."

"But...but...it can be a coincidence! Maybe we just haven't seen the connection between them!" she exclaimed, opening her eyes.

Conner blinked and then said, "All right," he retrieved some notes. "I want to point your attention to something: What happens when a person dies?"

Victoria appeared dazed. "I don't understand the question."

Conner asked kindly, "I meant what you do with the body."

Victoria shook her head and said, "Oh, well, funeral rites say that the body has to be cremated as soon as possible and the ashes have to be scattered in the field behind the Sinome..."

"Exactly," Conner said gravely. "The body is cremated, not buried. So there is no chance for an exhumation. And you have to do it as soon as possible in case of any side effects of the "disease" after death!" He paused. "And you know when this change to cremation started, right?"

Victoria was confused. "I don't know; it's been there forever. Natis requires us to cremate our bodies as fast as possible so that the spirits were able to reach Him in time before they got trapped here."

"Actually, Victoria, the cremation of bodies actually started about twenty years after Levitis first occurred, at a time when certain doctors were asking questions about Levitis and believed that they could glean facts from the bodies. They were denied access and a little time after there was a 'proclamation' from Natis which said that every Natish needed to be cremated from then on."

Victoria got up and raised a hand. "So wait," she said slowly, "You're saying that...all these deaths are connected to Natism?" And before Conner could respond, she burst out, "You're full of garbage! Natism is a pure religion! It teaches love, honesty, compassion! If whatever conspiracy theory you're spinning leads back to Natism, you're barking up the wrong tree!"

Conner stood his ground. "Okay, you believe in Natism, right? Then you should remember that I was declared a High Natish. And I saved Jon Peck's life, which is very rare, if not unheard of. So either you believe in that, which means Natis is on my side, and you should at least give what I'm saying some consideration, or you believe that Levitis is a lie, and that the very next day after I was declared "blessed" I was able to save Jon; then you should listen too."

Victoria stared at him. "Natism cannot be a lie. It can't," she said simply, a slight tremor in her face.

"I never said Natism was a lie, Victoria," Conner said gently. "All I'm saying is that maybe it is a result of people who thought they were doing it for the benefit of the community, of their religion. Maybe they were doing it for the right reasons in the wrong ways."

Victoria looked at him for a second before she straightened herself, nodded and sat down. "Fine. Let's see what you've got. How does a townsperson get Levitis?"

"Well," said Conner, "I'm pretty sure the doctor gets it to them somehow. Is there any way the doctor can come into contact with them at any given point of time?"

Victoria said slowly, "Well, everybody has a fairly routine medical check-up and the doctor can also schedule one for any of us if he feels we need it."

"And during these checks, does he give you anything?"

Victoria said reluctantly, "I know that he *does* give shots or medicines to people that he thinks needs them. Come to think of it..." She paused. "It's those people that he warns about it that are the ones affected."

"How does the doctor of the town get chosen?"

"An apprentice is chosen, and the apprentice is trained extensively. The apprenticeship is said to be done only under the town doctor and nowhere else since they need special training to combat Levitis. And the Father also helps in choosing the apprentice..." her voice trailed off as she realized the significance of what she was saying.

"Yes, one more link to the Sinome," Conner said aloud in line with what she was thinking.

When Victoria didn't say anything, Conner asked another question, "Which reminds me, who becomes the priest? I assume he's also selected by the Father and given special training under him?"

Victoria nodded. "The person who is chosen is said to have "special potential" and is chosen by Natis." There was a silence for a few seconds and Victoria said, "What? Out of questions?"

Conner smiled slightly, shook his head and said, "I was just thinking."

"If everything you say is true, what about Mr. Peck? Why was he saved? And why would the priest proclaim you a High Natish? What is all that about?"

Conner seemed uncertain for the first time that day. "I don't know about that, Victoria. I really don't."

There was another few seconds of silence before Victoria asked, "Where are you getting with all this, Conner? Why would the High Natish want so badly to keep us in town?"

Conner sighed and sat down next to Victoria. "I looked up the records. Levitis first occurred during a mass missionary movement, which almost wiped Natism out. People who stayed in Levion and converted to Natism were spared. Then whenever missionaries or "heretics" came into town, they were affected by Levitis. It was the same with the people who tried to leave. At the time, it was said to be the wrath of Natis, but looking at it now, we can of course view it in a different light. Soon people started adapting to the presence of Levitis in the town, and then I think it was used simply as a reminder to keep people faithful."

Victoria was nodding almost unconsciously. "The Day of Natis. Where Natis protected His followers from Levitis. We have an annual celebration on that day." She paused. "Every single priest and doctor, since Levitis became widespread, has died of it. What explanation do you have for that?"

Conner seemed thrown by the fact momentarily, but then shrugged. "Maybe they wanted to prove that no one was immune. Upped the fear factor?" Victoria didn't seem happy with that answer and muttered something under her breath after which there was silence for a while. Conner could see that she had something to say, so he waited. She didn't disappoint. "Levitis has been increasing over the past few decades. How does your wild theory fit into that?"

"I would assume something's changed that's making them take that move. Maybe it's the fact that no matter how hard you try and get used to a painful thing, it still comes back and pains you." He was looking pointedly at Victoria.

Victoria got it, was flustered for a second and then a sudden thought seemed to strike her, and her brow furrowed. "People have been talking about considering outside help, quietly of course, but in a small town, word travels fast. Some are saying that with these new advances, we could cure Levitis. Dr Clark attended a medical conference and they said that it's not possible but they would keep him updated."

Conner shook his head. "I doubt he went to any medical conference. He must have just said it to placate the townspeople."

"Why hasn't anyone figured all this out by now?"

"Nobody knew about these books, remember? In a lot of other history records, Levion is given less importance than it actually has, which has probably diverted a lot of attention from it. And until recently, everyone has accepted blindly that Natis is responsible. Anyone coming in from outside is not allowed here long enough to get any real information; there is no real mingling with anyone outside of town since all shopping and most of the jobs are here. I suspect that's the way it's supposed to be. A dome over the place wouldn't keep people in better."

"So how *did* you see all this? Why do you think that it has to be this way?!"

Conner shrugged. "I don't like it. I'm in a unique position right now. I have enough negativity to see the worst-case scenario in things, an author's imagination that helps me to think freely and connect the dots, but I'm starting to get faith to believe that I can change it, or at least try to. I said earlier that there is a reason for everything, it's all a story written by God, where even the smallest details matter, and that is true. There must be a reason for all those deaths, but we will never know them without knowing intricate details of every single person at that time. So that is not the point. The point is that now that I've found out about this, I feel that I have a responsibility to go ahead and try and stop it."

"But why? You said yourself that you believe in Natis now. Why can't you maybe believe that this is really what He wants?" asked Victoria, looking desperate to find a hole in Conner's theory.

"I *do* believe in Natis, Victoria, which is why I know that He would never sanction all this in His name."

Victoria stared at him for a second, and then it was as if the air seemed to go out of her. She sat back and blinked. "This is a lot to process." Conner nodded wordlessly. While she sat quietly, Conner looked her over. He had not forgotten about that night, and he really badly wanted to talk to her about her story - the rest of it - and get it off her chest, but he stayed quiet. This was hard enough for her; talking about that might just overwhelm her.

She finally looked at him and said, "So, even if all this is true, what are you going to do about it?"

"Well, first I'm going to confirm these facts."

"And how are you going to accomplish that?" Victoria asked with a raised eyebrow.

"By going straight to the source."

Chapter 15

Confessions of a Priest

There was a melancholy look in his eyes as he stared out over the town.

This was not the way it was supposed to go. This was not the way it was meant to be.

Suddenly he saw Victoria leave the inn. She thought that she was exiting from the hidden entrance, but nothing in Levion was hidden from Father Godfrey. It seemed, however, that something very important had happened outside Levion that had been unknown to him, and he had paid the price for that ignorance dearly. Conner also came out of the inn, ignoring the route Victoria had taken. He had not left the inn for two days, after which he was gone for another four, and now chose to have a conversation with Victoria the very day he had come back. Although the tempers in town had cooled down, he could see the townspeople turning to give him dirty looks. Even from here, though, Godfrey could see that Conner had a determined air about him and seemed to be heading towards the Sinome, ignoring everyone around him. Being close to Natis, Godfrey sometimes received divine intuition and he had a feeling he knew what Conner wanted to say. Godfrey accepted it.

He stepped away from the telescope and once again marvelled at the ingenuity of the builders of the Sinome. They had taken the plan for one of the towers of the castle that previously stood and remodelled it, making it more decorative and engraving it with the Natis Eye. But they had chosen the position and build of the tower that was perfectly placed to look out at the town. Then they had inserted two holes, one at the top and one in the middle. The one at the top was for stargazing, but the one in the middle was perfectly located for giving him a whole visual of the town. Later on, when telescopes were invented, priests had put in the telescope for easier viewing. The middle telescope was, quite literally, looking out the centre of the Natis Eye.

Normally remembering this would have made him smile, but today it didn't. He descended the stairs of the tower and then entered his room. He opened his drawer and took out a carefully preserved scroll, and unfurled it. The scroll was from the first great priest of the Sinome, whose name was also Father Godfrey. *How ironic. The man who preserved Natism has the same name as the one who might fail to preserve Natism.*

He sat down on his bed and starting reading it, although he knew the words by heart. It was a letter written by Father Godfrey that had been passed down from priest to priest, detailing the real events on the Day of Natis all those years ago. It was a message to the priests to do what was necessary, to sacrifice if needed. Scroll in hand; Father Godfrey remembered these past few days. He had talked to Nancy, tried to calm her down; he had reminded the townspeople of the fact that Jon Peck was still alive, and that he must pray to Natis for an answer. He had then retreated to his rooms and had become lost in thought. He got up and carefully replaced the scroll in the drawer.

He had planned a course of action for each set of circumstances, and hoped to Natis that Conner would let him choose the right one. He nodded to himself with renewed determination. He was not done yet, not by a long shot. Conner would be here soon, and the Father needed to prepare for his arrival.

****

Conner wanted to storm into the Sinome and go straight into the Father's chambers, but it was still a place of worship and so he gave it the respect it deserved. He walked slowly but purposefully to the Room of Secrets. There were a few people who eyed him angrily, and one or two who told him to stop, but he ignored them. He entered the Room; it was like he had been hit by a heat wave. It was sweltering in there. He tried to ignore the heat for now and was about to try and open the Father's door before it opened on its own. The Father stood in the doorway, a steely look on his face. "It's rude to barge in, you know."

"Well, I think rudeness is nothing compared to everything you've done," Conner said vehemently.

"There's that rudeness again. Sit down," the Father said, indicating the north chair, which gave the Father the position of power on the south one. Conner didn't move, but instead looked Godfrey in the eye.

"I said, sit down," said Godfrey in a low voice. Conner could see the menace in the man's eyes, so he complied in silence. The Father proceeded to sit on the south chair and said in a pleasant voice, "Thank you." Conner could see, however, that the menacing look remained, like a viper ready to strike.

There were a few moments of silence. The heat was really getting to Conner. He rubbed the sweat off his brow and composed himself before he said, "I don't know, *Father*, if you're even deserving of that title."

"Insults will get you nowhere, Conner," said Godfrey smoothly. "What do you think you know?"

"I know that Levitis isn't a real disease." Conner kept an eye on Godfrey to see his reaction. He was impressed because Godfrey's face was almost nonchalant when he answered, "Oh, really? And what are you basing this claim on?"

"I found the books at the library. The books you tried so hard to keep away from Levion. I connected the dots. I know the truth."

"Ah, those books," said Godfrey, resting back in his chair. There was a reminiscent and maybe even slightly mournful tone in his voice. "I was going to make Clark get them during the ceremony, but then we were rudely interrupted. Sometimes I wish we could have destroyed them earlier. They were written by one of our own. Foolish man. It was to show the future protectors of Natism their true history, in a way that only they could understand it. Putting it down in writing was too much of a risk, but at least he had the sense to keep it away from the town." He sighed. "There was a time when we had influence in the whole university, now only enough to convince the librarian that the books are under special protection and care."

Conner's head jerked back and he blinked rapidly, sending sweat flying. He tried to comprehend what was being said to him. "What? One of our own? Power in the university?" His eyes grew wide. "You're admitting you hid the books? You're not denying that Levitis is a lie?"

The Father shrugged and said, "What's the point? You're already convinced. Nothing I say will change your mind. So I might as well admit it. Yes, we did sacrifice all those people for the good of Natism and Levion."

Conner couldn't believe that it was as easy as this. All his arguments, all the proof he was going to put forward, everything in his head just crumbled to dust. Before he could say anything more, Godfrey said, "Now the question remains: Now that you know about it, what are you going to do about it?"

Conner was confused by this question, as if it was obvious. "Well, I'm going to expose you!"

Godfrey's lips twitched as if he was highly amused by the idea. "We'll get back to that," he said. Then he leaned forward and continued, "But do you know *why* we invented Levitis?" Before Conner could say anything, Godfrey cut him off. "Don't answer that question, because you can't. You can't possibly know about the sacrifices we had to make, and so let me tell you.

"Natism was a religion born out of chaos, a time when people really needed something to unite them, to bond them together; a time, essentially, of death and despair. Natism provided that bond, and it worked, for a time. Then, after a while, we decided to try and spread the knowledge of beautiful Natis elsewhere, but we were stopped. We were stopped by heretics, charlatans and so-called "missionaries". These missionaries not only prevented Natism from spreading, but they also came back to Levion and tried to convert some of our townspeople. And the worst part of it was: Some did convert and a lot more were considering it. After all we had done for them." Godfrey's face showed his disgust.

"So what were we to do?" he continued. "We were getting desperate and on the brink of extinction, so we devised a method - a method suitable enough to remind people of the death and despair that they had faced which we had saved them from and also ensured that the faithful stay faithful. So we invented this disease that affected only those who had stopped believing in Natism or opposed to it. And thus Levitis was born.

"Levitis brought back our old followers, plus some new ones. Things were peaceful for a while and then there was a new problem: People were getting discontent with the area, and so they wanted to leave. This was, once again, a threat to Natism. So Levitis affected people who wanted to leave, and we incorporated the principle of neighbourliness into Natism. Nobody left Levion."

The Father leaned forward even more. "Do you know what happens to someone who is on the brink of death, Conner? He lets go. He *lives* his life, truly lives it. He doesn't merely pass the time. And that's what we realized. Because of Levitis, people were aware that they could die the next day, and so they were happy. Levion was one of the happiest towns in all the land, and even better, they were the most devout. Every day of their life they believed was a gift from Natis. And isn't that the truth? Isn't every day a gift?"

He settled back in his chair. "We gave Leviites happiness and belief for a long time, Conner White. But then the tide started turning." He closed his eyes. "People slowly started getting disgruntled. All problems were...taken care of, one way or another. The seed, however, had taken root. Some people wanted to go out more often;

more and more students were determined to go to university. I was able to convince all of them, except Roger. I ensured that he swore never to talk about Levitis and that background information was falsified. I was worried that sooner or later, though, someone would find out about Levitis. I took on the role as Father in the middle of this difficult time. Levitis seemed to depress people further, so I needed a different way."

He opened his eyes and studied Conner closely. Conner seemed to paying rapt attention to his story, although he looked extremely hot and was sweating profusely. It *was* a hot day, but Godfrey didn't mind the heat. Before Godfrey could continue, Conner interjected, "Either you're delusional or you can't see facts right in front of you. Instead of creating a new "disease" and killing so many people, you could have won them back with love, respect and by showing them how you were *better* than others, not by threatening or bullying them. And if you already didn't know, no matter how much someone can tolerate a bad thing, even accept it and make it a positive, in the end, it will not change the burden of it and it will wear people down."

Father Godfrey did not comment on this; instead he smiled slightly and said, "Don't you want to know what solution I thought of, Conner?" He leaned forward slightly again. "It was you. The moment I found out about you and your reputation, I knew I could use you."

Conner's eyes widened in shock. "So you knew I was an author?"

"Of course I knew," said Godfrey, his smile broadening. "I make it a point to know everybody who comes here. Especially one who comes here at an odd time under unusual circumstances. It was easier because Clark was sure he had recognised you from a book jacket cover he had seen out of town. Sharp man, that Dr. Clark. I myself went and checked your room while you were with Jon. Mrs. Stewart knows I keep going up to her roof to "inspect the heavens". I have duplicates of all the inn room keys handy. Once I had confirmation, I knew I could proceed."

"You went through my things?!" Then he realised who he was talking to and stopped being shocked. "So how was I your... solution?"

"Well, I believed I could change you, give you some more confidence." Godfrey's eyes gleamed as he said this. "Imagine if I could tell the world that I had changed the great Conner White simply on the basis of my religion, Natism! How famous that religion would become! You could have gone and spread it elsewhere; people would have listened to a converted Conner White. People could have shifted or even visited other places, and I would have been at peace, knowing they would have been able to practice Natism there. Maybe more Sinomes could have sprung up! There would have been no need for Levitis! Dr. Clark would have developed a cure, and immunised everyone. I would be the priest who saved Natism! We would have gone down as Levion legends!" At this point, the Father's face turned angry. "And then that woman had to come and ruin it! She had never told me that she thought you were the one responsible for her son's suicide! Her husband was one of the few people in town who didn't die of Levitis, and that woman was too headstrong for her own good. If she had shared with me, things might have different today..." His voice trailed off.

After a few seconds, he raised his head and looked at Conner. "We can still do all that, you know," he said. "I can convince the townspeople that you're reformed now, that Natis has shown you the way. They will trust me; they will grow to trust you again. You can be the one who gives the inspiration to Clark to devise the cure. You can spread our message, Conner. After all, look at the change you've already achieved because of Natism, because of me."

Conner blinked and started sputtering, "Ex-excuse me? Because of you? I have-"

Godfrey raised a hand. "Who was it that made you a High Natish? Me. I was the one who made you believe that you were blessed, that you were capable."

"What about the light?"

Godfrey smiled widely. "A mechanism installed long ago, modified over time that was used to point out the blessed ones in the olden days. Only the priests knew about it, and we have long since stopped the practice, but I decided to put it back to use. You should feel privileged." Godfrey ignored Conner's amazed look and continued, "And since you've already figured out about Levitis, it won't come as a surprise to you that we were the ones that ensured that Jon would be saved.

"It really didn't matter what choice you made; either way Clark would have ensured that he was saved and that the credit would go to you. If you had chosen to kill him off quickly, Clark would have waited till Jon looked better, and said that he had chosen the right vial of medicine only because of the decision you had made. I would say you had divine sight and you would be a hero anyway." He paused to let this sink in. "But I knew you wouldn't. I could see the faith in your eyes; I knew that you were willing to give it a second chance just like you wanted to give yourself."

"So I was tricked," Conner muttered. "That means there wasn't anything to believe in."

"It doesn't have to be that way, you know," Godfrey said. "You believed in what you saw; you believed in Natism. Everything you made yourself believe was true. Don't doubt yourself, Conner. Believe that you can help Natism, because Natism has helped you get here. Do you think you would have become determined enough to confront me this way otherwise?" Conner's expression betrayed his answer, and Godfrey pushed on, "Conner, imagine what you could achieve. Imagine poor Roger. Don't you want to undo that wrong? Don't you want to spread hope and happiness after spreading despair and hopelessness all this time?"

Conner looked torn. He put his head in his hands for a few seconds, shook it, removed his hands and then said, "I don't know, Father. Can you please answer a few of my questions first?"

"Of course," said Godfrey, smiling amiably.

"Every single doctor and priest has died because of Levitis. Why?"

Godfrey smiled again. "Well, Conner, that is what keeps us strong. It is a rule of ours that we must die suffering worse than the worst Levitis case during our tenure. It also demonstrates the level of commitment that one has to have if he is to become a priest or a doctor, knowing that one day they would die in that terrible way."

"How do you prevent doctors coming here and diagnosing a patient differently? After all, you really can't stop all tourist doctors from coming here."

"Like I said, I do background checks on all patrons. If there is a doctor, we try and make sure he leaves quickly, and while he's here, nobody dies of Levitis. After all, there are always the sad tourists who come here, who are easily influenced by me and made to join the community by marrying someone here. Nobody who I've ever asked be part of our religion has denied me.

"During the tourist season, we try not to attract attention, and if we have to, the townspeople make sure to tell them it's a normal disease, and not Levitis. Our townspeople are generally discreet, and nobody is told about Levitis because it might spread fear and prevent tourism. Also, we have a very strict town code that ensures that nobody gets close to any outsiders unless a particular one is 'chosen by Natis to join our ranks'. Victoria, of course, seems to be the exception. She always seemed troubled but it's sad to see how much so."

"Yes, it must be killing you to have made that oversight, right?" said Conner with a small smirk. Godfrey controlled his anger. Conner then asked, "What's that *Death watch* board about?"

"That was a very clever move, actually. Every time a name goes on the board, there's a hidden button that rings a bell. The people have learnt to associate Natis with that bell, and that bell with Levitis. So the Leviites know that Natis is the one who punishes them with

Levitis, and I remind them that He is also the one who saves them from it."

Conner paused to let his subsequent admiration at the ingenuity and repulsion at the effect sink in. Then he asked, "Haven't you ever been found out? I mean, this has been going on for so many years now."

"There have been times, yes, when it has been close. But you must understand that the townspeople have utmost faith in us, believing that we are protecting them, which we are. Whatever problems have come up have been taken care of."

"I assume you mean killed," Conner said, his tone hard.

Godfrey leaned forward. "Contrary to what you believe, Conner, we are not murderers. We simply fulfil Natis' will; trying to make sure that our religion is preserved." He paused. "Now, your answer?"

Conner got up. Godfrey could see the look in his eyes and got up as well. "Again, it was never necessary. I've seen enough bullies in my life to know one when I see one. That's all you are, a big bully. It sickens me to see you sit here and talk calmly about death and murder like it's no big thing! You're talking about how clever you are for avoiding getting caught like you won the Award for Serial Killer of the Year! Then you say you're a man of Natis! And no matter what justification you put forth, you *are* a murderer of innocent people. I've been disgusted all the while I've been in your presence, and in case you didn't get the hint, I will *not* do *anything* side-by-side with you." He started to walk out when Godfrey blocked his way.

"Okay, Conner," he said.

Conner was startled. He just wanted to get out of this room away from this terrible man and the oppressive heat. "What?" he asked.

"It's all right, Conner. It's your decision."

Conner didn't know what to make of it. "Thank you?" he said unsurely.

Godfrey grinned. "I can see that you've been sweating profusely. Let me at least get you a glass of water. We are in a holy place, and I will show you that I can be hospitable."

Before Conner could react, Godfrey went past him and into his room at surprising speed. Conner could hear water being poured and soon Godfrey was back with a glass. Conner was actually pretty grateful for it, and if he wasn't feeling so hot, he probably wouldn't have accepted it and just walked out.

"Thank you," Conner said after gulping it down quickly and then turned to leave.

"What are you going to do, Conner?" asked Father Godfrey.

Conner turned slowly. "I'm going to expose you."

Father Godfrey smiled, and the calculating gleam was back in his eye. "I'm sure that they'll believe you. After all, I'm just their link to Natis while you're the ultra-trustworthy outsider, right?"

Now it was Conner's turn to smile. "Well, after they hear the words of their very link to Natis confessing, I believe the outsiders will gain some trust," he said in a triumphant voice as he held up his phone. "Yes, Father, I recorded our entire conversation."

****

Conner expected the Father to express fear, shock, disbelief or anger. What he *didn't* expect was Godfrey to start laughing, which is what happened. Godfrey threw his head back and let out loud blasts of laughter. Conner couldn't understand why. After a few seconds, he stopped and smiled at Conner. "I would advise you to check your phone."

Conner looked at his phone. The screen was blank. He pushed a few buttons, slapped it against his hand, but it refused to come on. He looked up at Godfrey, who was grinning at him.

"Poor naive Conner White. You really thought I would fall for such a cheap and obvious trick? I'm insulted." He stepped forward.

"You know, in the new generation, people tend to get distracted by all the shiny new objects they possess. So I went and got a nice, shiny gadget of my own." One more step. "What it does is cut out all electronic functioning. Not just radio waves, *all* functions. Pretty useful, don't you think?"

Godfrey was now right in front of Conner. "Don't try and go against me, Conner," Godfrey whispered. There was no smile now. "You will *always* lose. And don't think that you understand my motivations, because you never will. And don't you *dare* question my dedication to Natis, because you're just a whiny, two-bit writer who can't even man up and face the world. " He paused. "Seeing you're so disgusted with me, it is better you leave. Get out."

Conner took a step back. Suddenly Godfrey smiled, all amicable again and said, "Oh, and tell Victoria I said 'hi' when you meet her next. I'll have to make Clark pay her a visit. After all, we can't have people who conspire with evil running around town."

Conner did the only thing he could think of: he turned around and almost ran out of there with as much as dignity as he could muster, determined to get away as far as he could from those terrible eyes.

****

Conner's mind started working a little only when he was back in his room at the inn. He slumped down on his couch, a defeated look on his face. *What am I up against?* He had completely underestimated Father Godfrey. It was one thing to theorize about something; it was quite another to see it being admitted first-hand in an almost casual manner. Conner remembered Jon Peck and the pain he was in. Godfrey had caused that. He had admitted it. Conner had merely been a pawn; he saw that now. Godfrey had used him and was willing to do whatever it took for his cause. *How am I supposed to stop someone like that? Can I even do it? Am I in over my head?*

Conner stood up. He had sat too much. He stood in the centre of the room, deep in thought. It seemed that every time he had developed some resolve, someone had come in and destroyed it. It was as if it was not meant to be. *Was that true?*

Then suddenly he remembered Victoria, and Godfrey's threat. He made a move to call her, but before he could do anything, he had a strange feeling. The room started spinning and he felt weak and lightheaded. He dropped to his knees and tried to clutch the table but he ended up just banging his hand against it. He didn't have time to register the pain because the room just started spinning faster until he couldn't bear it anymore.

He had blacked out before his head hit the floor.

Chapter 16

Run

Victoria looked at Conner again with great apprehension and anxiety. The last time she had seen him was that morning when he was telling her about his wild theory. The scariest thing, however, was that Victoria was slowly getting convinced of it. The most convincing thing, however, was the fact that Conner was now lying on his bed, unconscious and presumably in intense pain, barely hours after he had said he was going to confront Father Godfrey.

A crowd of people were gathered at the foot of the bed, including the Peck family. Needless to say, not too many were looking unhappy at this latest development. Many were saying that this was Natis' divine retribution. Mrs. Stewart stood next to him, looking worried. It was by pure luck that she had found Conner unconscious on the floor. Conner had looked ruffled, and hadn't greeted her as he went to his room. She had gone to check on him. When he didn't answer his door, fearing something was wrong; she opened it with her key and had found him there. She had contacted Dr. Clark immediately. She had also called Victoria. By the time Victoria got there, a few people had already arrived, and a few came in with Dr. Clark, who had just entered.

The people gave way to Dr. Clark; he stepped to Conner's side and examined him. He checked his vitals, temperature and breathing. As he did so, he stated Conner's symptoms to himself in a low voice. It was almost as if there was satisfaction in his voice. His usual calm face was grave, perhaps to better convey the import of his words.

"I know that this man has made his mistakes, but I would advise none of you to judge him too harshly since he is dying."

Murmurs broke out among the group. Victoria stepped forward. "What does he have, doctor?"

Dr. Clark did not face her; instead he addressed the whole crowd, "I'm not sure at this point. I could give him a shot, but I don't know how much effect that will have."

"So give him a shot then," said Lindsey, Jon's daughter. The Pecks were of the opinion that although Conner might have made mistakes, he was still blessed because saving Jon's life had been proof enough for them.

"But it cannot be Levitis, can it?" Everyone's attention turned to Victoria, even the doctor's this time. "After all, Conner has been here much too short a time for Levitis to afflict him. Unless you will now say that it can spread easily to outsiders too, in which case, we will need to completely cut off contact with the outside world." By the time she had finished this, everyone was looking at Dr. Clark with shock and horror. Dr. Clark regarded Victoria, as if wondering what her intention was. Finally he said, "No, it's not Levitis. Like I said, I can't be sure what it is. But if I give him a shot, it might help his chances."

"But couldn't it also hinder his chances, Doctor?" Heads turned to Victoria. "If you misjudged it, it might make him die faster."

"It might, Miss Parks." Heads turned to the Doctor. "But it's a calculated risk."

"It's too much of a risk."

"And you're a doctor now?"

"I know enough to know that it could kill him."

"It could save him."

"It most probably won't."

"Oh, really?" asked Dr. Clark stonily, his eyes narrowing. "And what would you suggest I do?"

"Maybe you should figure out what his problem is. By taking his blood maybe?"

Dr. Clark laughed. "First you show concern and then you tell me to analyze his blood? By the time it's done and I've figured out a cure, he'll surely be dead." He paused. "And besides, why are you so interested in him?"

Everyone in the crowd had gotten a neck ache from bobbing their heads left to right rapidly between Dr. Clark and Victoria. Now their eyes shifted to another person: Conner. He had conveniently groaned at that exact moment and saved Victoria from answering. He tried to sit up and Victoria rushed to his side but Mrs. Stewart was closer and she laid him down, saying he needed to rest. However, many had noted Victoria's movement.

Conner opened his eyes a crack and muttered, "Listen to Victoria."

"What did he say?" someone in the crowd asked.

"Listen to Victoria," Conner said a little louder before he groaned again.

"The patient is delusional and-" The doctor started.

"Look, doctor, all you're doing is agitating him more, and that has got to be counter-productive. So just take his blood."

Dr. Clark stared at her for a second before he removed a sterilized syringe, quickly cleaned the area and started to draw blood. Conner groaned again and said, "No, don't let that man treat me!" Dr. Clark ignored him and transferred the blood into a vial. As soon as the vial was sealed, Victoria grabbed it.

"What are you doing, Miss Parks!" he exclaimed.

"I need this blood. He just said he didn't want you to treat him," she said, holding the vial close.

"He's a patient in extreme pain! He isn't thinking rationally and apparently neither are you!"

Mrs. Stewart came forward and whispered, "Victoria, what are you doing? Give it back to him. I thought you wanted to save him!"

Victoria whispered back furiously, "I do want to save him! That is why you have to let me do this, Mrs. Stewart! Please, there are terrible things that we have found out. You have to trust me."

Mrs. Stewart stared at Victoria before she looked at Dr. Clark, who was staring at both of them.

"Well?" The usual calm demeanour of Dr. Clark was breaking in the face of this opposition, which he was unused to. "This man is dying; can I have my vial back?"

"Take another vial," Mrs. Stewart said shortly.

"Excuse me?" Dr. Clark said, showing signs of anger now.

"I said, take another one! The man's not running out of blood, is he! Let her have her vial; you take yours! You said it yourself; he's running out of time!"

Dr. Clark stared at her, and then he went back to being his usual, calm self. He took another blood sample. He looked at Victoria and said, "If he dies because I didn't give him the shot, his blood is on your hands."

Victoria wanted to say that it was quite likely that his hands must be practically wrinkled because of blood, then. She held her tongue, though.

"Now get out, everyone!" called Mrs. Stewart. "This is not a circus!" Everyone started muttering and filing out, giving Victoria long glances. Before Mrs. Stewart could say anything, Victoria started, "Mrs. Stewart, please. You have to ensure that no one comes in here, especially not Dr. Clark. Please, you have to-"

"Victoria, what is this about? I trust you, but there are limits to what you can ask."

"Mrs. Stewart, I know it looks bad, but I promise I'll explain it to you once I get back. Please, do this for me, for Conner! You of all people know that Dr. Clark is not to be trusted!"

Mrs. Stewart stared at Victoria for a second, apparently thinking. Then she nodded shortly and said, "If Dr. Clark comes back with a cure and I think you're not going to make it, I'll let him administer it. You owe me a very good explanation." Then she glanced at Conner and said, "And he better not die, or it really will be his blood on your hands. Now do whatever you have to with the blood you're holding in your hands." So saying, she walked out.

Conner groaned and muttered, "Victoria..."

Victoria went to his side immediately. He muttered, "Father... confessed..."

"You have the recording?" asked Victoria breathlessly.

"Didn't...work..."

"That's fine, Conner. We'll try again after you're better. I'm going to get this blood analyzed and get you a cure as soon as possible. I'm leaving now. Conner, you're going to be all right." She rose slightly before he said, "Victoria..." after which she bent down and said, "Yes, Conner?"

"If...you...don't..." Victoria could understand what he was trying to say and shushed him. "It's all right, Conner. I don't hold anything against you."

Conner nodded slightly and then groaned. "Take...wallet...money... there."

Victoria looked in his pocket and found his wallet. There was a lot of money in there, which could come in use. She rose and said, "Now conserve your energy."

"Thank...you..." Conner muttered before he closed his eyes.

Victoria looked back at him lying there for a few seconds and there was only one word in her mind: *Run.*

****

And she did run. She ran all the way out of the inn to her house, making sure the vial was safe along the way. Within minutes, she had decided against going to Baronsville by train. There were only two fast trains going to Baronsville, one in the morning and one in the evening, for people with jobs in the city. All the ones now were too slow. The train to the university she didn't even think about, because it had too many stops and didn't go to Baronsville at any rate.

So she needed a car. Fortunately, she was one of the few in Levion who owned a car; the town was small enough to get anywhere by foot. There was a standing agreement that if you missed the train, you could borrow one of the cars as long as you brought it back safely, informed the owner and paid for gas. Mercifully, no one had borrowed the car today. She popped in to get the keys. She was almost at the door with them when she found her mother barring the exit.

"Where do you think you're going, Victoria?" she asked. She looked angry, which wasn't good.

"Mom...I have some very urgent work. Will you please...?"

"Please what?" her mother flared. "Will you push me aside like you did to Dr. Clark? You think I'm stupid or deaf? I heard what you did up there. I can see that you've been behaving stranger than usual since he got here. I've been cutting you some slack, but this is over the line. I can see that you're in love with the man but-"

"What!" Victoria exclaimed. "I'm not in love with him!"

"Then what are you doing? Why do you insist on embarrassing our family?" She stepped aside from the door. "You're really old enough to make your own decisions, but as long as you live under this roof, you have to factor us into your decisions. Now either you hand me that vial and we go and apologise to Dr. Clark, or you can take that and go wherever you want and not come back here."

Victoria looked at her mother for a few seconds. The decision was obvious and one she had been contemplating for a long time. She walked out of the door and got into the car, trying hard not to look back at her mother.

****

She drove out of town quickly, attracting stares along the way. She didn't care. She was just happy about the fact that she had gotten out of town without running anyone over. She then took a road that was not commonly used by the workers in the city so that she wouldn't be spotted by any of the townspeople.

Victoria knew these roads very well. She had loved exploring them when she was younger, and when she got upset, which had been often these past few years. She had found handy shortcuts, clearings and interesting flowers. Nature was really only the outside world Leviites were allowed to explore, and what a world it was. They always hated and loved Nature, because they assumed Levitis was a product of Nature. Now that Victoria was convinced otherwise, she felt an unbridled connection with the trees and plants around her that she had never felt before. Victoria had always felt safe here, away from humans and their schemes and intentions.

Victoria suddenly remembered her mother; she tried to push the thought away. It was not too hard. Victoria was slowly going towards the point of no-return, at which point she would have burned all her bridges. However, while she got to that point, she was also realizing something: She was okay with it.

She had cut herself off and started losing friends after the... unfortunate incident she had revealed to Conner the other night; she was happy about being alone.

The talk with Conner had been both good and bad. The good part was that it had let her express at least some of the emotions and thoughts she had had all this time. The bad part was that it brought up this swirl of feelings and memories that had always been under the surface and popped up at the most unexpected moments. It was one thing to pretend like they were not there and fight them when they came up, it was quite another to accept that they were there and try and fight them.

In any case, it had given her a different perspective. She didn't completely believe him, but a small part of her that had been shunned for a long time was slowly getting its voice back. Maybe she could start evaluating the way she had been living. She knew that this feeling would not last long, maybe just until the adrenaline stopped pumping, but she was hoping again, and that was suddenly a good thing.

Now if she was burning bridges, she knew it was for the right reasons. Conner had shown her a whole new land on this side of the bridge to explore, and if that meant leaving a few good things behind along with all the terrible things, she was willing to sacrifice it.

Sacrifice. Thinking of the word made her think of Levitis again. *Could it all be true?* She had always had great faith in her religion, even in the hardest of times. But the way Conner was putting it; it was apparently the people working for the betterment of it that were responsible, and not the religion itself. But all the followers wanted its betterment. So did that mean the followers, or the religion itself was at fault? That meant she, Victoria, was somehow responsible for all those deaths.

No, she decided. She couldn't be blamed for supporting something that someone else misused, unless she knew about it and didn't stop them. But she hadn't. And if a sexual assault victim who had a tendency for self-blame, paranoia and self-destructive tendencies could not convince herself that she was at fault for something, it was probably true.

She checked the time. She was still an hour away, and she didn't know how much time she had. She hated this; it made her feel helpless. In response to that feeling, she drove even faster and crashing was definitely a probability now.

She crossed a fork in the road that led to the university, and she thought of Roger, as she had every time someone mentioned the university since Roger died. Roger had been one of the people who had been nice to her even after she started losing all her friends. He was headstrong like his mother, and was the first person to go to university to study. He had paved a new way before he died and many were about to follow him there. However, after his death, everyone had gotten discouraged. Roger's mother had told everyone that he had met with an accident, so it had come as a shock to everyone when she had said that Roger had committed suicide, and apparently because he had read a book by Conner!

She had found that hard to process, but then she had remembered that Conner had admitted that someone had died because of him, and that he was trying to make up for it. She believed him when he had said that he hadn't been able to find anything on Roger since Roger had conceded to falsifying all his records when he went to university.

Still, it was hard for her to accept the reality. But it was also hard for her to forget Conner's eyes, the sincerity, and the honesty she saw in them. She had never truly seen that in a person. Or maybe she had never tried.

She stopped thinking for a few seconds...

And then: that image! Those hands groping, that minty breath as if making his breath fresh for her, expecting her to like it; and those eyes...those terrible eyes...

Victoria swerved just in time to avoid crashing into those trees. She hit the brakes and let out a huge gasp. The blood vial which she had kept in a plastic packet she had picked up from home was unharmed. Whenever she least expected it, that image would pop up. It was like some sort of terrifying jack-in-the-box that sprung out of its own accord at an easily startled person who was deathly afraid of clowns.

She took a minute to clear her mind, switched on some really loud music and gunned it.

She completed an hour's drive in half that time.

She drove the Baronsville streets, which were a bit more complicated, because there were actually other cars on them and real danger to human lives other than hers, both of which had been missing for the past hour and a half.

She had a good memory (something that had not always worked in her favour) and she remembered seeing a doctor who she had heard was quite reputed. She searched a bit, well aware of the ticking clock, and found his office. She ran to it and found a waiting room full of people. She went up to the receptionist and said, "I need to see the doctor, now!"

The receptionist eyed her and said, "So do the rest of these people, sweetie. And you certainly don't look unhealthier than any of them. You'll need to wait in line."

"You don't get it! There is a man dying who needs medical attention now! I need to get him a cure as soon as possible!" she yelled.

"You've got to calm down, ma'am. Now, where is this patient?"

"He's not here, but I have his blood here. Please, I need to see the doctor!"

Suddenly the inner door opened and a man in a white coat stepped out, who she presumed was Doctor Ron. "What's all the commotion about?" he asked.

The receptionist turned to him. "This woman here says she has a medical emergency. The patient isn't here, but she has his blood."

Dr. Ron turned to her and said, "Young lady, I don't know how long that blood will take to analyze and-"

Victoria stepped forward and said in a low voice, "I have money. I can pay you extra, just please give me a cure."

The doctor considered her and then told her to come in. He apologized to the patient inside and said that it was an emergency, and that he would finish up later. After the patient left, he turned to Victoria and said, "What is this medical emergency?"

"I think the person has been poisoned." When the doctor assumed a sceptical look, she stopped him and said, "Please just listen to the symptoms." And then she recited the symptoms she had heard the suddenly not-so-clever Dr. Clark reciting under his breath.

Dr. Ron narrowed his eyes. "Those symptoms could only have been found by someone with medical experience. Either you're a medical student trying to pull a fast one on me or-"

"No!" Victoria almost yelled. "I'm serious. The man has these symptoms, and here is his blood. The doctor doesn't have the tools for analysis and he suddenly got injured so he couldn't come here himself. Take the blood and analyze it, please." The lie came out smoothly, without thinking. She had got some good experience with lying for a few years, after all.

He didn't look convinced, but he took the vial. "I still don't know why they sent you, but from the symptoms you told me, I think I know what it is, and it's very serious. I have a lab here. I just need to run a quick test on this blood to be sure and, and then make the medicine. Wait outside. I'll tell you when I'm done."

Victoria exited the doctor's office. She didn't want to engage in small talk with any of the other patients, so she went outside.

She waited for a few minutes, tapping her foot impatiently and looking back into the clinic to see if the doctor was done. She turned back around and saw *him*.

He was across the streets with some people...who looked like they were his friends. There were two boys and a girl. Victoria tried to understand this scene. Those three people seemed to be...enjoying his presence. Victoria could almost see the scar and the glint of evil from those eyes all the way here. They suddenly started down the street. He started talking to the girl, and she laughed...and blushed? She was *charmed*? By *him*? Victoria could see his lust for the girl.

They stopped in front of what looked like this coffee shop. Then he gestured for the others to go in. They went in and he turned and started to walk towards Victoria. He smiled at her from afar, and it was as if Victoria's feet were glued to the ground. His smile grew bigger as he got closer to Victoria, until she could see the entire line of his exposed teeth when he was an inch away from her, and yet Victoria couldn't move.

"Hello, slut," he whispered, putting his mouth close to Victoria's ear. "I could see you admiring me from afar. I can see you want me; you want what you deserve."

Then he pulled back and leaned in to kiss Victoria...

The hand on Victoria's shoulder caused her to jump and almost shriek. It was the receptionist. "The doctor says he done and that you should come in immediately." Victoria looked over to the coffee shop. He was still there with his friends. She had imagined the last part, thankfully.

"Are you okay?" the receptionist asked. "I thought there was an emergency..."

It took the image of Conner dying to get her back to her senses temporarily. She didn't answer the receptionist and rushed into the doctor's office.

He said, "It was as I suspected. Your friend *has* been poisoned. It's mainly delivered through liquids. What was he mixed up in? I-"

"Can he be cured and how long does he have?" Victoria interrupted, desperate to leave as fast as possible.

Dr. Ron realized that there was no point talking, so he got up and gave her a few pills in a white container. "Give him those as soon as possible. These will cure him." Then he gave her different pills in a separate red container. "Give those to him an hour after you give him the first pills. Those will help him in his recovery, if you reach in time. He has only about five to six hours after the poison takes effect. I suggest you hurry."

"How much do I owe you?"

"Well, for the lab-"

"Give me a goddamned number!" Victoria exclaimed. She had the cure; she felt suffocated; she wanted to get out of his office and never see it again.

The doctor told her; she gave him the amount plus a little extra as promised and then exited fast. She ran into her car and started hyperventilating a little. She looked at the cure in her hand, and tried to calm herself down, to keep the emotions and thoughts under control. But even then they got through.

Even after paying the doctor, there was plenty of money in Conner's wallet. Levion wasn't far enough from this place. She needed to get farther away, as far as possible, and never come back. She looked in the rear view mirror. With horror, she saw that he was saying goodbye to his friends and coming her way. Victoria didn't know what else to do other than start the car as fast as possible and speed off.

****

Victoria managed to get out of Baronsville without killing anyone or causing any major property damage. She was now driving back to Levion at an extremely high speed, thoughts running through her head.

He has friends! That pervert has friends!

It was approaching evening now, and it was getting dark, leaving the surroundings looking ethereal in the twilight. Victoria, though, wasn't paying attention.

How can he have friends? Ever since he did what he did to me, I don't think I'm worthy of having a single friend! And he has so many who seem to like him!

She turned and then bared her teeth. This was a long stretch of road with no turns. She increased her speed.

He had been flirting with that girl! I was reluctant to talk to a boy for such a long time and he was acting casually around them, as if it was okay that he kept thinking about groping them against their will?

Then a particularly hard thought struck Victoria just as she made a hard turn at the end of the clean stretch of road and the side of the car struck a tree. Victoria didn't notice, nor care at that point.

What if that girl was his girlfriend? What if I'm the only person that he... liked in that way? She seemed to like him. Did she want to kiss him as well? Would that have satisfied him, or did he not get pleasure if he didn't force himself? Or did he just feel like doing that with me?

She sped up the car, doing so almost unconsciously.

Was I really a slut? Did I give him that vibe? Do I really seem that way? Am I? He seemed so popular and loved, how could someone like that be wrong, right? Why would he take me then if he could get anyone?

Her thoughts were cut short, however, when she had to swerve to make a turn. This time, however, her luck ran out and the side of her car hit the trees hard and sent the car spinning before finally crashing again and coming to a stop. Victoria had worn her seatbelt and was miraculously still conscious, although her head had hit the steering wheel. She was dazed for a few seconds, and tried to collect her bearings. Luckily, she was conscious enough to take Conner's medicine, which had also been unharmed. She had to get out of the car through the rear end door which was undamaged.

It was lucky that she didn't have a passenger, because he would probably have thrown up, peed in his pants, fainted, and then thrown up while he was unconscious, and that was before the crash.

Victoria stumbled some distance away from the crashed car and sat under a tree to catch her breath. Her mind numb, she surveyed her location. She had travelled quite far in a short time, but that was a result of extreme mental pressure. She felt something wet on her forehead and touched it. It was blood. She had a cut there, thankfully not too deep. She went back to the car, opened the trunk and took out a first-aid box. She cleaned up her wound and put a band-aid on, though she doubted that would help or hold for long.

Then she remembered what she was thinking about before she crashed, and everything started rushing back. She had always been scared of the night, and now that fear was returning in full swing. Her breath started coming in spurts. She squeezed her eyes shut and balled her hands into fists, trying to fight off her thoughts. However she didn't realize that the containers were in her hand, the lids of which scraped against her skin. Her reverie was broken and she looked down at the containers in her hand which reminded her why she had undertaken the journey to Baronsville in the first place. Conner was dying; he had little time left. An hour, an hour and a half maybe. She could have reached back to Levion with some time to spare if she had her car. Now, on foot, it would be cutting it very close and she would have to use every shortcut and trail she knew.

She cursed. Then suddenly she realized that the only reason that she was in this situation was because of *him*. Her whole life seemed to have been shaken by *him*, by that one terrible person.

She stood up. Yes, he was a terrible person. And yet she had let that one terrible person dominate her entire life. Was it right? Was it right that she hadn't been able to open up to anyone till Conner? Was it right that she had a warped view of all physical relationships? Was it right that because she couldn't fully trust anyone, she couldn't love anyone? Was it right that she had a big hollow hole which was supposed to be filled with relationships that she had practically dug by shunning all her friends in one way or another?

Victoria was at crossroads. She knew that the only way she could get to Conner in time was to run as fast as she could. Now the question remained: Was she going to be running *towards* something, or running *away* from something?

She looked towards the town and squared her shoulders. She had decided.

She was not going to run away anymore. Because even if she *was* a slut, she didn't deserve that. She didn't deserve to be treated that way by anybody. And it *wasn't* right that while she couldn't live a normal life, the perpetrator lived a happy, carefree existence with actual friends, admirers, maybe even a lover; things that she was denied. If that scum could lead a normal life after violating her, she didn't need to give him any power by letting it destroy her.

So she ran. And as she ran, it was as if she was leaving a great weight behind. She had not yet gotten over everything that had happened to her; she was still affected by it; that one moment of enlightenment wasn't enough to undo all that damage.

But she had made that first step in the long run: accepting that she could leave it all behind, accepting that she had the power to make it hurt less, the power to move on.

And as this weight lifted, her feet moved faster. It was as if her body knew that now it could run faster towards Conner, towards hope, towards belief.

Towards a better life.

****

Victoria stopped and panted. She had been running hard for almost an hour now; the town was yet half an hour away. She had been taking shortcuts, running through brambles, thorns, acquiring numerous cuts along the way, which she had ignored then, but they were really starting to sting now. Her legs were burning. She had always been a good runner, and had kept in shape, particularly because she believed that her livelihood was eventually going to depend on great shape and good looks.

She didn't know if she was going to get there in time, though, and if she was going to even make it and not collapse on the way. Right on time, she got a text and read it. It was Mrs. Stewart. It read:

Hurry up. Dr. Clark has forced himself in here with a few other people. I will have to let him give Conner what he says is a cure if Conner's condition worsens much more. It doesn't look like he has much time anyway.

Victoria cursed loudly. Well, there was more motivation if she really needed it. She sent a quick reply: Give me 20 minutes more. I will be there. Stall him, and don't let him touch Conner.

Victoria took a deep breath and started running again.

Fifteen minutes later, she was at the outskirts of town, but on the east end, where King's Hill was. To get to the inn, she had to go all the way to the west end of town. She skirted the base of the hill and paused for a second. She looked in the Natis Eye...

...Right at Father Godfrey. He had been sitting, observing the town and keeping a lookout for Victoria. He had hoped that she would not interfere, but she had and in a big way. It was possible that she could actually save him. Not if he had something to do with it. He sent a text off to Dr. Clark: She's almost there. Do it now.

Dr. Clark read this text and got up and said, "I can't wait any longer on your whims, Mrs. Stewart. I need to inject him now or this man will die."

"And I told you, a few more minutes," she said firmly.

Dr. Clark's lips curled slightly. "Well, I can't help it. I don't know how Miss Parks has brainwashed you, but I need to do my job." And saying so, he turned to his bag.

"I know the special relationship you share with Father Godfrey. And I'm sure that he'll not be pleased if I tell tourists about the existence of Levitis, and maybe ask for alternative remedies, or even ask about the benefits of converting to another religion. And I'm the only person who knows how to run the inn, so you can't even try to replace me."

Dr. Clark eyed her, then gestured towards the pale Conner, who didn't even seem to have enough strength to tremble, and said, "He can't wait long. I will give you two minutes, by which time I will have prepared the syringe."

Victoria was running hard. She had crossed half of the town.

Dr. Clark retrieved his syringe and his vial of medicine.

Victoria had crossed three-quarters of the town.

He inserted the syringe into the vial and drew the fluid inside.

She was now within sight of the inn.

He slowly tapped it and then squirted a little.

She was at the entrance of the inn.

"Can't wait any longer," he said.

She reached the steps.

He indicated to a few of the people to make sure Conner stayed still while he delivered the 'medicine'.

She was up the first flight of stairs.

He pressed around to detect a vein.

She was up the second flight.

He moved the syringe towards Conner's arm.

She was on the third floor.

Dr. Clark was about to insert the syringe into Conner's arm when...

The door burst open and Victoria ran through, practically tackling Dr. Clark to the floor, breaking the syringe and spilling his medicine. Before anyone could say anything, Victoria had opened the white container, put the medicine in Conner's mouth, raised his head and poured water down his throat, taking the medicine along with it.

All of them started talking simultaneously, including Dr. Clark who had exclaimed, "How dare you!" And then, "That was my only batch!" Most of their words, though, were a jumble to Victoria, who was only looking at Conner. There seemed to be no change; he appeared perfectly still. Everyone slowly stopped talking when Conner didn't move. A minute passed, then two, then five. People had started murmuring, but Victoria didn't care. He wasn't moving, he wasn't breathing. She had failed. Just when she thought she had succeeded, she had failed.

And then suddenly there was a small twitch. Then another. And then he had taken a deep breath. Victoria gasped, letting out the breath she didn't know she was holding. She let out a few tears, but these were not tears of sadness, which was all she had become used to. These were tears of joy. She handed the red bottle to Mrs. Stewart, who had come to stand next to her, and told her to give it to Conner after an hour. As soon as Mrs. Stewart nodded, her legs finally gave way and she collapsed out of exhaustion, her head hitting the bed right next to Conner's head.

The last thing she heard was Conner breathing.

Chapter 17

Where Are You, My Saviour?

When Victoria woke up, the sun was shining brightly. Her vision was blurry; she tried to figure out where she was. She was on a soft surface and her head was on a comfortable raised surface. It must be a bed. A bed at home. She was still feeling sleepy and cuddled up under the warm covers to go back to sleep when one of the memories of last night shot through her mind. Which meant she was...

Her eyes flew open and she sat up; she looked to her left. There was Conner, sitting on the bed with his legs under the covers, eating a cookie. She gave him a horrified look. He was in mid-bite; he smiled with his mouth full of chocolate cookie and said, "Hey!" Then noticing her horrified look, he chewed quickly and said, "You better look there first," pointing towards the centre of the bed.

Victoria turned to look and saw what appeared to be a partition of pillows between the two of them. Conner explained, "Mrs. Stewart wanted to monitor both of us together and she wanted you to be comfortable, so she kept you on the bed and partitioned us. She was up here an hour ago."

Victoria looked relieved to which Conner appeared hurt and said, "Hey, I'm not that bad a choice to wake up next to."

Victoria blinked and appeared at a loss for words. He hastily said, "I was joking, Victoria."

Victoria shook her head and said, "Sorry. A bit sleepy." She looked at him. "How long was I out?"

Conner replied, "Mrs. Stewart informed me that you were out since you saved my life last night. Thanks a lot for that, by the way." He smiled tenderly.

Victoria returned his smile and said, "I'm not going to say it was nothing, because it was really something."

Conner laughed and said, "Well, you're certainly going to have to tell me all about it then." He paused and said with his eyebrows raised, "Mrs. Stewart told me that you collapsed out of exhaustion, almost as if you had...run a lot. You didn't run to Baronsville and back, did you?"

At the mention of Baronsville, Victoria remembered the events that had taken place there and shuddered. Before Conner could ask, she said, "I'll tell you. Give me a while." Conner looked at her for a second and then nodded.

"So when did you wake up?"

"Middle of the night, actually. I looked around, trying to figure out what had happened to me and why you were sleeping on the other side of my bed. Everything was a blur. I was lying awake for some time before Mrs. Stewart came up to check on us and saw me awake. She told me that I needed to sleep and that she would explain everything in the morning. I slept; it wasn't that hard. My body had been hurting throughout the night, but it was decreasing.

"She did explain everything to me when I woke up, whatever she knew anyway, how she had found me collapsed; how she had called the doctor but you had interfered. From what she told me, you forced him to tell everyone that it couldn't be Levitis and then you managed to keep a vial of blood, effectively defying one of the most powerful people in your town. That was extremely brave."

Victoria blushed slightly and said, "You helped."

Conner laughed and said, "I helped? Oh, yes, Mrs. Stewart told me I said something. I was out of it; I can only remember vague images. Maybe I could hear at that time and realized what you needed and tried to help. The one thing I can remember clearly was intense pain, a burning throughout my body that was unbearable at times." He shook his head and then continued, "And then you returned a few hours later in the nick of time to save me from what we know was to be near-certain death."

Before Victoria could say anything, the main door opened. Both of them tensed until they saw Mrs. Stewart coming in. She came into the bedroom and said, "Oh, good! You both are awake." She said this with a smile, which seemed a bit forced. She turned to Victoria. "Are you all right? You seem better now."

Victoria smiled and said, "Much better now. Thank you so much, Mrs. Stewart."

"No problem. Come; let me give you some food." She started to move around when Conner said, "Something's wrong. What is it?"

She hesitated and then said, "It's about Victoria." Then she added hastily, "But it can wait."

Victoria said, "You can tell me now, Mrs. Stewart. It's alright. I'm fine and if Conner is the problem, it's fine for him to know, whatever it is."

She looked at Victoria and then sighed. "Your mother called. She wanted to know if you were fine. Once I said that you were, she said to tell you that she doesn't want you to go back there. They heard about what you did with Dr. Clark, and they think that you've embarrassed them and ruined the family name. She said she's sending over a bag of clothes. I'll send it up once it arrives." She paused and a curious look came over her face. "She also said that they found the car and that your father's never going to forgive you. Did you really wreck that car so badly?"

A troubled expression came to Victoria's face. She closed her eyes and shook her head lightly. Then she opened them and said, "Yes,

I didn't see the turn clearly and ran into the tree."

Mrs. Stewart nodded slowly, not looking fully convinced. "And, of course, there's another thing." She took a deep breath and continued in a hard voice, "I need answers. I've been deflecting questions from everyone in town, first about you, Conner, but now about Victoria as well. They ask me why I keep you two here, to kick you out. They claim they'll pool together the money and pay back Conner's advance payment for the month. I can't ignore them, especially considering I don't have any information from the two of you. I trust you two, but I need to know what's going on." She paused and then looked pointedly at both of them and said, "And if anything is, you know, going *on*."

Conner picked up on what she was saying first. With an embarrassed look on his face, he started shaking his head vigorously saying, "No no! Of course not. There's nothing like that between Victoria and me." Once Victoria figured out what Conner was saying, she mirrored Conner's embarrassed look and then started shaking her head as well. Mrs. Stewart raised her hands and they stopped. She had a relieved and slightly amused look on her face. "Well, that makes things easier, although you both are adults and I have no control over you." She paused and before she could continue, Conner let out a groan of pain, which brought her rushing to his side. "What happened, Conner?"

"I'm still getting these short bursts of pain," Conner said, wincing. "It'll pass in a while."

Mrs. Stewart nodded and said, "I'll be back in a while to check on you. And then, pain or not, you have to explain yourselves." She turned to Victoria. "There's some food. Have some. You need to regain your strength." So saying, she turned and left.

Victoria turned to Conner with a concerned expression on her face. "Where does it hurt?" she asked.

Conner straightened up and a small smile came to his lips. "Nowhere," he replied.

"Then why-?"

"You didn't seem like you were prepared for a talk right now. I wanted you to get everything off your chest first, if you want to, or at least rest for a while."

Victoria closed her eyes and said, "It's time to tell you the rest. Everything. But I need to prepare for it, please." She added quickly, "And don't worry. I'm not going to lose control like last time. I'm stronger now."

Conner smiled at her and said, "Good. Let's make you even stronger. I've already showered. You should eat something and shower. After that do you think you'll be ready?"

Victoria considered and then nodded. Before she went to the bathroom, she looked at Conner and said, "There's something different about you."

Conner smiled again and said, "Well, Father Godfrey was right about that, at least. Nearly dying makes you cherish life more." Before Victoria could ask, he said, "I'll tell you after you tell me."

Victoria made a face and then nodded. She got up to brush her teeth and shower and then she stopped. "I don't have my brush or anything to change into."

Right on cue, there was a knock on the door and Mrs. Stewart came in with a filled travelling bag. Conner proceeded to look sick as soon as she walked in and she asked him how he was feeling. He said that it was a bit better. She then explained that these were Victoria's clothes her mother had just dropped off. "Victoria is welcome to take any of her other stuff she's left at home," her mother had reportedly said.

Mrs. Stewart gave Victoria a sympathetic glance and left.

Victoria stared at the bag as if it contained a monster that was going to jump out at her as soon as she unzipped it.

Conner stood up. "Open it, Victoria," he said. "This is not the end of your family; you can still reconcile with them, if not now then later."

Victoria nodded slowly. She stepped forward, set the bag flat on the bed and was about to unzip it before she remembered *all* the clothes that were going to be inside the bag, and she involuntarily blushed. "I think I'll open it and take the clothes out in the bathroom," she said before she hurried into the bathroom carrying her bag with her, leaving a confused Conner standing there looking at the bathroom door. He thought for a second and then it hit him. Embarrassed himself, he sat back down on the bed. After a few minutes, he heard the sound of the shower. It brought to him the image of Victoria in the shower. That image stayed for a few seconds before he realized what he was doing, shook his head and got up, and moved to the couch, where he couldn't hear the shower.

Conner brought out the story and read it over. It was pretty obviously mirroring his life here in Levion. The big question now was: What was going to happen next? How was Conner supposed to proceed from here?

He considered this till he was interrupted by Victoria. She was standing in the doorway to the bedroom. She had changed. Conner had been so deep in thought that he hadn't heard her get out. She gave him a curious look and said, "Conner, I asked you what that is," pointing to the journal in his hand.

Conner didn't see any sense in lying to her. "It's a story I'm working on. A *good* story."

Victoria stepped forward. "Can I see?"

Conner pulled the journal back and said, "First you finish your story, then I'll show you."

Victoria sighed and sat down next to Conner. "It's not easy talking about this, Conner."

Conner got up, put the journal on the desk, sat back down and said, "Victoria, if you don't talk about this, it'll torment you forever. The very fact that you agreed to do it shows that you're willing to overcome this, to try and better yourself. I haven't thought of you as a 'bad' person; in fact I admire your strength and courage for getting through it."

Victoria's eyes were downcast and she said softly, "I'm not sure I even got through it."

Conner slowly extended his hand, put it below Victoria's chin and raised her head till her eyes were staring into his.

"Look into my eyes, Victoria. They're not going to hurt you; they're not going to do anything to you. You can see that in them. You can also see that I believe in you, and even if you say the worst things possible, my belief that you're a strong woman won't change."

Victoria looked and saw everything Conner had said, and more. She could see Conner's sadness, his guilt, his remorse. At the same time, he could see her sadness, her loneliness but above all, there was a fear, an overwhelming fear of terrible things that threatened to engulf her.

Victoria straightened up. "I remember where I left off. I think I'll continue from there."

Conner extended his hand and said, "Do you need to crush this again?" A smile tugged at the corners of his lips.

A faint smile came to Victoria's lips as well and she said, "No, not right now. If I do, I'll be sure to bring the ice-pack as well."

Then both smiled at each other for a second before Victoria's face became serious and she said, "Well, I guess I better start then." She took a deep breath and continued her story.

****

I managed to sneak home without anyone seeing me. It was not easy; I looked behind every five minutes to make sure I wasn't being followed. When I reached home, I went straight to my room and locked the door. I didn't talk to anyone that night - no calls, no messages. Whenever anyone from home knocked on my door, I said that I was sick and I had eaten so I didn't want anything.

I became a mute spectator to my own demise, looking at myself from the outside, unable to stop myself from hurtling down the path to destruction. A sixteen-year old girl barely kissed a few times, who was suddenly exposed to darkness, humiliation and whose innocence was destroyed. I had always been receptive to the outside world, sensitive you could call it, and this just broke my spirit to see that someone could violate me so easily and so...cheerfully.

I sat on my bed, crying. Suddenly, I got this feeling like my bed was too soft, too open. I felt the urge to hide, to protect myself. I went to the corner and folded my legs and put my hands around them...a foetal position, I guess. I don't know why I went into that position but it seemed comfortable and safe. I cried like that, softly, though at first. I didn't want my family to hear.

I was in shock...I didn't know what else to do. Whenever the crying worsened, I pushed myself further into the corner and squeezed my legs closer to me. All the lights were on but even then I couldn't close my eyes. Because every time I closed my eyes, that image came into my mind. I could feel him edging towards me, I could hear his footsteps. But whenever I opened them, there was nobody there that I could see, but it was like there was a presence lingering at the edge of my vision that seemed to dart away as soon as I looked at the spot. I kept eyeing the bathroom door, the other side of the bed, the partially open cupboard door. Anyone could have been hiding there, watching me. I had even closed the window tight and drawn the curtains, but couldn't someone break the window softly and come in? I didn't dare to get up and check. So I stayed there in mortal fear, crying, trying to keep my eyes open, looking at every possible opening.

That night passed by terribly. It's all a blur. I think I got exhausted enough to fall asleep there and then kept waking up with nightmares.

Needless to say, at dawn, I felt and looked terrible. I had school, but I really didn't want to go. I had no choice, though, because if I stayed home claiming to be sick, then Dr. Clark would have come and checked on me, and he would see that there was nothing wrong. We're all a bit paranoid about diseases here, as you can imagine.

Besides, it was the last day of school before summer. So I slowly built my resolve and got out of the corner. I had only a quick shower because I didn't want to stand so exposed for so long. It was extremely hot that day, but I wore a long-sleeved T-shirt and jeans. I didn't want to seem... slutty. I skipped breakfast, saying I had an upset stomach and that I would eat something light in school, which I didn't do. My parents asked me if anything was wrong, but I just made a lame joke and almost ran out of there.

School was another nightmare to go through. There was this gaggle of students around me, laughing, talking and smiling. Such empty, pointless banter. I avoided everyone who tried to talk to me, all my friends, all my classmates. But there was really one person I couldn't avoid: My boyfriend.

Yes, I did have a boyfriend then. We had just started dating a week and two days back, and I liked him. He was a really nice guy. As soon as I saw him, I froze. I didn't know what to do. I knew I wasn't going to tell him. That would have just driven him away. After all, I was dirty. I was a dirty slut.

He smiled at me and leaned forward to kiss me.

An image flashed in my mind. I jumped back and pushed him away. He looked at me, bewildered. He asked me what was wrong. "It seems like I am," was what I wanted to tell him. But I didn't. I claimed I was sick and didn't want him to catch it. He didn't look like he bought it but didn't ask any more questions, for which I was grateful. At the moment, anyway. Maybe if he had, things would have turned out different.

I used to be pretty studious, but that day I couldn't answer any questions, primarily because I wasn't paying attention. It was as if my brain was working in a stop-jerk fashion, not working for a few minutes before suddenly springing to life. The thoughts that caused it to spring to life were not pleasant thoughts, though. I barely managed to get all my homework down, and I had no idea how I would do any of it.

I gave my boyfriend some lame excuse about getting a head start on my homework and rushed home. I didn't know what I thought he would see, maybe some filth, maybe even he would think I was a slut. I wasn't sure if I was exuding that vibe.

Another reason I didn't stay back at the end of school: There was really no one I could be with. Boys of any kind were the last people I wanted to see, and the girls sitting around gossiping and discussing clothes wouldn't really understand, now would they? I didn't want to be with any of them. So I rushed home.

That was the beginning of the second-most terrible summer of my life.

I didn't go to any get-togethers or sleepovers or anything of that sort, claiming I was not in the mood. They tried to convince me, but that was when I started learning how to get evasive and give vague answers to people. After the shock wore off in the first few days, however, was when I really started thinking about what had happened.

I started avoiding everyone even more. My parents wondered what was wrong with me, but they assumed it was a phase. I stopped playing games with my younger brother, instead snapping at him and ignoring him. I never responded to any of my friends' messages, including my boyfriend's. I started exploring the surrounding forests more carefully because it was a place I knew was free of people. I was always afraid of someone sneaking up on me, so I studied the paths, became aware of all of them, and therefore knew all the secluded paths, areas and shortcuts in the forest.

I avoided both sexes for simple reasons. What if any boy would suddenly decide he wanted me and tried to touch me? When I looked at my girlfriends, it was potentially even worse. I saw their short dresses, makeup and pretty faces, and there was one thought that always came to my mind: What sluts. They're the real sluts, right? So why didn't anything happen to them?

Why didn't they get molested?

That was the one terrible thought that I couldn't get out of my mind. As much as I tried, I couldn't help wondering why me and not them. It was as if at times I was almost wishing for it to happen to them, so that they could stop being so happy and self-pleased, for them to know what I was going through. As soon as I thought these things, I hated myself for it, but I couldn't stop myself.

And then the question turned to whether I really was a slut. Had I attracted that...thing, that person? Had I unconsciously given off signals that I wanted that to be done to me? Did I give those signals off all the time? Was I giving them off now? I looked at myself, sitting in a clearing in the forest, and every movement of mine, every gesture, seemed perverted. Then another thought struck me: Had I consciously flirted with him, gave him a look, a wink? I didn't remember anything like that, nor did I behave like that on a daily basis.

Or did I? Did I do those things in daily life without realising it? Did I flirt with every guy here as well? Did they think of me as a slut as well?

My first kiss had been with someone who had turned out to be a player, though at the time I hadn't known it. So I had gotten a sort of reputation, which I was determined to eradicate. I had planned to go steady with a guy to prove that I wasn't the kind to just kiss and leave. I thought that what happened to me was a sign, that it showed me that maybe I was that kind.

By that time, I was already starting to feel like I was a slut. What if my boyfriend had been dating me just because I was one? I would have to check. I wouldn't tell him what had happened, though. I was too ashamed about that, disgusted at myself for having let it happen in the first place.

So when nobody was at home, I invited him over. He tried to ask me something, but I shushed him and led him up to my room. I was wearing a tank top and short shorts. I couldn't read his expression. Maybe it was shock, maybe it was appreciation. He didn't comment on my clothes, however. Once in my room, he tried to say something, but I started kissing him furiously. He seemed caught off-guard, but he consented after a second or two. He broke away and then managed to ask, "Victoria, what is going on?"

"What do you mean?" I had said.

"I mean, why have you been avoiding me? And why have you called me here so suddenly and what are we doing here?"

"We're doing what you wanted to do. It's why you started dating me, right? Because I'm a slut." And before he could say anything, I started

kissing him again. Then I stopped and took off my top, revealing a lacy bra. "Feel me up," I said. "You know you want to."

He had his mouth open. Maybe he was just shocked at what he was seeing. "What are you waiting for? Do it," I repeated.

He took a step back and shook his head.

"Why?" I asked him. "I'm a slut, right? Do it!" I didn't care what he did. I deserved it. I was a slut who had let someone else do more to me while I was dating him.

He shook his head and said, "I don't know what's going on, but I'm not going to do this. I didn't believe you were like this. If you ever want to talk, you can tell me, but until you do, I don't think I can date you. I'm sorry." Saying so, he turned and left. I couldn't read any of his expressions, except for one: disgust.

Then it hit me. I understood why he had not done anything to me. He was disgusted with me. He could see I was dirty. He didn't want to do anything to a dirty girl, a dirty whore. A cold shiver suddenly ran through me and I felt exposed. I hurriedly changed into something longer.

I don't know how much he told everyone, and I wasn't in the mood to talk to any of my friends. I was just thankful my family hadn't mentioned it. I was holed up in my room, mostly staring out into space or crying or hating myself. Sometimes I would go out into the forest so I could explore and continue doing all of that out there. Time passed quite quickly. Several times I would look at my watch and realize that hours had passed without me knowing it.

During the summer, I had visited the Sinome quite often as well. I prayed to Natis, asking Him if I was on the right path. I didn't get a sign. I didn't tell the Father what was wrong with me. I was afraid of what would happen. The Father might say I was corrupted, that I didn't deserve to be part of the Sinome. That was one thing I couldn't be an outcast in.

My parents tried talking to me several times to ask me what was wrong; a few of my closer friends also tried to get through to me, but failed. I deflected all their questions, and acted quite rudely to a few of them.

By the time school started, I'd like to say I was better, but the truth is I only seemed better. I used to cry on the inside. I didn't have to think anymore; mistrust, self-loathing, all of it was in-built into my actions now. I learnt how to fake smiles, how to make small talk and then disappear from the conversation. My studies suffered and all my teachers were concerned, but I didn't care.

At this time, I also started hooking up with guys. Not serious dating, just hook-ups with guys I made sure weren't going to tell too many people about me. After all, I had a rep, right? Might as well use it, but that didn't mean there was a need to spread it to my family, who might get nosy.

Still, it reached them, but it reached them after I failed my end of term exams and had to repeat the year. They asked me what I was doing, but I denied it all.

Even the Father called me to the Room of Secrets. He asked me what was wrong. I lied saying that nothing was wrong. He knew I was lying, but he simply said, "Whatever difficulty you are going through, either accept it completely or fight it completely. Don't stay stuck in the middle."

That advice stayed with me for a long time. I looked at my life, the loss of friends, the destruction of my studies, the intense pain and misery. I didn't want any of it. But the Father made me believe that it could be fought. Something in me kept telling me not to give up, so to silence it, I decided that I would try one last time, give it my all and if that didn't work, if I wasn't convinced, I would accept my life.

So every time I had a destructive thought, or felt angry or resentful, I tried to stop myself. I tried to convince myself that I was a good person and what had happened to me would never happen again, that I wasn't a slut. I didn't hook up with any boy for a month, and I think I was getting better. It had taken time to get over what happened to me, and I thought I was ready to move on. So I decided to take the ultimate test. I snuck off to Baronsville. This time, though, I didn't wear anything revealing.

Going to Baronsville at all, now that I think about it, was my first big mistake. My second was going there when it was dark. I thought going there and nothing happening would help me get over my fear. I wasn't ready for it yet. But there was someone there who was ready for me.

I saw the alley. I was terrified, my mind screamed for me to turn around, but I didn't. I kept walking, trying to keep the fear under bay. I had reached the half-way point, the point where it happened. And I stood there paralyzed. I couldn't go any further, unable to imagine what would happen if I walked any further and found him there. I found out soon enough because I turned around and started almost running back to the way I had entered; I found him there.

He seemed surprised to see me, but that terrible grin came to his face quickly. "Why hello, slut. I see you're back for more." Everything was the same about him, from his scar to his pale skin to his terrible eyes that made me feel as if I was going to be engulfed in darkness.

I tried to scream but no sound came out. I turned to run but he grabbed my right arm and turned me around roughly and slapped me with his right hand. "Don't try and run away this time, slut. Know your place!"

I couldn't break his grip which was now on my left arm, so I tried to hit him with my right but he just grabbed it midway and jerked it down. He let go of my left arm and pulled my hair. I tried pushing and scratching, but it hardly had any effect. He started kissing me. I can still remember the breath had the after-taste of mint, as if he had had a mint sometime ago. I kept moving my head from side to side as much as I could with my hair in his grip, and tried to make sure he couldn't get a grip on my lips.

He let go off my hair and squeezed my ass quickly, and then he went under my shirt and squeezed my breasts. "Nice, aren't they?" he whispered as I struggled. He returned to grabbing my constantly scratching left arm. I tried to stamp on his foot, but I realized that his feet were pressing mine to the ground, preventing me from lifting them. "Shall we go all the way this time?" His voice carried his tone of gleeful anticipation.

My blood froze as I realized what he meant and my terror and panic really took hold. I threw my head back and then slammed it into his head. This loosened his grip on my hands and legs, which allowed me to knee him in the groin and push him away. I punched him in the nose, though I don't know how effective that was. I didn't push my luck any further, instead turning to flee. He didn't chase after me this time, instead calling out to me, "You'll be back, slut! You know where to find me!"

At the end of the alleyway, it was almost as if I expected to find him there, blocking my path again. But he wasn't. There wasn't anybody there.

I ran back to the train station. I took the slowest train back for the simple reason that it was the most crowded. I didn't want to be alone at that moment, to be exposed, to be vulnerable. I wanted to blend into the crowd, to be just another face and not a singled out woman ready to be assaulted. I didn't care if I met people from Levion getting home (which incidentally I did), I didn't care if I couldn't cry in front of all those people. I just wanted to be forced to act natural, to act as if nothing was bothering me, to act as if my world wasn't shattering in the vain hope that acting like everything was fine would actually make it fine. I had gone to Baronsville to get over my fear, to show that I wasn't a slut. But then I had come really close to rape again. Was that a sign that I wasn't meant to get better? That I was a slut?

By the time I reached Levion, I was convinced of the fact. Before going home, however, I needed to do something. I needed to visit the forest, the trees. I needed to get some sense of calm and serenity before everything started spiralling. So I went into the forest and there, in the seclusion where I knew no one could find their way or hear me, I could finally let out my pent-up scream.

****

My parents found out that I had snuck off to Baronsville, and they grounded me. I didn't really care. I was going to stay at home anyway. I cried a lot, but not as much as before. But the pain was much more intense. This was because this time, my will to fight was lost. Father had said that either fight or accept. He hadn't known, of course, for what he was giving this advice. If only he had known. So now I had to accept. But accepting is not easy.

Misery for what had happened to me overcame me. I couldn't go anywhere without fear that someone would jump out of a corner and do something to me. The worst part was that I was not the worst off. I knew there would be someone out there who hadn't been as lucky as me, whose experiences would make mine feel like nothing. And I was terrified that I could be one of them one day. My only piece of luck was that I wasn't at that point. Yet.

I couldn't handle all the horror, paranoia and depression my life had become. One day, it became too much and I grabbed a paper cutter, the nearest thing to me, and I cut my wrist with it.

That was the first cut. The first in a long line of self-destructive physical activities. The things I did to myself were terrible. My life revolved around hiding the signs and marks from everybody and seeking that small relief in secret, but it really didn't end the pain.

And then it led to thoughts of the last destructive tendency: Suicide. I tried in smaller ways, though that never worked. Then one day, it escalated to the incident forever referred to as, "The accident".

I jumped from a roof.

I went to the tallest building in Levion and jumped. That day, my thoughts had become overwhelming and hurting myself just wasn't doing it. It was a cowardly act, a means of simply escaping all my problems though I didn't think of it as cowardly back then. I was to find out, though, that it was not as easy to escape as I thought.

I survived the fall, as any rational person could have told me I would. The only difference was that I had a few broken bones now. I claimed that I wanted to stargaze, and I had tripped and fallen. My love of nature was common knowledge, and I managed to convince them that it wasn't intentional and that I was merely stupid.

I was confined to bed for a few months, during which I had time to think. I couldn't cry or scream or show any sort of extreme emotion in front of my parents waiting on me, mostly my mother. However, a number of my neighbours also visited and expressed their sympathies. Some of my old friends also visited. They talked to me, updating me about what had been happening since I had stopped hanging out with them and saying that they missed me. They also asked me what had happened to me. I apologized to them, saying it was just a bad time and that I would love to hang out with them. I even apologized to my parents, telling them I would improve in my studies.

The truth was, I intended to do all this, but for different reasons than they thought. I had realized that hurting myself was akin to hurting everyone, because I could see how much the thought of me hurt had hurt my family. And I could see that they didn't completely believe the whole "stargazing" explanation. So I decided it was easier for everyone if I stopped putting up a fight, and gave up. So I did. I pretended to be alright with everything, faked all my interactions. I had missed another year of school because of my "accident" and I found it easier to start afresh with people who I didn't know personally.

So I took my classes, did my studies because I found that passing would get my parents off my back. I hooked up with more boys, but ensured that they told no one. I didn't want the news spreading at all because I couldn't be sure whether my parents were trying to keep tabs on me. Several times I could have gone all the way, and there were times I was gripped by this mortal fear that I would get my virginity torn by some rapist. But some part of me stopped from having sex, and I think I'm grateful for that.

I worked out too, to retain my figure. After all, if I wanted to leave Levion and be a prostitute, I had to be in shape. I believed that was what I was meant to do, because after all, people seemed to see only that in me, right? I figured there would be some cure for Levitis somewhere, or being safe in bed would prevent me from transmitting it. I also started to learn how to use my knife, just in case of emergencies because I heard clients often got rough.

And that was my life till a few days back. You know, something, though? All throughout, there was one thought that stuck with me and pushed me onward. In all the stories and books we hear and read growing up, the princess is always in danger, and the hero always swoops in and saves her. That's what I spent hours wondering, calling out: Where are you, my saviour?

That was what made me believe that I can't have true love, because if I could, wouldn't I have got some sign yet? That often was something that pushed me over the edge, because when it feels like you're the only one no one wants to save or even help, you have to try a different way by yourself.

Victoria stopped. She was out of breath and her narrative was at the end. At times it was more like she was letting a trapped monster out that had been eating her from the inside. She felt...relieved.

Some parts had been harder, but now she felt better. She had been lost in that time and now she returned to the present, and turned her attention to Conner, which gave her a start.

Conner looked even more zoned out than she assumed she had looked. His mouth was slightly open. As Victoria watched, tears slowly started rolling down his cheeks.

"Conner why are you crying?" she asked, putting her hand on his shoulder and shaking him.

He didn't snap out of his reverie; instead, he came out of it slowly, blinking a few times and looking at Victoria. When he spoke, his voice was shocked and trembling.

"I killed her, Victoria."

Chapter 18

Transforming Memories

The mind is complicated. It has the unenviable job of being a relatively small part of our body that guides our entire organism to brilliant actions. As such, it has to have its own survival mechanism too. It needs to adapt to situations as it sees them, so as to make sure the stability of the person is in no way affected.

Modifying memory is an important way of adaptation for the mind, achieved through the subconscious. As we grow older, we often find that there are things we don't remember clearly, parts of our history we can't recollect or even certain memories that are later proven to be completely untrue. Our subconscious modifies these memories, sometimes represses them, keeps them from our conscious mind, and allows us to recollect only at the point where it knows it will be least damaging to us. Or at least until the mind is faced with a situation in which it is better to remember.

It seemed that Conner White's subconscious had apparently decided it was time to bring back some memories.

Conner was in that moment of perfect clarity: where you can see your life laid out in front of you bare, the kind they say you get just before your death. It was as if he was reliving his life, but this time as he passed through his life, flashes of images and words came forth, all explaining things he had never previously known the answers to.

Victoria stared at Conner, completely confused. "You killed somebody? Sophie? What are you saying, Conner?" Victoria also felt a little peeved that she had poured out some of her worst secrets to this man, and he was here blabbering nonsense.

Conner sensed Victoria's anger, and said, "I'm sorry, Victoria. It's just that you made me realize something and I'm just really shocked." Thoughts and emotions surged into Conner's head even as he was speaking.

"What did I make you realize?" asked a perplexed Victoria.

Conner stood up. He couldn't sit. He wanted to run, he wanted to jump; he wanted to just let this feeling last, this moment of euphoria when you were aware of everything, every crack in wood, every hair on the skin. He wanted to let out all the emotions he didn't know he had that had suddenly come to the surface. Tears came unbidden to his eyes, the only outlet for his emotions.

Victoria stood up too, worried now. Was Conner breaking down?

Before Victoria could say anything, Conner raised a hand and indicated to her to take her seat, which she did slowly, keeping an eye on him.

Conner didn't make a move to wipe his tears. Instead he said, "I wasn't talking about Sophie, Victoria. I was talking about my first girlfriend. She committed suicide, but I never found out the reason why." He looked her directly in the eye. "Until now."

Victoria took a second to register what Conner was implying before she gasped and said, "You mean...?"

Conner nodded and said, "Yes. The same thing that happened to you happened to her."

"How can you know that now, after all this time?"

The tears stopped falling and Conner nervously started pacing. He was experiencing a whole spectrum of emotions. Depending on what Conner was thinking, some emotions were more intense than the others, but the other emotions were there in the background, ready to jump to the forefront. The emotion most intense right now was the thrill of revelation.

"I know it seems strange," Conner said in a slightly excited voice. "But you seem to have triggered certain memories, and putting those memories in perspective has explained a lot."

"Like what?" asked Victoria, now curious.

Conner stopped pacing and his voice turned sad. "Well, when you were talking about how you avoid everyone, sit at home and cry, I remembered that she had started becoming reticent for the past few months. She told me she was just getting sick very often, and when I visited her, she certainly looked sick. Now that sickness seemed more mentally induced. Her friends also told me that she had been behaving strangely with them, not returning phone calls or texts."

Conner paused for a second, closed his eyes and then continued, "It was the little things that you mentioned that she had started doing. She started commenting on people's clothes and their attitudes, things she had never done before while she herself started wearing longer clothes. She started avoiding all boys except me." Conner's brow furrowed. "And there was something else: she seemed disgusted (or was it scared) by the colour grey." He was cut off by a sharp intake of breath by Victoria, which caused him to open his eyes.

"I can't handle the sight or smell of mint, and dark striped t-shirts terrify me," Victoria said, touching the chain of her necklace.

Conner waited till she indicated to continue. "Her behaviour towards me had also become strange, but I didn't think too much of it. She had always been a bit insecure, but the insecurity really increased during this time. She was constantly asking me if I was going to stay with her, whether she was good-looking enough for me. Several times she would ask me whether there was something wrong with her. I assured her that she was great, but somehow I don't think she was convinced. There were days when she didn't seem to want to be touched anywhere; on other days she was overly aggressive."

Conner put his hands to his eyes, lightly pressing them. His voice was full of pain. "Towards the end, her behaviour became even more erratic. Subtle jerks of her hand to hide her wrist from me. Sharp objects around that she immediately put away as soon as I walked in. Pills I had never seen before, apparently medication which she was taking because she fell ill so frequently. She also started talking about endings and said that we would be together forever; now I realize she meant forever for her, which wasn't to be very long." Conner moved his hand and opened his eyes wide. "Oh God. Once she asked if we could have sex, saying that she would like to try it at least once. I got confused, saying that we would have a lot of time in the future, and that it wasn't necessary to do it right now. She said that it was better that I was the one to do it and nobody else. I said I would; we hadn't been dating for long enough. I could see that there was something more, something she wasn't telling me, but I couldn't get it out of her. A few days later, she was gone."

"How did you not see it, Conner? And the day that it happened, didn't you know something was wrong?" Victoria asked with anger in her voice. "You could have still comforted her, saved her. Yet you were there as her boyfriend and you didn't help her in any way!"

Conner didn't flinch; he didn't try and defend himself. He simply nodded. "I was away for a family vacation for a week or two. After I came back, she was acting strange. That was the only time it could have happened." He closed his eyes again. "I was blind and stupid. She was so convincing about everything, and I just believed her. I was just so happy having her; I didn't want to accept that something was wrong."

Victoria stared at Conner, still fuming before something stuck her. "Why aren't you more upset about this? You're infamous for being pessimistic and negative. How are you not getting angry at yourself, getting depressed or saying terrible things about yourself after realizing something so monumental? Not that I want you to, I'm just wondering," she hastily added.

Conner raised his head to the sky, closed his eyes and stayed there for a few seconds, letting all his emotions stabilize and flow to the ground, and return to the earth. Then he looked at Victoria and smiled. It was the most genuine smile Victoria had seen on his face.

"You haven't realized it yet, Victoria. Something so monumental, as you put it, could not have gone by unnoticed by me over such a long period of time. It was in the back of my mind all along, and it was because of that that I have been this way all my life. I did feel responsible for her death, and all my anger, all my guilt I buried was slowly influencing all my thoughts and decisions until it became a way of life for me. My writing is the only way to release those emotions, and the subject material of my writing is an expression of my emotions which show how much I truly blame myself. Also, I've been so angry at myself that I've been trying to project that feeling of hopelessness on others as well so that they know what I'm feeling, as if they could share my pain and somehow end it.

"So Victoria, I'm done punishing myself. I made a mistake, and I've suffered for it. And punishing myself has done no one any good, and it's definitely not what she would have wanted." He paused and looked Victoria straight in the eye. "And I think you should do the same. Get out from the weight of this torment by believing that it can be lifted."

Victoria looked down, wanting to believe what Conner was saying, but she just couldn't. "It's not as easy for me as it is for you, Conner."

"Why?" asked Conner forcefully, causing Victoria to jerk her head up. "Because you think you deserved everything that you got?"

Victoria didn't say anything, but her eyes confirmed Conner's statement.

"Okay, Victoria. I might not know about you, but I knew Linda. She was an amazing girl, and from what I've said, she had at least half the same reactions as you. She even got farther than you and managed to kill herself. So why was that? Why did she feel like her life was so bad that she had to do that? Was it because something bad happened to her? Earthquakes, hurricanes, floods - all of these tragedies occur in people's lives. People try to rebuild. So why don't they kill themselves? Simple: They don't hold themselves responsible for the tragedy; they just realize that they have to move on.

"So Linda and you, and God knows how many others respond terribly because you feel like you're responsible in some way for it. So here I am telling you - *You are not responsible."* Conner said these last four words with particular emphasis, enunciating every syllable.

Victoria got up fast and looked at him with fury. "How would you know, huh?"

"You think I can't understand because I've never gone through it? Then help me understand. Let me see if I understand why you think you're responsible," Conner said quietly, but with great force. "You thought you were a slut. Let me go through why. You say you 'might' have encouraged him, flirted or even made eye contact or anything with him. Now I want you to think, did you? Or is it just your mind trying to put that feeling there just because you think it *will* be there?"

Victoria looked stunned. She blinked and stayed quiet. She had no answer.

"And even if you had, do you really think even your closest friend in the world would automatically get the right to do anything he wants to you just because you were nice or looked nice?"

Victoria shook her head slowly. "I might not have done that, but I still looked like a slut," she said quietly.

"So you say you looked like a slut. Tell me, the second time it happened to you, were you wearing anything provocative or revealing? You said that you wore modest clothes, right?"

"Yes, but by then he already knew that I was a slut and knew...what was beneath the clothes." Victoria looked down in pain.

"So, what, you think you were giving off this vibe because of the clothes you wore? Let me point something out to you. Please don't panic now; I'm just demonstrating." Saying so, he stepped back and removed his shirt.

Victoria stepped back. "What are you doing, Conner?" she exclaimed, startled.

"I'm not going to do anything," he said, raising his hands. "I just want you to look at me. I work out, and you can see the effect."

Victoria looked and saw that Conner indeed did work out; his arms and chest muscles were developed well, not too much; he had still managed not to look bulky. It was a nice effect, she had to admit, to herself, at least. To Conner she said, "Why are you showing me this, Conner?"

Conner put his shirt back on and said, "I've always tried to maintain at least a decent figure, because I've believed that I was a little good-looking, and didn't want to lose that. So would you have thought badly of me if I tried to look good?"

Victoria shook her head. Conner continued, "And now suppose I wore a vest showing off my arms and shorts showing off my legs; would you call me a man-whore?"

Victoria was startled. She shook her head without really thinking what Conner was talking about. Then realization dawned and her eyes widened.

"Exactly," Conner said. "So why is it that you think that if you want to look good or wear what you're comfortable in, you automatically become a slut?"

"I...I...Because..." Victoria was at a loss for words. "Because if I wear stuff like that, it's more likely that it'll happen because it's like I'm tempting them?"

"Yeah, so when I was standing there with my shirt off, did you automatically think of raping me? You have the knife. Did you think of threatening me with it and making me do as you please?"

Seeing Victoria's shocked look, he didn't wait for a response, but continued, "The thought must have never even occurred to you. That's the point. The thought has to occur to you, and that's the important part: The thought. The second time you weren't wearing anything immodest, and yet he attacked you. It didn't matter what you were wearing, he would have made up a justification regardless. When someone does something bad, they can justify it however they want, that's all it is: a justification. And people who want to do terrible things will do it for reasons as simple as 'I wanted to' or as complicated as 'I had to.'" Conner's voice quietened. "If someone does something bad to you, it doesn't make you dirty, it makes them dirty." He paused for a second.

Victoria stepped back, as if physically struck by Conner's words, but more by what they meant. Conner's words made sense, and somehow she had always known them. But to hear them and realize they were true was a completely different story. She had to re-evaluate her whole life, her self-worth. She sat back on the couch, her eyes wide as the full import of everything that happened over the past few years really crashed on her.

Conner seemed to sense this, and he sat down next to her and waited. It was a few minutes before she started, her voice trembling, "I lost so much, Conner. I destroyed relationships, I destroyed friendships, I ruined my career; I almost died! I changed my whole life around that one belief, and now I see how wrong that was." She looked at Conner with pleading eyes. "I've been so affected by this; am I ever going to have a normal relationship again? Will I find love? Will anyone love me? You suddenly seem to have all the answers, right? Tell me."

Conner took Victoria's hand and said, "Victoria, you're a beautiful, smart, nice girl. There will be many out there who will definitely love you. It's not too late to change. You can and will find love. And Victoria, there might not have been a saviour in your life, but even if there was, how would you know? You didn't let anyone in. How can anyone help you if you choose not to let them help you? You need to first decide whether you want to be saved, and then if you think you're worth it. Because you have to believe that you are worth it, and so much more, for it to happen."

"What about Mike? Why did he go?" Victoria whispered.

"Victoria, he was overwhelmed and he ran away. He probably just couldn't understand what was happening, and left. People fear what they don't understand. I'm not defending him, I'm just saying that you were affected badly; he couldn't see why, and it affected him too. You did come on him pretty strong."

Victoria looked down and closed her eyes. She suddenly opened them and turned to Conner with fear written all over her face. "What about those images?" she said with fear in her eyes. "How can I stop those images, even if I don't think I'm responsible? They're still terrible."

"It'll take time. They'll fade away, if you simply let them. Learn to accept what happened to you, and try to leave whatever you can of it behind."

Victoria's fear slowly faded and she said, "So you really think I can do it, Conner? You think I can finally leave this behind? I can move on?"

Conner gently raised Victoria's head as he had done before till she was looking at him and said, "Yes, Victoria. I believe in you."

Victoria became quiet. "There's something else, though," she said softly more to herself than to Conner. "Something that I think I just fully realized myself while I was talking right now. The second time, when I saw those eyes coming down that alley, I...I think I lost something." She didn't say anything for a whole minute before continuing softer than before, "I think a part of me lost faith."

She was quiet. "My faith. Natism. A Leviite's greatest treasure. Our strongest belief. I don't think I admitted it to myself. But I always knew. I had a feeling at the back of my mind. A feeling where I didn't believe anymore that someone was always going to be there watching over me, that everything that was happening made sense, that at the end of the day I was going to be fine. I didn't have that one belief that had made up my entire core anymore. And that broke me more than anything. Because I hated myself. I hated that I felt that way. I buried that feeling deeper than anything else, but that self-hatred drove me to such extents that wouldn't have been possible otherwise. No matter how much I tried to love Natism after, no matter how much ever I tried to honour Natis, that feeling made me doubt myself and I felt guilty for having it there."

She turned to Conner, tears streaming down her cheeks. But these weren't hysterical tears. These were the tears of quiet acceptance, when something you've been trying to deny for a long time finally settles in your mind, like the loss of a friend.

Conner sat down next to her and waited for her to continue. "I just couldn't see a reason for it all, Conner. I couldn't see a reason for it all to happen. Why such terrible things and why me? I hadn't been a bad person. I didn't deserve it. If Natis does things for a reason, why did He do that to me? It seemed so senseless." She paused and then looked down. "I just didn't understand, and I still don't. You gave that speech about how everything is connected, but I don't see how this is. I doubt even you have an answer to that."

Victoria didn't want to look at Conner. She was sure she would see his inability to answer written all over his face. Instead she heard his smile through his voice, "Actually, I believe I do have that answer."

Victoria's head shot towards him in disbelief. He was indeed smiling and before she could say anything he continued, "When outsiders come into this town, they are not to be trusted, made friends with or given any more information about the town than is absolutely necessary. Now, when I came into the town, you helped me. You've helped me to an extent that no Leviite would normally have. And you could only do that if you were dissociated or disillusioned with Levion in some way. And you were, and the way Natis chose to make that happen was through what happened to you."

Victoria couldn't say anything. So many thoughts and arguments were rushing into her head, but they just wouldn't come out.

"You might think that there are many other ways that this could have happened, but one event could have stopped you from going down several other paths that might have proved worse for you in the long run.

"All I know for sure is, Victoria, that if that hadn't happened to you, we wouldn't be sitting here across from each other. The truth about Levitis would never have been discovered and many more would have died. It doesn't mean that you like your past; simply accept it."

Victoria stared out into space for a minute or two before she closed her eyes. She felt overwhelmed. Then a glow started spreading inside of her, a glow that warmed her completely and she knew that Natis had returned to her. She was happy. She wanted to cry with joy, to leap, to run. To run to a destination which she could now see more clearly. Instead she hugged Conner.

Conner was surprised, but he hugged her back. "Thank you," she whispered.

"No, Victoria, thank you," he whispered back. They stayed there for a few seconds before Victoria pulled back and asked, "Why are you thanking me?"

"Even I learned how terribly I was leading my life, the burden of guilt and despair I was carrying around, and now even I can move on from that. Without you, that might never have happened. So I have to thank you as well."

Victoria smiled at him. Then she straightened and there was a renewed energy about her. "So, what now?"

Conner mirrored this position and said, "Well, now we save the town of Levion."

Chapter 19

Inspiration, Surprise Allies, Secret Plans-
It's a Real War Alright

Before they did anything else, Victoria wanted to read Conner's story, so he showed it to her. Victoria read *The Dark Alley* silently and said that it was beautiful. She then read the one that Conner had started writing after that and said, "This is…familiar. And incomplete."

Conner nodded. "I'll finish it soon."

"Do you know how it's going to end?"

"I think I have a fair idea."

With that, Conner put the stories away.

The first thing they had to do was to decide what they were going to tell Mrs. Stewart, and figure out what they could expect if they told her the truth. After some discussion, they agreed that she deserved to know the truth, especially after all she had done. Conner then updated Victoria on what Father had said in their meeting, and how Father had foiled Conner's plan. Victoria's mouth opened wider and wider.

"I can't believe that they went to such extents to…control us," she said at the end of it.

"They used good things to justify bad actions; it doesn't mean you have to ruin your image of the good things, right?"

Victoria nodded. "And that glass of water at the end..."

"...Was probably spiked with the poison," Conner finished grimly.

"It's never that hot in the Room. Could he have purposely kept the air-conditioning down so that you drank the water?"

"It seems that way."

"And that jamming device...now I understand why I can't get reception in the Sinome sometimes."

"We really underestimated the Father, which was stupid considering all we even suspected him of doing. We have to be more careful."

Before Victoria could ask anything else, there was a knock on the door. Both of them got up, steeling themselves. They walked to the door; Conner nodded to Victoria and opened it. Mrs. Stewart seemed surprised to see both of them at the door. "You both are fine now?"

"It seems so," said Conner, smiling at Victoria. His smile quickly faded as he turned to Mrs. Stewart. "Come in, we have a lot to talk about."

****

Conner narrated the entire account to her, at points adding extra information that he had discovered from the Father. Conner decided against telling her how the Father had tricked her and entered his room. Victoria also added her comments and information that Conner had forgotten to mention. She also mentioned little things to Mrs. Stewart, things that Conner as an outsider would never be able to understand, but which Mrs. Stewart understood immediately. Mrs. Stewart's face remained expressionless throughout and when Conner finished, she didn't say a word for a few minutes.

"Can I see those books you got information from?" she finally asked.

Conner nodded and then went into the bedroom to search. After a few minutes of frantic searching, Conner came back open-mouthed.

"They're not there!" he exclaimed.

Victoria also got up to search, but Mrs. Stewart raised a hand. "Don't bother," she said. "I think I know where it is. Dr. Clark spent an awful lot of time in there, remember? I'm pretty sure I saw him interested in a book, which I didn't see later. I didn't really see him take it, so I couldn't say anything."

Conner and Victoria eyed her uneasily. "You do believe us, don't you, Mrs. Stewart?" Conner asked.

She raised her head to look at him with piercing eyes. Without her jovial smile and pleasant demeanour, she seemed kind of intimidating. "Yes, I do, Conner. It would explain a lot, better than the explanations we've been fed all our life." She got up. "It's a lot to process, Conner, and I have to think about it. Thank you for telling me. I think it might get me closure." And uttering this ambiguous statement, she left, closing the door behind her.

Conner turned to Victoria, "What do you think?" he asked.

"Don't worry," Victoria said, smiling. "She's solid. It's just very hard to think that all this is possible."

"Or maybe it's very possible but you all are just blinded by everything you already think is true to see what really is true?"

Victoria chose to ignore this. Instead she said, "I need to use the bathroom." So she turned and walked towards the bathroom. When she was almost at the entrance, however, she tripped and fell straight onto the floor. Conner saw this and rushed to her side. He helped her up, asking if she was okay. She nodded, rubbing her shoulder. "Wait a second," she said after a minute. She got down on her knees and reached into a corner of the bathroom, right under the toilet and her hand came out holding a small red-coloured shard of glass. "Why do you have this here?"

"Ah, I must have missed that. Give it to me; I'll throw it away," Conner said, slightly embarrassed.

Victoria pulled her hand away. "You had a girl over here? Who was it and when was this?" Victoria asked suspiciously.

"Well," said Conner, "Rosaline was here."

"What? Why would she be here?" Victoria asked, clearly not believing Conner.

So Conner told her what had happened when Rosaline was here, including the part where she admitted the mayor was using her to gain information.

Victoria laughed aloud. "That does sound like Rosaline. She keeps trying to portray this aura of poise, but she never really lets anyone see how smart she actually is. She prefers to keep them in the dark, letting them think she's some kind of bimbo so they underestimate her. She tried to run for mayor; unfortunately this town didn't let go of its "traditions" and elect her. She's the one who runs everything anyway through her husband, though that poor man has no idea. I can imagine her trying to get information out of you by playing the victim."

Conner felt stupid at having been duped so easily. "Don't worry about it," Victoria consoled him. "She has that effect. But there's one part of your story that doesn't make any sense, and that's this," she said, raising the shard.

"What? Rosaline is too prim and proper to drop a bottle?"

Victoria laughed again. "Ah, the hurt ego of a man. No, I mean this is not the kind Rosaline usually uses. Don't look at me that way; in a small town where you're restricted from going out, you tend to keep track of whatever new cosmetics you can buy in town. Rosaline buys all of her beauty products specially-made, all very expensive. She would never come down to our level and buy something that we common folk use, which this is. I would recognize this tinted red colour anywhere."

"So why would she be carrying around a bottle that she never even used?" asked Conner, confused.

Victoria hit upon the solution. "Because she intended to break the bottle and didn't want to waste her expensive stuff. So that means that she wanted to draw you in here and clean up, which means..."

"...That she wanted to check something in the room without me there! My story was out, and she asked me about it!"

"So that means she knew that you were not who you said you were long before Nancy told us!"

Conner nodded, but he was still not sure where this was headed. "But if she knew who I was, why didn't she confront me or expose me?"

Victoria said, "There must be a reason. Rosaline always uses what she has. She could help us if it helped her get power. Want to go make sure we can use her before she tries to use us?"

Conner said sheepishly, "Yes, I would usually say, 'Let's go to the source,' but every time I have, I wish the job could have been outsourced instead."

Victoria smiled and said, "Well, this time you have me with you. Let's go pay the *real* Mayor of Levion a visit."

****

When they left the inn, they felt like they were looking at the town differently, as if everything had changed or at least their view of everything had changed. The townspeople had put aside their anger towards Conner, preferring to regard him with a cool distrust, which they now applied to Victoria as well, after they heard that she had defied Dr. Clark, the protector of their lives! Victoria seemed unfazed by this, though. She explained to Conner that Rosaline spent her time in the house, though she periodically checked in on the Mayor. Rosaline deliberately didn't stay in the office full-time so as not to make anyone suspicious.

"How do you know all this if she never shows it?" asked Conner, amazed.

"I used to idolize Rosaline when I was younger," said Victoria with a small smile. "She was this beautiful woman who I could see was so ambitious. I knew she wouldn't let anything slide past her, so I started observing what she did on a daily basis and tried figuring out why she did it. I respected her, even though I didn't really approve of her methods. Then other things came in the way, and I stopped thinking of her."

Conner nodded. He wanted to point out that Rosaline and Victoria seemed to be very different people and Victoria seemed like a better person, but he held his tongue. They reached the mayor's house and knocked on the door. It was opened within minutes by Rosaline, who didn't seem surprised to see them. "Why, it's Conner...White and Victoria Parks. What an interesting pair visiting me! Please, come in." She said this in a cordial fashion and stepped aside to let them in.

They stepped inside and she led them to her living room. It was very artfully decorated, and it had an elegant feel to it. They sat on the sofa and she sat on an armchair opposite them. "Can I get the two of you anything to eat or drink? One of my cookies that you love so much, Conner?"

Victoria didn't want Rosaline to work her magic once again on Conner, so she leaned forward and said, "Let's just get down to business."

Rosaline gave her an arched smile and said, "I like the sound of that."

"I know you tricked me when you visited me. You wanted to read my story and I have a feeling you knew who I was as well," Conner said.

"Me? Trick you? How would I do that?" she said, appearing hurt.

"Mrs. Dobbs, it won't work. Even if Conner gets fooled by you, I won't."

Ignoring Conner's hurt look, Rosaline turned to Victoria and considered her. She assumed a serious expression and said, "You seem to be clever. I heard about you saving Conner yourself. That seemed bold, though I don't know the reason behind it, which might make it stupid." She smiled again, "And call me Rosaline. I have a feeling we're going to be good friends."

Victoria smiled back. "Okay, Rosaline. I have a feeling you want something from us. What is it?"

Rosaline gave such a feline smile that Conner could almost imagine a tail flicking lazily behind her. "You seem to know something about me, dear," she said to Victoria. "So it will come as no surprise to you that I desperately wanted to be mayor of this town." Here, her face and voice grew hard. "All I want is the benefit of this town, but I can't do that if the people don't want to let go of the past. And it's not helped by the fact that Father and Dr. Clark seem to hold more power than I do! I want to bring in doctors of repute to help cure Levitis, so that we can finally expand, so that we can maximize our potential! I also know that it's impossible under the present circumstances because I realize the power of the people *really* in control." Then her voice devolved into one with terrible, seething anger. "And I hate it."

A few seconds later the real, terrifying face of Rosaline was replaced once again with the charming, poised veneer she wore on a daily basis. "So, unless you can give me this, you have nothing of substance to offer."

"What would you say if I were to tell you that I could cure Levitis, plus have connections in a construction company that would start negotiation with you when it is to your convenience after Levitis is cured and expansion is possible?" Conner asked.

"I would say you were high," Rosaline said shortly.

Conner laughed. "Well, it is true, Rosaline. I can do all that. All you have to do is agree to do what we ask you to."

"And what do you want me to do?" she asked cautiously.

"We don't know yet," Conner admitted. "But we'll tell you soon enough."

Rosaline raised an eyebrow and then turned to Victoria. "I like you. Tell me, is he on the level?"

Victoria nodded. "Completely. We *can* achieve all that."

Rosaline considered this and then said, "I would want to ask how, but I doubt you will tell me, and I suppose it is better that way." She looked at Victoria and smiled. "It's lucky you were here. You should have seen this one the last time we met. Like putty in my hands." Ignoring Conner's embarrassment and indignation, she rose and the other two rose with her. She looked at Conner and said, "I would do *anything* for that to come true. So let's see if you can make this miracle come true, even if you're not the High Natish anymore."

****

When they reached the inn, Mrs. Stewart was waiting for them. "Where did the two of you go?" she asked.

Conner opened his mouth to answer but she raised a hand. "Victoria will fill me in. I need to talk to her alone, Conner. She's a Leviite herself, so I need to get her take on all of this happening. I'm sorry, please don't take this personally."

Conner nodded and took a step back. "I completely understand," he said. "I'll take a walk. It'll help me think of the next step." He nodded at Victoria, who looked a bit surprised but went with Mrs. Stewart regardless.

Conner started walking at a measured pace, not too fast nor too slow. He didn't go near the main town, skirting the outskirts. The townspeople shot him dark, furtive looks and he ignored them. *A beautiful relationship*, Conner thought wryly.

After about fifteen minutes, a boy of about twenty ran up to him and asked, "You're Conner White, aren't you?"

Conner looked at the boy who had asked this clearly rhetorical question, since he was the foreigner running around wrecking havoc. "Yes, and who might you be?" he asked, bracing himself for a fight.

"My name is Harold Cage," the boy said, apparently mustering up courage. "And I see you've become close to Victoria. You better not have done anything to her, or you-"

"Whoa, whoa!" Conner exclaimed, putting his hands up. "I'm not doing anything to Victoria. I care for her deeply, and I only want the best for her." As Harold stepped away, startled, Conner put his hands down and examined him. "And apparently, that's what you want as well."

Harold lowered his head and nodded.

"Victoria never mentioned you," commented Conner curiously.

"Doesn't surprise me," Harold said ruefully.

"Secret admirer?"

Harold laughed as if the idea genuinely amused him. "Quite the opposite actually. Victoria knows how I feel about her. She just completely misinterprets it." Before Conner could ask, he continued in a slightly sad voice, "She thinks I'm some kind of crazy stalker, but what she doesn't realize is that I like her, and I want to help her through whatever she's going through. I was friends with Mike, her ex, and he told me how she had acted with him. I knew something was wrong, but I could never bring that up, obviously. She would just freak. So I showed her my affection in the hope that she would realize that she had a friend in me, that she could turn to me, but she misinterpreted it. By the time I realized what I was doing wrong, she had stopped listening to me completely. It was a big mess."

Conner looked at this boy who obviously liked Victoria very much and wanted to help her, but wasn't able to. He put his hands on Harold's shoulders and said, "Chin up. I'll talk to Victoria. But if I do, I might need some help from you on another matter, but which Victoria will really appreciate. Will you help?"

Harold was extremely surprised at this but he nodded enthusiastically. "Yes! Thank you!" Conner got his number, nodded to him. As Harold walked away, Conner remembered something and stopped him. On Conner's question, Harold gave him the answer, somewhat reluctantly. Conner promised he needed it for a good reason, and he started walking towards his destination.

Conner reached the house he was looking for, took a deep breath and knocked on the door. It was lucky no one else was in the vicinity.

A woman opened the door and on seeing Conner, immediately adopted an angry expression.

"What in the name of Natis do you think you're doing here?" she hissed. "How dare you, after all the hurt you've caused her already?"

"Please, I just want to talk to her," Conner said softly.

"For what? So you can convince her to kill herself as well?" the woman was almost yelling now.

"Look, I want to apologize to Nancy, to-" Conner started desperately but was cut off by a tired voice from inside the house. "What's all the ruckus, Beth? You know I don't want any visitors and-" Nancy herself had come to the door and she was staring at Conner.

"I was just getting rid of him, Nancy," the woman named Beth hurriedly told her and then turned back to Conner, ready to berate him once again. Conner seemed ready to launch into a speech of his own when Nancy cut both of them off.

"Let him come in, Beth. Let me see what he has to say."

Beth stared at her. "Are you sure, Nancy? This is-"

"I know who this is, Beth," said Nancy tiredly. "Let's get this over with."

Beth shot Conner a dirty look and said, "Well, I'm going to be in the other room. You tell me if you need anything."

"I think we'd better do this right here, Mr. White. Too many sharp objects in the house." Conner wanted to assume she was joking, but she had a matter-of-fact look on her face.

"Okay," Conner said, taking a deep breath. "I'm here to apologize. For writing those books, for pushing your son to that extent. I'm really sorry."

Nancy blinked. "Okay, continue. Tell me your justifications, tell me how horrid your life has been, and how it is somehow okay in the world for you to write all this," she said, her voice bitter.

"There are none," Conner said flatly.

"Excuse me?" Nancy asked, bewildered for the first time since she opened the door.

"There are no justifications. My biggest mistakes didn't make me write my books; my books were my mistakes. They're my life's work, and they caused someone to take his own life. That itself is terrible. And on top of that, my wife also lived an unhappy life because of me, and died knowing that I was hurting people, including myself, my whole family, and yet she couldn't stop me. So I know a little of how you feel and I want to tell you that I'm deeply sorry, even though I know that won't bring your son back."

Nancy stayed quiet for a few minutes, simply looking at Conner. She finally said, "I can't forgive you. She paused and she looked as if she was thinking something over. "I think I'll move. There's nothing except memories of dead family members here. Thank you, Conner, for at least trying." So saying, she turned and shut the door on Conner's face. Dazed, Conner stood there for a minute when he got a text from Victoria telling him to come back to the inn.

When Conner got there, he met Mrs. Stewart and Victoria at the front desk. Mrs. Stewart greeted him with a soft smile, which Conner took as a good sign, considering Mrs. Stewart hadn't smiled at him for some time now.

"I've discussed it with Victoria," she said. "And although I hate it, I have to agree with your findings. Especially when you consider the fact that even though neither the Father nor the Doctor likes me, I'm still alive because I've never gone for check-ups after I started defying them. Come to think of it, I've seen people who were considered "unpleasant" die pretty quickly, and it was always cited as Natis' wrath. We never realized, as you said, that Natis would never want that." She paused and then said, "Let's go up to the room and strategize. I'll close up everything here."

As Mrs. Stewart went about closing up the inn, Conner whispered to Victoria, "She's taking it quite well."

Victoria snorted and said, "You should have seen her when she was with me. She was devastated. She didn't want to believe it, but I showed her the discrepancies. She just doesn't like showing anyone what she's really feeling. I suppose that's what happens when you're a woman running something as big as the inn all alone."

Conner nodded. Mrs. Stewart finished and then led them up. They went into Conner's room. Before they started their discussion, Conner told them of his conversation with Nancy. They were shocked, but glad Nancy had taken it better than expected. Then they started their discussion.

It was a long and tiring discussion. They decided on a few key points fairly quickly though. Even though this whole thing was essentially because Fathers throughout the ages had deceived the townspeople, they needed to deceive the townspeople one last time to make everything right. There was no way that the Leviites could know the truth; it would destroy the very roots of their basis of life. Their deception needed to be strong enough so that the Father would not be able to refute it. The Father was at an advantage, because they couldn't expose his methods of deception.

They also needed a way to stop Godfrey or Clark from poisoning the minds of the people again and hurting them. Though that was a difficult part, nobody even talked about hurting them. Levitis could only be "cured" if Dr. Clark wasn't there to spread it, and Leviites could only reach their true potential if Father Godfrey stopped stifling them.

Slowly a plan started to form. It was a few hours before they had a rough idea of what they had to do. It was dangerous, reckless and a little crazy. Then again, wasn't this whole thing mad?

"Okay, can we decide what day we're going to do this?" Conner asked.

"The Day of Natis," Victoria answered immediately. "It will be perfect for the plan, and it seems fitting, doesn't it?"

Conner and Mrs. Stewart nodded in agreement. Mrs. Stewart got up. "I need to check on a few things. I'll be back."

Victoria rose too. "And I need to make a phone call."

Conner nodded absently. He was thinking of something that he really needed to do, but which he wasn't going to share with the other two because he knew that they would never get on board with his plan.

Victoria went out of Conner's earshot and looked at the number that she had managed to get from a friend she was still on talking terms with. She took a deep breath and dialled it.

The person on the other line picked up within a few rings. A cautious voice said, "Hello? Who is this?"

"Is this Megan White?" Victoria asked.

There was a silence on the other end before Megan's voice suddenly turned cold. "I don't know who this is and how you got my number, but if you want to know something about my father, I don't know where he is or-"

"Listen to me, please. I know where your father is and I've recently come to know him very well. Please hear me out for a few minutes." Victoria told Megan about how Conner had changed, how he had genuinely been trying. She said some more about him before she asked Megan for a favour - the real reason she had called.

Megan listened quietly to this stranger who had called her out of the blue and considered what she was saying. "I'll look into what you've asked me." She paused and then added quietly, "And if what you're saying is true, thank you for telling me." She hung up.

Megan stared at her phone, desperately hoping that everything she had just heard was true.

Chapter 20

OMN!

It was two days before the Day of Natis. Conner looked out at the setting sun, apparently deep in thought. There was a knock on the door. Conner opened the door to see a burly man wearing a golden badge on his chest at his door. Behind him were, as usual, some townspeople tagging along. Didn't these people have better things to do?

"I'm Sheriff Dade; I don't believe we've formally met," the burly man said.

"Yes, what can I do for you, Sheriff?" Conner said in an annoyed tone of voice.

"I'm sorry, Mr. White, but I have to arrest you."

"On what grounds?" Conner exclaimed, startled.

"Conspiracy to do the townspeople, the town and the Sinome harm," Sheriff Dade said in a monotone and produced a pair of handcuffs.

"But that's preposterous! I haven't done any of that! These claims are baseless! On whose orders are you doing this? " he yelled, stepping back.

Sheriff Dade stepped forward and snapped the handcuffs on Conner's wrists. "I'm sorry, but I've been instructed directly by Father Godfrey. Please don't try to resist. Co-operation will make this easier."

Conner stopped struggling the moment he heard Father Godfrey's name. A look of comprehension came over his face and he said, "Ah. Father Godfrey put you up to this? Now it makes sense. Father Godfrey hates me." Saying these words, Conner started walking without being told and people hurried to catch up with him, including the surprised Sheriff.

As Conner was climbing down the steps he exclaimed, "Father Godfrey doesn't like the fact that Natis is now on my side and not his!"

Sheriff Dade seemed confused by this (an intelligent sheriff was probably not the best thing in a serial killer's town) but he hit Conner and said, "Less talking, more walking." Everyone else in the line had heard what Conner said and they started texting. One boy in particular, was texting more than others.

OMN! Dis Conner guy is gng crazeeeeee! Cum to da inn, man![1]

When they reached the bottom, Mrs. Stewart was there, looking furious. "I tried to stop him, Conner! I'm sorry!"

Conner stopped, smiled at her, a wide, flowing smile. "It does not matter. I have Natis on my side." Then he continued walking.

By the time they left the inn, a crowd was gathering, watching Conner handcuffed and walking to the station. Conner just kept walking, smiling and occasionally waving at people. Suddenly, Conner stopped. A few people crashed into him, but he didn't budge. He just kept staring out into the distance, and then his eyes and mouth opened wide, a look of pure terror on his face. Then he crumpled onto the floor. Everyone surged around him, surrounding him in a circle. Sheriff Dade looked at him, panicked. "What's happening? What should I do?"

After a few minutes, Conner's eyes opened slowly. Conner rose to his feet, refusing help. There was a silence as everyone stared at

---

1 Author's note: For all those who can't read text "language", or the other (smarter) ones who prefer *not* to, this translated means: Oh My Natis! This Conner guy is going crazy! Come (This was a rather unfortunate spelling error) to the inn, person! (man doesn't always refer to a "man")

him and then he proclaimed, "Tonight I am going to die! There is an evil in this town that wants to do me harm! Natis save me!"

He dropped to his knees and closed his eyes. Everyone assumed he had fainted (or whatever had happened to him earlier) and they gasped. A few stepped forward. But they stopped when he brought his hands together and started to utter words rapidly under his breath. He was praying, and everyone seemed breathless with amazement at this utterly odd spectacle. A relative stranger praying to their God, claiming to be His messenger, in the middle of the street with hands cuffed together.

"What is the meaning of this?" A cold, harsh voice cut through the murmurs. It was Dr. Clark. The crowd quickly parted to let him through. He grabbed Conner's arm roughly and lifted him. "What is this debacle?" Dr. Clark asked the Sheriff. "Why aren't you escorting him, like you're supposed to?"

Seeing the usually calm Dr. Clark angry scared the hell out of the Sheriff and it was quite evident. The big man paled (an amusing sight) and grabbed Conner's arm. "I'm sorry, sir. I'll do it right away."

Conner's eyes opened, but his hands didn't part. He looked at Dr. Clark and said, "Let's hope I won't be seeing you again tonight, Dr. Clark." Conner didn't let the accusatory note in his voice get too diminished. Sheriff Dade pulled his arm, not wanting any more anger from Dr. Clark. Conner closed his eyes and continued praying. The crowd, much bigger than before, walked as well. Conner looked crazy, which made him appealing. After all, isn't there at least a little craziness in every great thing?

Just before they reached the station, Conner opened his eyes and yelled out again, "If I die, know that Natis wants you to start truly believing in Him again!"

"Shut your mouth," Sheriff Dade said gruffly, pushing him into the station. He unlocked the holding cell and shoved Conner into it. He took out his key to unlock Conner's handcuffs when an authoritative voice commanded, "Let those handcuffs be on."

It was Father Godfrey. The crowd once again parted, giving him passage. "Search him, confiscate his items, lock his cell and leave the room, please. All of you leave," he said when he came in front of Conner.

Sheriff Dade took Conner's belongings, put them in a drawer, locked the drawer and the door. While he was doing this, Conner said in a voice loud enough for everyone present to hear, "Natis disapproves of what you're doing, Father. Your power has corrupted you."

Godfrey turned to Dade, who stood frozen on the spot and said, "Didn't you hear me? Leave." Everybody shuffled out quietly until it was just Father Godfrey and Conner.

"You couldn't have just left, Conner? It would have been so much easier. You had to stay and poke your nose into everything," Father Godfrey whispered. Conner didn't say a word. "You know who gave you up, though? Your supposed ally, Rosaline. She told me you were plotting against me and warned me to it. I suppose I'll owe her a favour. After all, she knows who has the real power in town." Conner's face revealed a hint of dismay before he straightened it. Father Godfrey caught it and laughed. "What? You thought promises of curing Levitis would get you anywhere? She knew it was stupid and realized that she could strike a better deal with me."

"Although," he continued, "I have to admit what you did right now was clever. I can't harm you tonight because people will take you to be some kind of martyr. Well, you can't keep saying that because then people will think you're a loony. And besides, it's not hard to get access to your food." He smiled at Conner, who didn't react.

Father Godfrey studied Conner as if he were under a microscope. Finally he said, "I don't think you really understand what you were trying to do, Conner. You don't realize the benefits of our society. There is almost zero percent crime and unemployment. Everyone who wants a job is gainfully employed. They have a strong kinship. They have a strong religion. I'm like a real father to most of them; I listen to all of their problems, and nobody here needs a therapist. Everyone is happy."

"Extreme happiness comes at an extreme price," Conner said simply.

Father smiled as if Conner had made a very amusing statement. He stepped back and started walking away. "I'll pray to Natis to have mercy on your soul," Conner called.

Godfrey turned and said sneeringly, "There's no one here to perform for, Conner."

"That was no performance. That was the truth."

This time Father Godfrey didn't have anything to say. He simply turned and left the station. "Keep an eye on him," he said gruffly to Sheriff Dade and then continued on to the Sinome. He didn't need to say anything to the Leviites. Conner wouldn't die during the night, and the Leviites would regard him as a madman. Yes, Father Godfrey felt he was at the very top, and no one could touch him.

What he had forgotten was that the bigger they are, the harder they fall.

****

After Conner was locked up, the night was relatively quiet. It was an eerie, anticipatory silence, like the calm before the storm. Most Leviites stayed awake. The adults were talking while the teenagers and young adults were texting. The boy who had given them the early info on Conner soon encouraged them to join the parents in their discussion. He reminded them that someday soon they would have to make the decisions so they better know what was going on, and that they prayed to Natis too. Besides, shouldn't they have some say? Maybe they would get some freedom with this new change! That guy Harold sure is smart, many of them thought as they went to talk to their parents.

Dr. Clark had to stay awake because of strict orders from Father Godfrey, who himself was staying awake and keeping watch all night from the Tower Eye to make sure that there was no mischief afoot.

After a while, people finally stopped waiting. They started to retire to bed and Dr. Clark and Father Godfrey became even more confident that nothing could happen that could influence the town.

BOOM!

That was the sound that every Leviite heard in the middle of the night, a sound louder than the town bell; it woke them all from their sleep. Father Godfrey immediately turned his telescope to the area where it had occurred. It was around the edge of town, where there was mainly forest. He couldn't make out any human figures there. Meanwhile, while the children were kept in the house, the adults had come out of their houses and were huddled together, some worried whether there had been an explosion of some kind, and everyone wondering what the hell was going on. The elder children, at least, came out of the houses as the night progressed.

Father Godfrey quickly moved his telescope to the police station. Sheriff Dade had rushed out and was looking wildly around, but it seemed Conner was still inside. Father Godfrey figured this was a ploy and so decided to stay put. What happened next was a tad bit harder for him to get a grip on.

People of Levion! It is I, NATIS! A powerful, booming (literally booming) voice rang out clearly. And it didn't just come from the place where the first boom had come, it echoed around the entire area around the first one. *Do not come closer! You will not be able to handle my presence!*

Father Godfrey had to go and see what this was about, if only to refute the claims that this was Natis. Surely Natis would come to him first! So he left his post at the telescope and started rushing as fast as he could to the throng that had started gathering in the centre, some looking up to the Sinome for guidance.

Do not look towards that traitorous Godfrey! The voice boomed, sounding angrier. *He betrayed my trust, and he and the ones before him have been misguiding you for generations!*

Everyone gasped. Godfrey froze in his tracks half-way down the hill. Everyone turned to stare at him, some suspicious, some unbelieving, but most just looking for an explanation. Father Godfrey continued down the hill, with Dr. Clark coming to help him.

Ah, look! Godfrey's faithful helper is going to assist him. Go on Clark, help your master.

Dr. Clark stopped and looked back out towards the trees where the voice came from, but didn't see anything as before. "Go see what's in there, Clark," Godfrey whispered. Dr. Clark nodded and ran off into the trees. A few minutes later there was a barely perceptible sound, and then Dr. Clark screamed. A few people instinctively rushed forward, but they were stopped by others who realized the danger.

I warned you! The voice rang out, only this time it came from a completely different area, causing everyone to turn their heads wildly. *That is what happens to people who defy me! Go on, pick him up and get him back. You're not the ones who deserve the pain.*

Two Leviites looked unsurely at each other, took a deep breath and ran to where Dr. Clark had fallen, and was slowly twitching. Without looking around, they quickly picked him up and ran back as fast as they could, where they dropped him to the ground. Everybody thronged around him, though keeping their distance, as if he was infected.

Father Godfrey pushed past them and knelt next to Clark. Something had burnt a hole through his shirt and onto his stomach as well. It was blackened and Clark was still unconscious.

He is not dead. The voice came from both, the original as well as the new area now. *Instead of tending to him, you should see who is* really *missing from your ranks!* Heads turned, parents rushed home to check on their children. Father Godfrey's blood ran cold. He turned around to see Sheriff Dade standing there with the others. "What are you doing here?" he screamed, his voice cutting through all the others. "Where is Conner White?!"

Conner White, the only true High Natish in your town, is with me now.

They stood there, stunned, and before they could do anything, they heard another sound. This sound was more familiar to them, but it was because of its familiarity, that it struck deeper fear in the hearts of every Leviite than even the supposed voice of Natis could. It was the sound of the Sinome bell, which since time immemorial had signified the death or imminent death of a townsperson.

"Conner!" a girl screamed and started running off towards the police station. It was not Victoria, but Lindsey Peck and then her parents, who were considerably slower. "What are you doing? Go, you miserable oaf!" screamed Godfrey when he saw that the Sheriff was standing there, the events proving too much for his brain. The Sheriff started running and Godfrey ordered someone to take care of Clark and then carried on as fast as he could. All the other Leviites who could run started running as well, faster when they heard Lindsey's shriek of terror.

Sheriff Dade surprisingly was one of the fastest. When he entered the station, he saw Lindsey standing opened mouthed, staring at something. He went a little further and saw what she was looking at. This resulted in him throwing up all over the floor, causing Lindsey to jump and move aside. Jon Peck came in along with a few others. They saw everything; one or two threw up as well. Jon exited the station and told the incoming Leviites to make sure the children stayed out. A few minutes later, Father Godfrey, looking like he was on the verge of collapse, came as well. "What's going on?" he asked breathlessly.

Jon threw him a suspicious look, but indicated that Godfrey should follow. A few others came in as well.

Father Godfrey walked in, stepping through vomit, but the sight in front of him had mesmerized him, and not in the good way. Conner's cell door was wide open, his mattress and pillow had been ripped. The most terrifying part, however, was the writing on the wall. Literally. There, a dark red substance had been used to write five words in two lines:

Evil comes.

Natis save me.

A girl screamed. It was Victoria. She shoved everyone aside and went right to the cell and screamed, "Conner! No!"

Her legs trembling, she took a drop of the still-dripping red substance and smelled it. "It's blood!" she shrieked. "You killed him!" She pointed to Father Godfrey. She dropped to her knees right in the large pool of blood in front of Conner's cell, her face distraught and agonized. "He wanted to save us, and you killed him," she repeated. This time she wasn't looking at Godfrey, but simply staring out into space.

Father Godfrey ignored her and looked at the pool of blood instead. He dipped his finger in himself and smelled it. It did smell like blood. Then he suddenly spotted a stray drop. He looked around and saw another. Some part of the floor was covered in vomit, but he looked towards the exit and saw a smudged one. He ordered everyone to move aside and he managed to find a few more till the exit of the police station.

Everyone outside was murmuring; people having seen what was inside were telling the ones who hadn't. Godfrey pushed them aside, following the blood trail. The ones, who were inside with him and had seen the blood trail, followed him, including Victoria who looked dishevelled and was sticky with blood.

Suddenly Godfrey stopped. He seemed to be staring at something on the ground. He looked around and there were no other blood spots anywhere. Someone who had the good sense to bring a flashlight had been guiding Godfrey and now shone his light on the end of the trail.

It was a large Natis eye, drawn in blood.

****

The rest of the night was organized chaos. Father Godfrey tried to take over, but suddenly everyone seemed unwilling to trust their purported religious leader. So Mayor Frank took charge of the townspeople, and Father *couldn't* interfere, which was completely unprecedented. This whole night had been like a wet dream for Mayor Frank. It had been terrifying and shocking, but what really could top Natis *Himself* coming and telling the townspeople that Father Godfrey was not to be trusted? His wife, in a moment of rare insight, had advised him that he should hang back and let Father Godfrey be at the forefront and seem responsible for everything. Now, he would be responsible for the cleanup of Godfrey's mess! Mayor Frank had to stop himself from appearing ecstatic at the possible death of someone.

He organized groups of townspeople to search the surrounding area for any signs of Conner. Most of them were reluctant and scared. They were afraid of incurring the wrath of Natis. That was when Rosaline stepped forward and assured them that Natis would not harm them, convinced them that the danger had passed and that He wasn't unfair to inflict harm on them unnecessarily. Mayor Frank just stared at his wife charming people to her side effortlessly and he became strangely angry. He had just gotten power; he wasn't going to let it go to her so easily and so suddenly. He would take care of her later.

So the townspeople went off in search of Conner, being divided in such a way that they covered maximum area in minimum time. They were also not to go too far, because it was dark and dangerous, and there was no way Conner could have gotten so far if he really had lost that much blood. There was one team that was also sent to search the rooms of the inn, because the Father put forth the idea that he might have "magically" appeared there.

The funny thing, however, was that nobody knew whether they were searching for Conner because he was an escaped prisoner, or because his life was in danger. They just knew that this outsider had come in and things had changed a lot, to the extent that Natis proclaimed to them - something that had never happened before - that Conner White was important. So they searched.

The townspeople didn't feel safe going back to their homes, so Rosaline organized an impromptu neighbourhood watch, and assigned them shifts and quadrants as well. They, too, were uneasy because they didn't really know what they were looking for.

It was difficult to decide what to do with Dr. Clark. After all, what were you supposed to do when the only person with medical experience gets hurt? Unknown to them, however, Father Godfrey knew what to do. This eventuality had been accounted for long ago, and all priests over the years had to know how to diagnose and treat most basic illnesses and injuries. Father Godfrey told them to put him in his home and apply some basic burn ointment and he would be fine. They were unsure of whether to listen to Father Godfrey (which frustrated him), but Rosaline gave them the go-ahead, and so they went without question. (This frustrated him even more).

Father Godfrey gruffly said that he needed to see if anything had happened to the *Death watch* board which might have set off the bell, and he needed two good trackers to see if there were any marks indicating where the perpetrator had gone. Without waiting for anyone to respond, he turned and set off towards King's Hill. Rosaline indicated to the men that they should go, and they set off behind Godfrey.

They scanned the shortest route that would be taken by Conner if he was to climb the hill, but there were no tracks on that route. They finally reached the top and examined the *Death Watch* board. There was a big hole in the centre. When they shone their flashlight on the board, there was a name written: Conner White. The trackers shuddered while Godfrey just got angry. Then they noticed another weird thing. Directly below the board, there was a large circle in the grass rimmed by broken glass. And within the boundaries of that circle, the grass was completely trampled. Outside that circle, however, there were no indications of footsteps.

"How is that possible, you nincompoops?!" Father Godfrey yelled. He snatched the flashlight and started scanning the ground with it himself. Suddenly, he came upon some trampled grass and triumphantly exclaimed, "Ha! What's that?"

One of the men put his head down and looked as if he was controlling a laugh. He finally adapted a straight face and said, "Those are our tracks, Father."

Godfrey gave him a murderous look and threw the flashlight down in anger. "Well, search the rest of the hill! Report to me if you find anything!" Saying so, he stomped off into the Sinome.

Godfrey walked down the long aisle into his room and started climbing up the steps to the tower of the Eye. Halfway up, though, he collapsed. He managed to catch hold of the banister which prevented him from rolling straight down the stairs. He sat on the stairs and leaned back. He hadn't realized until that moment how exhausted he was. He might have a fiery temperament and mind, but his body was still old. These last few days, and especially tonight, where he had been pushed to his physical and mental limits, had really taken a toll on him. He closed his eyes for a minute or two, took some deep breaths and then got up. He couldn't afford to fall asleep, not when an infidel was trying to use Natis for his own purposes! That was just not right. He climbed the steps and sat in front of the telescope, looking for anything that would give him a hint as to where Conner White was.

****

Nobody found any trace of Conner. It was like he had disappeared from the Natis Eye drawn in blood. There was no sign either as to who had written Conner's name on *Death Watch* and had rung the bell. The people of Levion did not sleep that night, as if they knew that no dream could match the reality that they had seen. They all waited, tense, for the voice of Natis to be heard again, for someone to come with the news that Conner White was safe and sound. Neither of these things happened though. After the search parties had been called off, and everyone was in their homes for some "rest", it was said that you could hear the wind blowing the dew drops off the grass in the early morning.

Dr. Clark regained consciousness after a while; he couldn't remember anything that happened to him. He claimed he just stepped into that patch of trees, and he had experienced intense pain; his muscles had felt limp and disconnected, and he had collapsed. He had said this just as he had woken up, when he was not able to comprehend the implications of what he was saying. This news added fuel to the fire of conversation going around, saying that Dr. Clark had suffered "Divine punishment".

And that fire was raging. Now that the shock had worn off a little, people were trying to analyze what had happened. It was the perfect time to talk and discuss. Everyone, including school children and workers, were given the day off on the Day of Natis, as well as the days before and after it.

They wondered whether it had really been Natis, or if someone was trying to bring down Father Godfrey. People opposed to this theory asked who would want to do something like that and why would they? They wondered where Conner had gone, why he was so important and the strange things that had started happening since he had arrived, the *Death Watch* board message and the track left only below the board. Conspiracy theories flew like *Rosaline Chocolate Cookies* did when near-diabetic children were around them.

Soon, they started to question *why* Natis would have said that. *Were* they being misguided? Could they have done better with their life? Could there be a better way of living?

These questions burned through the day and most of the next night, when, for obvious reasons, nobody slept. They burned in the bar (where the helpful bartender added some more logs), they burned in homes (where text messages pointed out that this could be the beginning to a much better and more liberated future); they burned for so long that the smoke almost choked Father Godfrey, who was getting increasingly dismayed at the fact that, for once, things were spiralling out of his control.

Finally, it was the Day of Natis.

At 10 a.m. sharp, everyone filed into the Sinome, wearing their absolute best. Everyone had their ornament depicting Natis displayed proudly. However, no one was happy. They all wanted answers, because the answers they were coming up with right now were not satisfactory to them.

Within half an hour, everyone was seated. The Day of Natis was a special day, and it was not good to waste time on such a holy day. Father Godfrey got onto the raised platform and surveyed the crowd. The reactions were very mixed; Father Godfrey was not pleased. However, he was sure he had a speech ready to sway them. He cleared his throat and got ready to deliver it.

Suddenly, the door slammed open and all heads turned. Standing silhouetted, against the light, wearing the same clothes and hands bound in the same handcuffs, was Conner White.

Chapter 21

These Authors

And Their Metaphors

Conner seemed not to notice all the eyes staring at him. He put his handcuffed hands behind his head, looked up to the sky reverently, closed his eyes and called out, "Natis deliver me from these chains!"

He stood still for a few seconds, and then one hand came forward, free of the handcuff, and then the other one as well, leaving the handcuffs to drop behind Conner, and he nonchalantly kicked them away with the back of his foot. Then he walked onward down the long aisle as if nothing had happened, all eyes following him, every ear tensed for some sound other than those of his echoing footsteps. Father Godfrey stared at him, with a feeling he had never felt before: a feeling of impotence, of not knowing what to do.

Conner walked up to the platform and vaulted onto it. He looked out at the crowd as if for the first time. He then addressed them, his voice reaching the ears of all Leviites, although from all directions, the effect he assumed the builders of the Sinome were going for though he doubted they ever intended it for use of anyone like him.

"People of Levion! I, Conner White, today have come to tell you that you have a great evil in your midst! That evil tried to kill me, but the great Natis has saved me and brought me here to deliver this message! And that evil has taken the form of that man over there." This time, it was Conner's turn to point at Father Godfrey.

"This is blasphemy!" Godfrey yelled, enraged. "How dare you try and use His name against me, that too in His sacred place? How do we know that this isn't a big act that you've concocted to destroy my reputation? How do we know *you* are really not the evil here?"

"You know what - you're right. Why don't we let the people of Levion decide? We'll both make our speeches and then they can decide who they want to trust, right?"

Godfrey smiled his subtly wicked smile. Conner had foolishly given him an opening, and now it was time to strike back. *There's no way they will choose Conner over me when it comes down to plain and simple debate, no tricks.* Godfrey's smile grew bigger as he thought to himself.

"I think I shall go first," Conner said, coming right next to Godfrey.

Godfrey immediately shook his head. Conner wasn't going to get what he wanted. "No, I've been here longer, and I shall go first," he announced.

"But what happened to you in the woods, Conner?" someone called out. "We want to know."

The others murmured assent.

Conner put his hands up, stepped back graciously and tried to conceal a smile. "No, Father Godfrey has insisted he go first, so let him go first. Nobody can say I wasn't considerate."

Godfrey caught the smile, and realized that Conner *had* got what he wanted, and once again at his expense. He walked to Conner and whispered, "You better have a good story ready."

Conner whispered back, "I'm an author. I always have a good story ready."

Godfrey just glared at him and went to the front of the platform, standing in the centre, the same way he did whenever he was delivering a sermon to the Leviites. He put on one of his winning smiles, the calm ones that help to reassure whoever came to ask him for help. "Hello, children of Natis," he said in his smooth voice. "You know, many of you are my children too; after all I am your Father." He smiled, putting some of them at ease. It was just Father Godfrey talking to them like he did every week, and not some intense debate where the fate of their entire town hung in the balance. Not that at all.

"You know, I feel like a real father to some of you. I've seen so many of you grow up, so many of you have to come to me when you need me. I've shown you the true way to Natis. Joe," he indicated to an athletic-looking man in his thirties, "Didn't you realize with me that you didn't want to compete with your brother, the mayor, and that you wanted to become a farmer?" After the man nodded slowly, Godfrey turned to a woman in the back. "Jane, didn't I convince your family to let you get married to a different person?" The woman nodded and Godfrey addressed all of them, "And haven't all of you, at some point or the other, come to me because you needed help in some way or the other because a family member had been affected by Levitis?" Nobody could refute this fact. At the very mention of the word, their faces saddened because of some bad memory associated with it. Godfrey gave them a few seconds to mourn here before he continued.

"But aside from Levitis, tell me, what major problems have any of you faced? Natis has blessed you, and I have ensured that He continued blessing you. Outside this town, what is there? Destruction, unhappiness, chaos? Here you have love, peace, security, family, happiness, neighbourliness, Natis! What more could you want from life? Everything you could possibly need is provided here! And the only reason that it is provided is because Natis watches over you, and who is it that has the direct connection to Natis? Me."

Godfrey's voice increased in urgency now. "Ask yourselves this: I have been taking care of you for most of your lives. Why would you trust this outsider more than me?" Here his head dropped and his voice lowered, but not so much that he went unheard, "I admit, I misread the signs when he first came here. When the light shone on him, it was not to tell me that he was a messenger of Natis, rather it was a warning that Natis was trying to send me! When he 'saved' the life of Jon Peck, he was actually tapped into Levitis, an evil force, and forced it to relent!"

From the murmurs and scared looks in the crowd, Father Godfrey knew that he was turning them against Conner. He moved in for the kill. "And then is that whole thing with poor Roger. Can you, as a Leviite, trust a man who killed one of your own, a boy, no less? Tell me how that man is doing the work of Natis if what he does is cause death?" His voice was raised, the loudest Conner had ever heard it. "So join me, Leviites to expel this intruder and return to our lives where we can go on worshipping Natis without his dirty tricks present to mislead or hoodwink us!"

A lot of people clapped, some even got up and cheered. Everyone seemed to be suddenly back on Father Godfrey's side. Almost everyone, anyway.

"Silence!" A woman with a voice of authority yelled. A woman named Rosaline, that is. "Everyone sit down. We have always been a fair people and shall remain so now. We agreed to let Conner White speak, and speak he shall. After he is done, we'll decide what to do what him." Her lips curved, as if she was wondering what kind of torture to put Conner through later, but her eyes clearly said to him, "Your move. Better make it count." After a few minutes, they quietened down and sat in their seats, though many acted as if they weren't going to even bother to listen. Father Godfrey smiled, his arrogance returning swiftly. "Yes, why not? Go on, Conner, say your piece. And please tell us what happened to you these past two days. We're all dying to know."

His tone clearly indicated that he thought it was just going to be a fanciful story.

Conner ignored him, stepped to the front and said, "Thank you, Rosaline. Your fairness, and the fairness of the townspeople, is appreciated." He took a deep breath and closed his eyes for a few seconds. He stepped back till he was almost touching the wall and his head was almost in the centre of the pupil of the Eye. Then he opened them, and with renewed vitality started, "People of Levion. You may think that by now I need no introduction, but I would like to introduce myself to you. Father Godfrey here is at an advantage; you know him all your life, whereas you never properly got the chance to know me. But first, you say you want to know what happened to me. The truth is that I'm not sure myself."

Godfrey scoffed, but Conner ignored him again. "I was in my room when I was hauled to the police station on trumped-up charges. You all know what I said, and it was completely true. I knew something was going to happen to me that night. So when I was sitting there, I heard the voice of Natis just like everyone else, trying to warn you, and I was happy. While I was praying, I heard a voice beside me and before I could open my eyes, I was attacked. I fought back blindly, my eyes glued shut. I got cut badly and I was bleeding. Suddenly I saw a light so bright, I was lucky my eyes were closed. After a few seconds, it dissipated and after a minute, I opened my eyes. My side was bleeding badly, my mattress and pillow was ripped.

"I took some blood and wrote that brief message on the wall so that you all would realize where I had gone in case I didn't make it. I could see the cell door was unlocked. I tried to walk out, but I fell and started bleeding out in front of the cell. I realize I needed something to stop the bleeding, so I ripped out part of the mattress and put pressure on my side with it. Then I slowly walked out, feeling something guiding me. I didn't call to anyone, or anything of that sort. I simply walked till I felt that I had to stop and pray. After what seemed like a few minutes, I'm here at the front door of the Sinome, my wounds completely healed.

"Why did Father Godfrey proclaim me as a High Natish in the first place, if he didn't see my potential? He got scared of it, fearing I might be more in Natis' favour than he; he disowned me and cursed me."

Many shook their heads in disbelief, not knowing what to make of this story. Father Godfrey's influence was still strong on them. Conner closed his eyes for a minute. Everyone stared at him, wondering what he was doing. Suddenly he whipped around, putting his hand on the centre of the Natis eye and screamed, "We have to leave! There is a place we have to go! After we go there, everything will be revealed." Conner got down from the platform and started walking down the aisle. Halfway through, he looked at everyone and cried out, a bit angrily, "Come on! This is not some trick! We have to go there, or something terrible will happen! If I'm wrong, I'll say no more." Conner tapped his foot impatiently. "COME!" he screamed at them.

Nobody had seen Conner so agitated before and even Father Godfrey looked a little worried. "All right, let's humour him," he said reluctantly. As people started shuffling out of their seats, Conner practically ran to the entrance, and got them all out. they got out faster than they had gotten settled in. Conner ensured that everyone had left, and then led them down the hill.

Once he reached the bottom, he started leading them down the roads, making quick turns, completely assured of his path. After about ten minutes of walking, by which time impatience has spread, Conner stopped. "This is the spot," he said. Then he started looking around. It looked like an ordinary enough part of the town, the only difference being that one building was painted brick red, whereas Conner has never seen any of the other houses painted that colour. "Can anybody see anything here?" he asked the crowd, which had suddenly become deadly silent.

One man stepped forward. "I'm the head of the volunteer fire brigade. This is where we meet to practice."

Almost right on cue, someone screamed, "Fire!"

Everyone turned to look at King's Hill, where the person was pointing.

The Sinome was burning.

****

"Come on, boys! This is what we trained for!" the head of the volunteer fire brigade announced and started organizing his men quickly. "Make sure no one except us goes next to the blaze!"

Soon some men started carrying a large portable tank specially stored for such situations towards the hill. The others took buckets and hurried after them. Father Godfrey, who seemed unable to comprehend that his precious Sinome was burning, suddenly snapped into action. He started walking as fast as he could towards the Sinome, tripping a few times, but picking himself up and walking regardless, gaining speed as he walked.

Conner saw this and started running after him. By the time Godfrey had reached the top, so had Conner. The fire-fighters were trying desperately to control the blaze, which was hard because although the stone itself couldn't burn, the wooden supports were burning fast.

Godfrey saw their hopeless faces and ran (as much as he could run) into the Sinome. "NO!" Conner screamed. To the men he yelled, "Keep fighting it! I'll try and get him!" Without waiting for a response, he rushed in after Godfrey.

The fire was raging all around Conner. Most of the benches, made completely of wood, were ablaze. Conner, through smoke, saw Father Godfrey at the end of the aisle already, apparently heading for his chambers. Conner covered his mouth, bent down to get below the heaviest smoke, and started walking as fast as he could without getting out of breath towards the end of the aisle. Conner looked around as much as he could. The only reason that the ceiling hadn't fallen on him was because the support beams holding it up were strong, a few made of stone.

The Room of Secrets was more wooden, so the walls were catching fire faster. It seemed like the area beyond it was much worse affected. Conner went into Godfrey's chambers and this was confirmed to be true.

Most of the Father's room was ablaze. The Father himself was standing in front of a desk with a book in his hands. To be more accurate, a burning book in his hands. Godfrey's face was pale and he looked as if he was going to collapse any moment. This was probably from all the smoke that he seemed to be ignoring, but to Conner it seemed as if it was because of that book in his hands. Conner smacked the book away and took Godfrey by the shoulder, dragging him out. Godfrey barely seemed to register his presence. Conner had a hard time covering his own mouth and Godfrey's mouth, and at the same time, trying to drag Godfrey.

Conner heard a deep rumbling and then suddenly there was a collection of loud crashing sounds one after the other. Unbeknownst to Conner, the wooden stairs in the tower with the Natis Eye had completely burned up, leaving the tower to collapse. This caused the Father's room to collapse just as Conner entered the Room of Secrets. Conner uncovered his mouth and smacked the now-burning table aside and resumed dragging Godfrey, who seemed to be walking a bit now. Conner could feel the flames closing in, the searing heat threatening to burn his skin. Then he realized that some of his skin *was* burning. Some of his forearm was on fire and he quickly patted it away.

Between the table pushing and extinguishing his forearm, his mouth and nose had been left dangerously exposed to smoke for too long. His vision was getting hazy, but he pushed on. He was barely out of the Room before it collapsed. Conner ducked low and made Godfrey do the same, and they walked further, although now it was much slower. They were only a little way down the aisle when there was another loud sound as before, only this time it was followed by the *boom* of a much bigger object as it fell down from a tremendous height. The bell tower had collapsed.

Conner had a vision of the Natis Eye painted on the wall behind the altar with fire spread all along its lines, making it seem even more searing than usual.

Halfway through the aisle, Conner could feel his strength sapping away. Father Godfrey had stopped trying, how long ago he did not know. He dropped down to the floor because the smoke had become too thick to even walk upright in. Conner crawled forward dragging the Father by one arm for as long as he could before he too couldn't move. Conner could hear screams outside, footsteps close. But none of these facts registered because all he could feel was the heat crawling against his skin, the smoke slowly suffocating him. All he could think about was that, at least he had tried. His life wouldn't have been a complete mess.

Strong arms grabbed his shoulders and someone else grabbed his feet and started carrying him out. Then they dropped him onto the grass in the fresh air, but Conner was already unconscious by then.

****

When Conner woke up, he found that there was some sort of mask pressing against his mouth. His mind was foggy and he tried to look around, but some sort of pressure was being applied to the mask. Conner shifted his eyes to see one of the men from the volunteer fire brigade holding the mask over his face. He had a reassuring look on his face and said in a calm voice, "You're going to be all right. Just breathe in deeply."

Conner kept breathing in the oxygen until he remembered everything that had happened and he started struggling. He pulled off the mask and asked breathlessly, "Father Godfrey. Did he make it?"

By this time, one or two more men came to subdue Conner, and the mask was put back on. But from the looks on their faces, Conner could see that he hadn't. Conner let his head rest back and breathed in deeply. He squeezed his eyes shut and waited for a few minutes till he felt better. Then he opened his eyes and lifted himself up, pulling off his mask. "I'm fine. I'm much better now," he said, holding up a hand to calm down the men tending to him. Conner slowly got to his feet and looked around.

All that remained of the Sinome was a clump of charred stones with a lot of wood debris inside its remains. Some smaller fires were still being put out. The majority of the townspeople, however, were standing over a prone figure on the ground. Some looked shocked, some confused, probably at the completely unexplained death; but the look of sadness was unanimous among all. No matter what reservations they had forming over the past two days, this man lying there had been important in some way or the other to all of them.

One person not among the crowd was Victoria. She was standing in front of the ruins, her eyes fixed on Conner. They carried within them a swirl of emotions, one that Conner was not ready to face at the moment. It was time to change the fate of Levion.

Conner started walking towards the body. As he did, he felt parts of his hands and legs sting. He looked down at himself for the first time since he regained consciousness and found that a lot of his clothes had burnt away, and there appeared to be something applied to his burnt skin. Conner ignored this pain and as he got close to the body, he saw something that had been blocked by the crowd, Godfrey's most faithful follower, Dr. Clark, on his knees before the corpse. The usually calm and straight-faced Dr. Clark was crying, his head on Godfrey's chest.

Conner didn't pay attention to anyone around him as he took Clark's arm gently. Dr. Clark resisted. "Come on, he wouldn't want to see you like this," Conner said softly.

Dr. Clark recognized Conner's voice and straightened up immediately. His face was livid. "You're responsible for this! You engineered this whole thing; it's because of you that he's dead!" Saying so, he stepped forward to punch Conner. Conner calmly caught his hand and pushed him back slightly. "I risked my life to try and save him. I wouldn't have done that if I had intended it to happen."

Dr. Clark snarled, "You knew that the Sinome was going to burn; you took us out of there. Why did you do that? You don't care about us; you should have just left us there! I should have been in there instead, but I collapsed halfway up because of what you did to me!"

"I did not know this was going to happen, Clark," Conner said quietly. "I just led everyone out because I knew that I had to. And I didn't do anything to you; I was on the other side of town in my jail cell."

"So you say," spat Clark. Conner didn't move. Instead he said, "Okay, Clark. I'm sorry."

Stares all around. Nobody knew exactly what he meant. Was he confessing to killing Father Godfrey?

"I'm sorry, Clark," Conner repeated. He turned to the crowd. "I'm sorry, people of Levion." He turned to the body on the ground. "I'm sorry, Father."

Victoria came up to him and touched him on the shoulder. "What are you sorry about, Conner?" she asked, softly, almost cautiously, as if scared of the reply.

"I'm sorry because I did want to set off a fire, but not like this. I didn't realize there were better ways to do it." He stepped forward and stood near Godfrey's body. "I wanted to set a fire, but in your hearts. There are some things that you needed to realize, that you needed to know. But I went about it the wrong way.

"I prayed to Natis to give me some way to tell you, and the result was what you have witnessed the past few days culminating at this point. You may wonder what has brought this on. Well, Father Godfrey and all the priests have been the cause for Levitis continuing in this town to this very day."

This really set off the crowd. They could listen to Conner patiently, give him a chance because the circumstances seemed to demand it, but this time he had gone so far as to accuse Godfrey of being responsible for Levitis, the most destructive force in their world! Some came forward, looking ready to beat up Conner. Conner, however, stood his ground. "You can do as you please with me. But that will just help in repeating the cycle and Levitis will forever plague you." They eyed him with hostility, but stopped nonetheless. Dr. Clark himself was eying Conner, waiting to see what he would do next. Conner had no doubt that Clark would silence him if he started revealing the true secret of Levitis. But for now, he just looked on.

"All your life, what have you been told Levitis is? Natis uses it to make sure you stay faithful, to make sure you stay in Levion and fulfil your bonds of brotherhood and stay loyal to your town, your family and your friends? What if I was to tell you that was not true? What if I was to tell you the true name of Levitis?"

The anticipation was palpable as the townspeople waited for Conner's answer.

"Fear. That's what Levitis is. Fear. Now let me ask you a few things, Joe." He turned to the man Father Godfrey had addressed earlier. "You say that you didn't want to become mayor. But did you really want to become a farmer? Did you want to do something that perhaps people don't do here? Didn't all of you at some point?" Conner looked around for a second before he said, "Jane, you say you got married to somebody else. But did you get married out of love, or was it just another arranged marriage because you couldn't go beyond Levion to look for love?"

Conner seemed to be in sync with the crowd now, feeling their emotions, feeding off them. "You all say you've never really had any real problems. Well, I ask you, what is so great about that? You've never felt heartbreak or great sorrow, anger, curiosity or loneliness. That seems to be a good deal? Well, look on the flipside. You've never known that feeling of triumph when you finally overcome them! You've never felt the joy of finding true love; you've never known what it's like to feel great joy or happiness; you have never experienced these intense emotions! Just imagine being able to go anywhere you want, or feel anything, or even feel *something*!

"Look at you; you're dressed the same way, you have the same mannerisms, the same reactions; it feels as if some of you even have the same features! Where is the individuality? Is being like everyone else so important that you sacrifice everything you have, everything you *are*?" He fiercely pointed to the blocks out in the field. "Those blocks don't just symbolize walls of ages past. They symbolize walls present even now. Walls that you need to break. There is no progress. There is Levitis.

"Levitis causes more than just death. It causes fear. Levitis kills more than just people; it kills your will to live. It makes you wonder why you should do anything extraordinary because you know that you might die because of it, because you are not conforming. So Levitis kills you long before you actually die.

"Now you may think that Natis is responsible for this fear mongering, for all of you being trapped here. But that's not true. Natis has never been responsible for any of this, and His name should not even be mentioned in connection with any of this, because it is the priests who are truly responsible. They were scared themselves, so they found a way to transmit this fear to you. They believed that they were protecting you. But they didn't realize that they were doing you more harm than good. Evil caught onto this fear, and Levitis was born.

"When I first came here, I was lost and scared as well. But I was trying to overcome my fear. That is why I was able to save Jon. Because I brought hope, hope for me, hope for Levion. And slowly I managed to overcome my fear, and today I stand before you, a changed man. All of your life you've faced fear. What you can achieve when you overcome this fear is much more than you would have ever imagined. So if I, one man, could change so much after overcoming mine, imagine what an entire town could do!

"Remember, you don't need to be exactly the same to be united. Levitis can't kill you only if you believe that it can't. I promise you, people of Levion, there will be no more Levitis!"

Conner looked down at the corpse of Father Godfrey. "Levion tradition says we have to cremate the body almost immediately. Why don't we burn him along with the remaining ruins of the

Sinome? It would have been what he wanted." A few seem surprised by the change of pace, but they listened to Conner and quickly arranged a makeshift pyre. Dr. Clark looked at Conner and nodded. Conner understood. Today nothing more would be said, in memory of Father Godfrey. Whatever differences they had could be settled tomorrow.

The question about who was going to light the pyre arose. Some said Conner should do it, but Conner gave the torch to Clark. Clark wordlessly took it and as he was lighting it, Conner exclaimed, "Let all our fear and doubt burn along with this body, and may we get the strength to defeat Levitis once and for all." With that, the pyre caught fire quickly, and the Leviites watched their past burn away. Earlier, they would have wondered if this or any sort of change would be good for them.

But now they knew that from these ashes, a new life would emerge.

Chapter 22

Final Strikes

Conner looked out of the window at the town, which had become his favourite activity. Only, he was sure that he, or anybody else for that matter, had never seen it quite like it was now. Even though it was evening, the town was alive. Everyone was walking about and talking to each other. From what Conner could see, they were excited, though some seemed anxious. But they all didn't look the same anymore. They looked different, yet seemed to blend in together. Like a true community.

There was a knock on his door. Conner opened it; Victoria stood in front of him. She didn't say a word to him; she simply went past him and sat down on the couch. Conner closed the door and sat down next to her. They both sat down, unspeaking, until Victoria said, "You intended to burn down the Sinome all along."

She didn't look at Conner. It wasn't an accusation, it wasn't a question. It was a simple statement.

Conner nodded. "Yes. I knew that was one thing you wouldn't be able to agree with, so I didn't say anything."

"How did you do it?"

"I used this little device that catches fire after a specific amount of time. I set it to half an hour.""Why?"

"There was too much in there. Too many secrets, too many tools of manipulation, things I must not have even known about. I couldn't possibly destroy or dismantle all of those, and if the Leviites found those, it would be disastrous. And it would have cut off the Father's power."

"You didn't mean for him to die." Again, it wasn't a question, just a statement.

"No, I didn't. There was something in there he desperately needed to recover, a book of some kind. He was holding it while it burned before his eyes."

"I guess we'll never know what he risked his life for."

"I guess we won't."

Victoria got up and went to the window. "You've caused a real stir out there. For the first time in life, my fellow townspeople seem... animated. Like they actually want to do something with their lives, like they can move on. Like they're not scared."

Conner got up and stood next to her.

"Did you mean what you said? Could we have got to this point without using Natis the way they have done?"

"I don't know. All I know is that if we deceive people for greater good, someone else will do the same. And it'll continue to be a big cycle until someone breaks it by realizing that taking others' opinions will help realize not what is good, but what is best, for everyone."

Victoria nodded and stood quietly, watching the townspeople run about, like mice recently released from their cage.

"Did you complete your story?" Victoria asked.

"I completed it that very night I showed it to you."

A curious look came across Victoria's face. "But everything you had written till then was a reflection of what had happened. How could you write it when you hadn't been through it yet?"

"I felt confident enough to write my own ending."

Victoria paused for a few seconds before she nodded and asked, "Can I read it?" "Not right now. But don't worry. No matter what happens now, it will come to you."

Victoria didn't say anything.

After some silence, Conner said, "It isn't over yet, you know."

Victoria finally looked at Conner. "Yes, I know."

Conner looked at her as well. "There's a good chance I won't make it back."

Victoria nodded. Both of them didn't say anything for a long while, just looked at each other.

"Conner," Victoria started slowly. "I really don't know what will happen to me. I still feel inadequate, incomplete and broken. I don't think anyone will accept me in the state I am. I doubt I'll ever get love."

"What about Harold?"

Victoria turned slightly cold. "I told you before; he's not the person you think he is."

"And what is he, then? Besides being somebody who wants to help you and obviously loves you?"

Victoria stayed silent.

"And it's not true that nobody loves you," he said, looking into her eyes. "I love you."

Victoria just stared into his blue eyes, wishing that it was true. He leaned forward, waiting to see if she would pull back. But she didn't. So he kissed her.

At first, Victoria felt terror on feeling his lips on hers. Then she remembered Conner's blue eyes, his comforting face and realized she was kissing someone she loved as well. So she kissed back, and it was a feeling she had never experienced before, didn't know was possible. A feeling that went beyond lust; a feeling so magical that she now understood it; the feeling of pure love.

When they finally separated, Conner smiled at Victoria and said, "All the kisses before this one don't matter anymore. You can live your life, knowing that there is someone out there who loves you and someone else who will love you, because there will always be that someone for everyone."

Victoria nodded and smiled too. It was a smile of joy, one that was very rare for her. "Conner," she said, still smiling. "I've sort of been holding out something from you too." She paused and then continued, "I called Megan the other day."

Conner started. "Megan? My daughter? Why?"

"I got her number through a mutual friend. I needed to check something, and she was the best person to do it. And she did it; she reported back with the results some time ago. I can't even imagine how you'll react."

Conner looked impatient and anxious. "Well? What is it?"

"I asked her to look into Roger's death. Get the case file if possible. She pointed out some irregularities to the campus police, who were anxious to rule it off as suicide quickly and avoid media publicity. Turns out it was staged to look like suicide."

Conner sat down, seemingly unable to stand. "So...what are you saying?"

"You, the person who was running around trying to figure everything couldn't guess that Father Godfrey and Dr. Clark were going to try to stop their biggest threat." Conner looked like he was having a hard time taking this in. "It wasn't your fault, Conner. You weren't responsible."

"I wasn't responsible," Conner whispered quietly. "I wasn't responsible."

Conner got up and the full extent of the revelation struck him. "I wasn't responsible!" he yelled. "I wasn't!"

Victoria smiled at Conner's elation. Conner turned to her and hugged her tight. "Thank you," he whispered. "Thank you so much."

After Conner released her, her face turned serious again. "And Conner...that decision you asked me to make...I did. I want to do it."

Conner realized immediately what she was talking about. His face turned serious as well and he checked his watch. There was time. "Take your clothes and let's go do yours. Then we'll come back and I'll finish off mine," he said.

"Let's do it," Victoria agreed. She went in and made the preparations. She came out carrying a bag.

They both looked at each other. "If I don't make it back, tell Mrs. Stewart goodbye from me," Conner said quietly.

Victoria nodded and said, "Of course."

"I want you to go make up with your parents. I'm sending over a gift which will help smooth things over." He paused while Victoria nodded. "And can you do me one more favour? That statue in the square; can you ask Rosaline to fix it? Even if they don't know exactly what the face is like, it'll be better than that incomplete one there. Good people should be remembered in whatever way they can be."

Victoria seemed surprised by his suggestion, but nodded.

By unspoken assent, they started walking towards the door. Conner looked back at his room, his home for the past month, for what might be the last time. Then he shut the door.

****

He licks his lips. That girl who just came up and knocked on his door was so good-looking, after all. God knows what she was selling; all he knew was that there was just enough of her skin, that he wanted her. Lust rises up within him. Sluts need to get what they deserve, he thinks. He runs down the stairs, hoping that she uses his favourite short-cut. He just steps out of the apartment building to see her walking into the alley. He smiles and pops a mint. He thinks he's going to have fun.

Think again.

The girl runs soundlessly past me, as she was instructed. He can't see her. He assumes that it's because of the darkness. He looks up at the sky and grins. It's as if he's thanking God that this alley is not lit, so that he may inflict the punishment he is meant to. Imagine, thanking God as if He wanted this!

Footsteps start down the alley. He tries to blend in the shadows, but he doesn't realize that, ironically enough, because of him, I can blend into the shadows better than him. Seeing his face in the dim light terrifies me. It brings back such horrible memories; it makes me want to turn and flee. My breathing almost stops. But I don't flee. I stand my ground. I remember everything Conner has said and it gives me strength. I think of Conner, waiting close by, ready to jump in if things seem like they'll go awry. I calm my breathing. This is the moment.

I step out of the shadows. The rapist is startled and he seems surprised to see me. Then he breaks into a grin. "You just can't get enough of me. This time, though, you won't get away," he says.

He's about to jump forward and my terror almost makes me run again. But my survival instinct overrides it and I raise my trembling hands quickly and press the button.

The coil jumps from the Taser and hits him square in the chest. A current of electricity goes through him, and he's on the floor within seconds, flopping like a fish. He's unconscious. Conner suddenly steps out of the shadows, a big rock in his hands. "I was just about to clock him; you looked like you weren't able to handle it."

I nod mutely. I can't take my eyes off the person on the floor. He must be twenty years old. How long ago did he start, even if he started with me? Four years? Four years of putting women through unspeakable torture. Conner's asking me what I want to do. I say that this much isn't enough. I tell him to step back and stay ready if necessary.

I continue to stare at the man; can I call him a man? No real man would ever do this, I've come to realize. More like a beast. So I stare at the beast on the floor and I'm not that scared anymore. He looks so powerless, sprawled there. I drop my taser and pick up a piece of wood. It's elongated and tapered to a sharp point. I kick the beast a few times, and I've given him a low voltage, so he wakes up, though looking a bit dazed.

"What's going on?" he says groggily. He looks at me and fury comes into his eyes. "What have you done to me, you whore?" he cries and tries to move, but the effects of the taser are still present, so he can't move.

Seeing his fury, rage builds up inside me as well. How dare he get angry at me? If he thinks he is the victim, I'm going to make sure he becomes one.

"You know what? You have no control right now. You have no power." I lean in closer so I can see his disgusting face twitch when I look into the eyes which have tormented me for so long and say, "You can't hurt me, you coward." After which I spit in his face.

I can see the fear and then rage as he tries to move his arms and legs, which he seems to be regaining control of a little. "Oh, you still think you can get to me? Let me remedy that." I position my foot so he can see what I'm about to do, and then I look at the terror in his eyes as I kick him straight in the groin.

I put the stick of wood in his mouth, so he can't scream, the way he made sure I couldn't scream. His hands instinctively try to cover his groin, but they're still too stunned to move. I step back when he looks like he's stopped screaming. Suddenly there's rage on his face and he gets up, his hands trying to grab me. But I'm ready. I slam the flat end of the stick against his chest. And I slam it again and again. Then I step back. Tears are rolling down my cheeks. Maybe because all the anger, all the hurt I've been facing for so long is finally getting out.

Suddenly I feel the soles of my shoes getting wet. I look down and see there's a small pool formed. It is urine, I realize. He has peed in his pants. I look at his face and tears are rolling down his eyes. "Please stop," he says softly, almost begging me. "Please. I'll do anything."

I look at the terror in his eyes, and it is almost like I am seeing some of my own terror reflected back at me. The same terror that I felt, the same way I wanted this beast to stop. I feel almost repulsed at myself. I drop the stick and pick up the taser. "Don't worry," I say to him. "The worst is yet to come." And thus saying, I increase the voltage on the taser and use it on him.

Conner comes into view. His face seems to have no expression on it, but that's probably because I can't see it clearly. "The pain he's feeling is nothing compared to the pain I felt all those years, the pain he has probably made others feel. But by doing this, I'm bringing myself down to his level. So let's get him something worse," I say.

Conner nods, not saying a word. He comes next to me and hugs me and I break down crying. I think I can hear some footsteps moving away at the far end of the alley but I don't care. I just want to cry before I face the hardest part.

****

There was a knock on the door. Dr. Clark opened it, knowing who would be there. Conner, without asking to be invited in, brushed past Clark into the living room and sat down on one of the few chairs there.

Conner looked around the living room. It was sparsely furnished, as if Clark had just let the design and decorations from the previous hundred years or so simply clump together. There was a long table in the centre, which had numerous cracks as well as small chinks, which Conner estimated came from a knife thrown on the table. There were four chairs, one at each end of the table. It was pretty obvious that Clark didn't expect, or want, much company. The walls were painted in a depressing grey, but the painting was poor, because you could see splotches of other colours peeking out at random intervals if you looked hard enough.

"I see you're admiring my interior design," Clark said, sitting opposite Conner in the north-eastern chair.

"Or lack of it," Conner noted. Then he focused back on Clark and said, "Okay, let's get to it then."

Clark's face had the ghost of a smile for a few seconds before it flickered away and indicating the room, he said, "Yes, that would be best. As you can see, I'm not one for pleasantries."

"And I'm sick of playing these games. Or being played. So I'm going to ask you flat-out: Are you going to disappear quietly?"

An amused smile curled on Clark's lips. "Disappear? Are you going to kill me and bury me in my backyard?"

"No," said Conner with an ironical smile. "I'm not you."

Dr. Clark gave an acknowledging nod but maintained the amused smile on his face.

"So here is my proposal," Conner said, leaning forward. "I'll give you money to go set up in a deserted part of the country. You keep your nose clean and live the rest of your days in peace; hopefully you'll repent all the deaths you caused, but you can't stay here."

Dr. Clark raised his eyebrows. "And suddenly you're one to judge that? You've been doing a lot of that nowadays. Before I even consider your ridiculous proposal, satisfy my curiosity. How did you manage the voice of Natis, and the blood? You must have had help."

Conner sighed. He had hoped he wouldn't have to talk about this. He leaned back, keeping a wary eye on the not-so-good doctor. "Rosaline convinced Father Godfrey that he should arrest me, when she was really on our side, and it was what we had planned. It also gave him a chance to believe he was doing something while we prepared. My business contacts helped to get the equipment we needed, a lot of them prototypes, and Victoria's intricate knowledge of the forest helped us to place them. Small speakers which played pre-recorded messages were set up. When we were ready, Mrs. Stewart set them off according to the texts she received from Rosaline.

"The person who recorded those messages, an acquaintance, thought it was a joke.

"He had a terrifying voice, which we magnified further. Mrs. Stewart was the one who tasered you, and I'm sure she felt good taking revenge for her husband's death. On the other side of town, Victoria brought me a copy of the cell key we had acquired from Rosaline earlier, and we opened my cell door. I had cut myself some days earlier, which is when I got the idea. I collected my blood and we mixed it with animal blood and paint. Then we painted the message, dropped the blood out carefully, and then finally drew the Natis eye. Victoria knew how to cover up tracks, so she did. She was the one who rang the bell without leaving any tracks. I was in the basement of the inn for the next day and a half.

"That handcuff was a simple manipulation of the key behind the back. The speech was completely from the heart."

Conner stopped, looking at Dr. Clark to gauge his reaction. There was none. Dr. Clark had his impenetrable mask on. "And the fire?" he asked in an even voice.

Conner simply shrugged and said, "I just knew I had to lead them out at that point. Don't ask me why."

Dr. Clark, who had been impassive throughout, gave an ironical smirk at the last comment, which he clearly didn't believe. He got up and said, "Come. I want to show you something." And without waiting for Conner, started walking down a long hallway, passing closed doors until they reached a flight of stairs leading downwards. It was dark going down, and Conner made sure to check his footing as he walked. They came to what Conner estimated to be a steel-reinforced door. Clark pressed some glowing numbers on a keypad next to the door and pushed it open. Conner had a really bad feeling, but he couldn't turn tail and run at this point, now could he? So he took a deep breath and stepped through the door.

Taking a deep breath turned out to be useless to Conner, since he let it out as soon as he saw what was in the room. He barely registered the door shutting behind him as he took in his surroundings. The walls were white, matching the white of the doctor's coat. This was not shabbily painted like the living room, however. It was very neat and had a sort of sterilized look about it. There was also a ventilation shaft in the upper right corner of the north wall.

Several patches seemed to be freshly painted, as if to cover up something. This was on the parts that Conner could see of the wall, that is. Because the walls were covered with numerous charts labelling chemicals and chemical formulas. There was a small chalkboard in one corner, with a string of numbers and alphabets written on it. A large chart right opposite the door that listed a long list of chemical formulas on one side and on the other contained... ailments. Conner realized that these were symptoms induced in a person when this formula was inserted in the body.

There was a long cabinet near the door and three long wooden tables that lined the three walls. There were a large variety of scientific instruments organized neatly on the tables. There were Bunsen burners, beakers, retorts, microscopes and a lot of other things Conner couldn't name. The east also had a large number of sealed glass cylinders with liquids of different colours inside them. Conner recognized them as the "medicine" Dr. Clark used. There were also a large number of syringes, including five that looked more like shots than syringes. They were each filled with four different colours, pink, two purple, clear and green.

Conner suddenly realized that Dr. Clark had been watching him while he studied everything around him, and Conner could see that he was enjoying Conner's attention to what Conner assumed was his life's work and the work of many before him.

"You actually have an evil lair," Conner commented drily.

At this point, Clark actually broke into a grin. He moved to the centre of the room and quickly became serious. "So, Conner, tell me. Why aren't you trying to convince me that you're really a messenger of Natis; that I should believe in you?"

Conner remained silent, but kept eye contact with Clark.

"That's right," Clark said softly, "You aren't trying because you know I'm firm in my belief. So firm that I've been killing for it most of my life. So what were you going to do, Conner? Send me somewhere far away and then get me locked up there on some trumped-up charges? Thought I'd simply fade away? You know what I'm going to do instead? Kill you. You will be the first in a string of new Levitis victims. That'll put them in their place. First, I'll start with Victoria for her meddling. I'll make sure that one is painful."

Conner knew that Clark was just trying to incite him so he didn't move; he just waited for Clark to make one.

"I assume you know how we pick doctors here, Conner. But you know what's really needed, other than great intelligence, aptitude for science and intense devotion? Apathy and love of violence. So I'm basically a mad genius, which is why I know I'll be the one who leaves this room alive and not you."

That was when Clark made his move. He darted left to grab one of the syringes. Conner was watching for this and jumped forward. Clark managed to grab the syringe with the pink liquid (which he assumed caused death) before Conner rammed it into him and tried to wrestle control of it. Conner elbowed Clark in the face, which disoriented the other, giving Conner the advantage for a few seconds. This was then taken from him when Clark punched Conner in the stomach, which made him stagger back a little. Unfortunately for Clark, he did it with the hand that was holding the syringe, thus smashing it.

Conner tried to make a grab for the purple syringe, the one that caused Levitis, but Clark caught him and tried to push him away. Conner resisted, instead pushing Clark against the west wall. Clark crashed against some of the instruments there, pouring some chemicals onto the floor. Conner used this opportunity to grab a Levitis syringe. As Clark recovered and tried to attack Conner, Conner rammed the syringe into his arm and pressed the plunger.

The effects were almost instantaneous. Clark stumbled and then fell, his head below the east table, his body slightly convulsing.

Immediate silence. Conner felt like collapsing. It was over. This would presumably give Clark the illness, killing him the same way he killed so many others. Conner closed his eyes for a minute to calm himself down before he realized that something was wrong. He opened his eyes and examined Clark's body. Everything was as expected...until he came to Clark's eyes. The eyes were clenched shut, not naturally shut as when one has fainted. Clenched eyes meant bad memories, bad dreams or...

Before Conner could stop him, Clark had raised himself up, grabbed a Levitis syringe and plunged it into Conner's arm. He smiled at Conner, an evil, wicked grin before he fainted for good this time.

...or gathering strength. Conner had misjudged Clark, as he had misjudged way too much. Only this time it was costing him his life for sure. Conner's vision got blurry, and he fell to the floor, one more fallen object among the chemicals and glass.

Conner fought against it. The weakness, the crippling pain burning through his body. It was extremely hard, maybe a little too hard. He wanted to give up, to give in to all the pain, so that it would finally end, so he could finally move on. And besides, what hope did he have by attempting to stay alive? Who was coming to save him?

Then something in his mind sparked. He could save himself. An image flashed: Dr. Clark injecting a green liquid into Jon Peck to save his life. The green one was the cure. There was a syringe with the cure on the table! Conner had to make his way to it.

He was on his back, so the first thing was to get into a crawling position. Every pore in his body screamed, "NO" at even the thought of it, but Conner gathered up his strength and flipped over. He was facing the opposite direction from the table with the syringes, so he had to turn to face it. The chemical on the floor helped by providing some much needed traction. Even doing this had exhausted Conner. His body was on fire, but he put one arm weakly forward and pushed himself. He barely covered any distance. He wanted to close his eyes, to gather his strength as Clark had, but he was afraid that if he closed his eyes, he wouldn't open them again.

Conner dragged himself a little more before the smell of something rancid reached his nose. It must be the chemicals finally reacting, even his dull mind realized. One more reason to hurry, if he didn't have enough already. An image of Sophie came to his mind. Sophie, who he had hurt so much in life. She would have been so proud of him today. Conner smiled slightly and dragged himself a little, ignoring the glass scraping against him. Then Conner thought of Megan and realized how much he wanted to see her proud of him. Looking into her eyes would be just like looking into Sophie's eyes, and he needed to see that.

He dragged himself further, trying hard to block out the pain in his body, to only think of the pride in Megan and Sophie's shared blue eyes. Conner reached directly under the table where he was sure the syringes lay. Clark's proximity to the spot confirmed it. As Conner tried to pull himself up, he found he couldn't. There was not enough strength in his body; it had all been drained. He was barely hanging on as it was.

He didn't think his hands could hang on to both together. If he used his last bit of strength to get up and grab the right syringe, he wouldn't be able to inject himself with it. So he had to pick one while lying on the floor and inject himself. The problem was, there were two and if he picked the wrong one, he wouldn't be able to retrieve the other in time. He was on the verge of fainting. So he stretched his arm slowly and pawed for a second before he felt two syringes side-by-side. He tried to pick up both; they were heavy and hence full.

Here was where Conner needed luck. So he prayed, took hold of a syringe and brought it down. His vision was badly blurred and the bad smell was intensifying. He couldn't see what colour the liquid in the syringe was.

Conner steadied himself, inserted the needle into what he hoped was a vein and depressed the plunger.

The last few drops entered Conner's blood just as the syringe dropped out and Conner fainted.

Chapter 23

Believe

The people of Levion gathered in the square, talking quietly amongst themselves. The children had been sent to school, since the adults had a lot of plans to make. The rumour mill, however, hadn't and wouldn't shut down.

According to the fire chief (who suddenly had a lot of work on his hands) there seemed to have been some sort of explosion in Dr. Clark's lab, which had resulted in a fire. Dr. Clark's ancestral house had been situated in a remote part of town, and by the time the fire chief got the call, most of it had already burned down. He assumed that there was at least one body in the rubble, though he couldn't tell for sure, and he couldn't do an intensive search at the moment in case of residual effects left by the chemicals. So he gave strict instructions to his fire-fighters not to tell anyone till morning, and even then not to approach the site.

Victoria was also in the square, extremely worried. She had gotten no message from Conner, and she feared the worst. The previous night, she had gone back home to talk to her parents. She had explained to them the mental distress she had gone through over the years without telling them the reason for this, her interaction with Conner and all the help he had given her, and finally, with tears in her eyes, she promised to change for the better. Her parents, visibly upset by this point, asked her what it was that had caused her so much grief. Victoria promised that she would tell them if she could, though when she was ready.

That was the point when Victoria's father got a call. Apparently someone had arranged for a complete fix-up and upgrade for his car. That had been Conner's "gift". Her father was ecstatic. Victoria wanted to go to the inn to wait for Conner, but she couldn't tell her parents this, and they made sure that she stayed at home. They were probably worried about what she would do if they let her out of their sight.

Victoria had just found out about the fire and she was at her wit's end. She spotted Mrs. Stewart entering the square and ran to her. Mrs. Stewart had been busy talking to the townspeople for ways to increase tourism and hadn't managed to get away. She answered Victoria's unspoken question with a shake of her head. "He isn't in his room, Victoria," she said gently. "He might have come back when I wasn't there, but nothing in his room seems disturbed."

Victoria wanted to cry, but she controlled herself. "He wanted me to say goodbye to you," she said softly.

Mrs. Stewart wanted to tell Victoria that it would be okay, that he would come back, but she knew that it wasn't possible. She had to control her tears as well. Rosaline approached the two of them, her face grave. This was strange, because Rosaline never seemed upset about anything. As they soon found out, though, it wasn't about Conner.

"Victoria, I need to talk to you about something. I think you would prefer if we talked in private," Rosaline said, glancing at Mrs. Stewart.

"I'm good here, Rosaline. What's this about?" Victoria asked her brow furrowing.

Rosaline still seemed unsure. She took them away from earshot of the others and continued, "You made a trip to Baronsville last night with Conner, didn't you?"

Victoria panicked, but she tried not to let it show. "Yes, I did, but how do you know and why does it matter?"

Rosaline's worried expression really scared Victoria. If Rosaline was worried and showing it, it must be something really bad. "What happened, Rosaline?" Victoria asked, resisting the urge to shake Rosaline.

"Arthur Barker was in Baronsville yesterday. He was there to check out a few of the shops, maybe get new ideas now that he can expand even further. In any case, he was going to this little out-of-the-way shop that he knew, when," she paused, "When, apparently he saw you and a man that resembled Conner White in an alley torturing some boy. He says he recognized your voice."

Victoria suddenly remembered the sound of footsteps moving away. They must have been Barker's. When Mrs. Stewart saw that Victoria seemed unable to reply, she broke in fiercely, "How does he know that was Victoria's voice? And why has he bothered to come to you about this when he doesn't have proof? What point is it besmirching this poor girl's name? Why-"

Rosaline put up a hand. "I asked him the same thing," she said. "He said he wasn't going to say anything, until he saw an article in the *Baronsville Times*. It showed you reporting someone for three cases of sexual assault." Mrs. Stewart gasped and Victoria's face instantly paled. "I'm pretty sure that the only reason that it was printed was because Conner was a witness to the third one. Barker, the pompous idiot, claims that the third didn't occur, and you were the one that hurt that boy."

Victoria looked unsteady, so Rosaline gripped her shoulders, the determination returning to her eyes, "Listen to me, I need to know for sure; did that boy do anything to you before last night?" Victoria looked like she was about to throw up, which was enough for Mrs. Stewart and Rosaline. They both started to spout a string of unmentionable curses. Rosaline looked at Victoria and said, "Victoria, I'll go there and make sure he doesn't tell anyone else. I'll revoke his license if I have to. I'll ban people from going to Baronsville for a few days, so that they can't read this issue, I'll-" Victoria raised a hand and indicated towards the crowd.

A few of them were throwing furtive glances towards the three of them, with varying expressions that Victoria couldn't understand in her state of mind. "They're just wondering what we're doing here, Victoria," said Mrs. Stewart soothingly. "Nobody knows."

"Then why is that one reading a newspaper with her mouth open?" Victoria muttered before she bent down, bile coming up her throat. "Hey!" Mrs. Stewart yelled and grabbed the newspaper from the woman reading it and then started saying something incoherent while Rosaline walked off toward Barker, who was talking animatedly to another townsperson.

Victoria forced herself to calm down. She could see that there was no way to control this, and that even two very smart women hadn't been able to stop it. She had known from the start that it was possible that her town would find out, but she never imagined it would be in this way. What must they be thinking of her? All sorts of thoughts came into her mind, and she wanted to throw up. She thought of Conner, of what he would say, and she calmed herself down. It had to be done, she decided. The only other option would be to run away, and she was done with that.

Victoria looked at the trees, the greenery, and it calmed her down like always. Then she walked back to the square.

As they saw her walking towards the broken statue, they quietened down. Mrs. Stewart rushed to her side. "Victoria, what are you doing?"

Victoria ignored her, mainly because she was saving up her words, and climbed onto the pedestal where the half-statue stood. It didn't take up much space, so she could stand comfortably. "People of Levion," she called, although everyone was already listening. "I'll get right to it, because if you haven't already heard it, you'll hear it soon enough. I was sexually assaulted. Twice."

Instant whispers and murmurs. "Please," Victoria said, raising a hand. "Don't say anything until I complete." Everyone stopped, though it was apparent that it was killing a few of them. Victoria could see her parents, Harold and a lot of classmates who used to be her friends. They had varying expressions of shock and horror on their faces. Victoria couldn't bear to look at them, so she shifted her gaze to a girl on the edge of the crowd. She had dark hair and her face seemed familiar, though Victoria knew that she wasn't from town. Her face was comforting, and she was smiling. It wasn't a rude or snarky smile; it radiated warmth. She nodded slightly, as if to tell Victoria to carry on.

"Yesterday, I finally got the courage to face him," Victoria said, her voice a little stronger now. "I turned him in. I had the clothes from the nights he attacked me, I hoped they could pull enough evidence from that but I was worried that they couldn't. So last night I fabricated the attack attempt so that they could at least hold him on that while the media attention from Conner acting as a witness gets that bastard's name out there, which will hopefully get more people to come forward. Yes, I beat him in an attempt to get some closure, but I realized that making sure that he was locked up and protecting others was more important. But trust me, that beating was nothing compared to what I went through," She paused, out of breath. She looked back to that girl in the crowd and her small smile was encouraging.

"To say it was terrible would be an understatement," said Victoria, "I alienated myself from everyone around me, losing almost all my friends in the process, hurting so many of them. My studies were badly affected, I lost interest in life. I lost my boyfriend. I destroyed my relationship with my parents; I don't know if I'll ever get it back," She turned briefly to her mother and father. Her mother was crying, and her father had tears in his eyes. "I'm sorry for not getting better for your sake." She turned to her friends. "Sorry for not confiding in any of you." She turned to Harold. "Sorry for not giving you a chance." She knew she had tears in her eyes, but it didn't matter.

"But you know what I'm not sorry for?" Victoria exclaimed, standing up straighter. "I'm not sorry for what happened to me.

And there was one person who changed that, and his name was Conner White. He made me believe in myself, in my self-worth. He showed me how I could have a better future, a better life. Look at all of you; he changed the course of our entire town! He proved that no matter how bad you are or think you are, you can always do some good. He had faith in me, and I like to think that by having faith in him, I made him believe. Without him, I would not be here. So wherever he is, I want to thank him. I want to thank him for believing and making me believe." Victoria looked at the girl at the edge of the crowd and saw that she was crying as well. "So my fellow Leviites, do with me as you will. If you want to shun me, shun me. If you want to treat me like a dirty outcast, do it. It doesn't matter. I'm confident that I don't deserve it."

Victoria stopped. She didn't know what more to say. She put her head down, ready to move past the crowd when someone said, "We're not to going to do that, Victoria."

Victoria looked up to see who the speaker was and saw that it was Mike. "I'm sorry I didn't realize what you were going through, Victoria. I got scared that I couldn't help you, and I'm ashamed to say that I avoided you, and have been avoiding you ever since. I was too scared to figure out what the problem was. "

"Nobody's going to shun you, Victoria," Mrs. Stewart said. There were murmurs of assent.

"You were the victim. You're not any sort of dirty outcast."

"It could have happened to any one of us, Victoria," a man from the crowd said. "It could happen to our sisters, our daughters. We'll treat you with the same consideration we would treat them with, because we're all family here, including you." This was followed by a rumble of assent.

"We understand now, Victoria, and we're sorry we didn't understand," one of Victoria's friends said.

"Even after I know this, I'm still going to want to be with you, Victoria," Harold said.

"And you're still going to be our daughter, Victoria. We still love you. We didn't know and I'm so sorry we let you go through this alone," Victoria's father came forward and said, tears in his eyes.

Victoria had stepped down from the statue, and her parent's comment finally made her completely break down. Her father came and hugged her and her mother joined in, then Harold and soon everyone surrounded her, overwhelming her with their love. Victoria had been hoping for, but never really expecting this.

Conner had been right.

After a few minutes when they broke up, Victoria went through the crowd to find the familiar dark-haired girl but she couldn't, and nobody seemed to have noticed her. Victoria suddenly realized who the girl reminded her of.

Megan White went back to her father at the edge of town and recounted all that had happened. Conner smiled. "I'm so proud of her," he said.

"And I'm proud of you," Megan said and hugged Conner. Conner hugged her back. They stayed that way for a few minutes before Conner looked into her eyes and saw pride, the sort of pride that he had never seen in his daughter's eyes, and it reminded him so much of his wife that tears came to his eyes. Megan just looked back at him, understanding.

After a while, they started walking. Conner told her that he had just found out that two more girls had come in to report the rapist, so even without Victoria's evidence, the pervert was going away for a long time.

"I'm glad," Megan said. Then she looked back to the town and said, "Why aren't you telling them you're alive?"

Conner had shot himself with the right syringe, and had woken up in what he estimated as a few minutes. He had barely escaped the explosion caused by the chemicals mixing, and the consequent fire. He was glad, though, that everything had burned. There was no way that someone would use those formulas for evil again.

"What's the point of those goodbyes? Victoria doesn't need me right now. She needs to push forward on her own. I've done all I can for her. I need to push forward on a journey of my own for now. Maybe someday, I'll meet her again. But for now, let's go home."

Megan nodded and Conner put his arm around her shoulders and they started walking away from the town of Levion.

****

Victoria went up to the inn and checked Conner's room. Mrs. Stewart was almost right; everything remained untouched in the room. Except for one critical thing. No matter how much Victoria searched, she couldn't find Conner's story. She chuckled to herself and shook her head. Then she remembered something and went to talk to Rosaline, leaving Conner's room, but carrying with her the knowledge that Conner would be with her in her heart always.

****

Later, Victoria stood in the forest alone. Even though this wasn't a new experience for her, it felt different. Her hands hung loose by her side; they weren't held ready to grab her pocketknife at the first sign of danger. Her body was relaxed, and when she looked up at the blue sky and the green leaves, she smiled, for no reason at all. She closed her eyes and felt the cool breeze and something washed over her. It was a magical feeling that made her feel nothing at all. It made her want to do nothing and yet feel able to do everything. It was a feeling of peace.

Suddenly, the breeze picked up and it whipped against Victoria's face. This didn't dampen her spirits; in fact it made her face broaden into a grin. She stretched a little and then started walking against the wind, which eventually turned into a run.

As she ran, the wind lashed against almost every part of her skin, even under her past some of her clothes to the skin underneath. But she didn't feel violated. She didn't stop. Instead she let out a laugh and ran harder.

The wind responded in kind, hitting her skin harder, so hard that it seemed like her skin was flaking off as a result.

Victoria realized this and she let out a laugh of pure joy, not bothering to stop and look back at the parts of her that were being left behind and blown away, hopefully to get lost forever.

Epilogue

In the months that passed, Levion changed. Its people became more open; they started going to Baronsville more often. Rosaline was elected mayor and helped bring in many changes. More tourists came into the town and Mrs. Stewart suddenly got an offer from a construction company to help her expand at a very generous price. The stone blocks all around were removed for good. Rosaline started adding new houses, and more people came to call Levion home. Arthur Barker expanded even more and started considering franchising in Baronsville. The Sinome was rebuilt, and it was more glorious than it had ever been. Natism not only survived, it flourished. The hardworking people of Levion became happier, and Levion came to be regarded as one of the fastest-growing towns in the country.

Victoria managed to battle her demons fairly well, and she had a good relationship with her boyfriend, Harold. She made new friends and regained a lot of old ones. She was studying to do a degree in psychology. She had become more open with her family, and her home life was also pleasant. She was happy, truly happy. The only thing she wondered about was where Conner White had gone, but she knew that when the time came, she would find out.

One day, that time came. There was a delivery in the mail for her, a book. The title was *Lessons Levion Taught Me* by Conner White. She was shocked but eagerly opened it and read the first story.

It was dark. He was trying to think about why it was dark, but he couldn't figure it out. Then he realized his eyes were closed. He tried opening them but all he saw was more darkness so he pressed them shut. Slowly he felt as if he was regaining feeling in the rest of his body. Both his arms were outstretched; the left hand was against something hard, and his right was against something sticky. His legs were spread, and he could feel socks but not shoes. He now realized that he was completely flat on the ground. He now lifted his head and opened his eyes.

He was lying on a patch of damp grass. He got up into a sitting position slowly, and blinked his eyes. He looked around him. It seemed like a small clearing, and there was a small opening by which he could see a road. A small amount of light filtered in through the openings in the leaves. He stood up shakily. He blinked his eyes and tried to think. Where was he? Then he blinked again. Who was he? He couldn't remember anything about who he was or what he was doing on the ground in what looked like a forest.

He looked at where his head was resting. There was a small rock there. He felt his head. There was a bump there. He felt that there might be a connection between that and his memory loss, but he didn't know exactly what.

He went through the opening in the trees. It was the early morning sun. There was a dirt road which led in both directions. He looked at himself more carefully. He was wearing a coat and a plain shirt, and simple trousers. He didn't know what year this was, so he had to assume this was what all the people wore. His pockets were empty, looking as if they had been turned out. He looked in both directions. What was he supposed to do?

He sat down, resting against the tree, trying to regain some part of his memory. He figured that somebody might come down this road and he could get some help. But neither of those things happened. After a while, he got up. He decided it was better to move somewhere. Once again, he thought about which direction to go. Suddenly something caught his eye. It was a mark on the other side of the road. It seemed to be tracks of a wheel going east. He started to follow the tracks. The tracks were not consistent and it seemed that the vehicle, whatever it was, was on the verge of toppling.

And so it was. Some way day the road, the man found ruins of what seemed to be a horse drawn carriage. It seemed to have crashed. He wondered if it was his and whether he had lost control and been thrown out of it. He searched the debris but could find no clues, other than some confused horse tracks, which meant that the horse had probably escaped. There were no bodies either, which probably meant he was travelling alone, or there were survivors nearby. He yelled out, "Hello!"

There was no response. Nobody was nearby. He shrugged and started walking. It was probably going to be a very long walk.

It had been a long walk, but suddenly a town was visible in the distance. His pace picked up; he was very sweaty and tired but now he got a burst of energy. He sped up. Soon he saw three men. He hailed them. They looked surprised to see a man so far away from town.

"Yes?" one of them asked, "What is it you desire?"

"I am lost," he said. "I don't know where I am, and I have suffered an injury which seems to have made me forget how I got here."

They looked at each other. Then the second one asked, "So, do you have a name, injured stranger?"

A pause. It was better to decide a name so he wasn't deemed completely crazy. "Of course. My name is Marvin."

They looked at him with stunned gazes. The man who we shall now refer to as Marvin eyed them curiously. "Something wrong?" he asked.

They muttered to each other and then the first man, apparently the leader, stepped forward and extended his hand. "It's nothing. I'm Tyson and these are my friends, Pierce and Daniel," he said, pointing to the second and third man respectively. "Come on, maybe we can get you some help in our town."

Marvin nodded gratefully and they started walking.

"So aren't you hungry?" asked Daniel, speaking for the first time since Marvin had met them.

Marvin shook his head. "Well...no. Somehow I know the name of the herbs that are edible, and I've eaten enough of them to keep my hunger down."

They looked sceptical but before they could say anything, they were able to hear a commotion up ahead. They sped up and came up to a crowd of people that had gathered around a man who was on the floor, writhing and screaming. The people saw them come and the man who was standing over him, who was apparently the doctor, looked at Tyson and said in a grave voice, "Poisoned, just like the others."

Tyson knelt down next to him, looking worried. "Is there nothing we can do?"

The doctor shook his head gravely. "I can try giving this, but I don't know if it will work." He held up a small green plant.

Something about the writhing man was familiar to Marvin. He pushed aside the people and knelt down next to the writhing man and examined him. He suddenly stood up, snatched the plant and announced, "That will only kill him faster. I know what this man is suffering from."

And ignoring the surprised glances of the onlookers, he moved the head in such a position that the writhing man could get better air. He heard whispered conversation between the doctor and Tyson. Instead of listening, he rushed to the forest and started searching frantically around for something. The people stared at him instead of the writhing man. Suddenly Marvin seemed to have found what he was looking for. He grabbed a few leaves and started crushing them together as he walked towards the writhing man. The doctor blocked his path. "What experience do you have?"

Marvin pushed him aside, knelt down and put the crushed leaves in the man's mouth, tilting his head so that he managed to swallow it. Everyone waited to see what would happen. After a few seconds, the writhing man screamed. A few strong men came and took hold of Marvin, while the doctor said, "He has given him poison which has made him suffer!"

Marvin ignored all of this, watching the man on the ground. After ignoring the doctor for a few seconds, he indicated with his head, "Look."

The man had stopped writhing, and everyone was stunned. Marvin broke free from the now-loosened grips, and propped the man's head up against the nearby well.

He seemed to be regaining colour in his face. Everyone gathered around to see if he was really feeling better. The doctor checked him and said, "Yes, he's much better."

There was a murmur around the crowd. "I understand you can't remember anything about your past?" asked the doctor. "But yet you can remember sicknesses and their remedies?"

Marvin nodded. "I'm not sure how it happened. I hit my head after a violent crash, I think."

The doctor thought for a while and then said, "I think only your personal memories, like friends, places, etc. are forgotten. Maybe some trigger will make you recall them. Do you know what you call yourself?"

A hesitation. "Marvin."

There was a flurry around the crowd. The name "Marvin" seemed to have some kind of meaning to these people. Suddenly the poisoned man groaned. Everyone's attentions turned to him once more and the doctor hurriedly exclaimed, "Give him some water!"

As Tyson stepped forward to draw the water, Marvin exclaimed, "Stop!"

Tyson stopped and looked at him. "You said there were others poisoned?" Marvin asked.

Tyson nodded. Marvin stepped forward and drew water from the well. He sniffed it and sipped a bit of it. Then he spat that out and threw all the water on the ground. Everyone was, once again, surprised.

"This water is the source of your poison!" he exclaimed. "Does anyone know whether the poisoned victims had drunk this well water?"

Slowly people started giving affirmative responses. Suddenly one person said, "I've kept it home for using later on."

Marvin's eyes widened and he said, "Go run ahead and tell them to stop! If they are sick, take a few leaves of this herb, crush them up and feed this to them! Quickly!"

Marvin brought several of those herbs and gave them to Tyson who rushed off with some other people.

The rest started walking quickly towards the village, two men giving support to the ill man. After a while, everyone was checked. They were a few others poisoned, but they were all saved. After everyone was confirmed safe, they stood around looking at Marvin reverently.

"You're a saint!" one of them screamed.

Marvin was taken aback. "I'm no saint."

One old man who was standing at the back of the proceedings all day, suddenly came forward and said, "Marvin was the name of our saint. You appear out of nowhere and save our town, bearing his name. You are his reincarnation."

And then they all hailed a very bewildered Saint Marvin.

Saint Marvin was very confused. He had just been doing something to save a man's life, even though it felt very unusual to him. Wasn't he supposed to have felt familiar with saving people if he knew all about cures?

At any rate, people were praising him wherever he went. He had no money; nevertheless they gave him food and a place to stay. One of the people he had saved from dying had been the local innkeeper, and he got a room. It was not impressive, but Marvin had a feeling that he had stayed in worse places. Anything more than vague feelings eluded him, though.

Suddenly there was a lot of noise coming from the square. Somebody yelled, "That's Saint Marvin!"

Marvin was curious to see what was going on. He set off towards the square. Everyone seemed to be gathered around a man who was holding a poster. Marvin went closer and saw that it was an artist's drawing of what seemed to be a picture of...him.

The man holding the poster suddenly saw Marvin and shouted, "That's him" before producing a pistol and pointing it at Marvin.

"His name is not Marvin," sneered the man holding the pistol, who seemed to be a sheriff. "His name is Oscar Gibson. He's a mass murderer. Poisons people. Knows every kind of poison there is."

Marvin, or Oscar, suddenly had flashes of memory. People dying while he stood over them, watching his poison take effect. Tortured souls giving up all sorts of information, begging for an antidote.

"He was finally caught and being transferred to a faraway prison when he found a way to disrupt the carriage's path. The carriage driver and two guards were found gravely injured. He seemed to have been thrown out, but we couldn't find him. And now we have."

Everybody turned to look at Marvin. All these images were slowly coming back to his mind. Someone said, "So that's how he knew how to cure us and is so well-versed in poisons."

At the sheriff's prompting, a pair of strong arms grabbed Marvin's arms. "When you didn't know who I was, you accepted me. Now that you've seen the bad I've done in the past, you forget all the good?" asked Marvin in a pleading voice.

Nobody seemed to be listening. "Please!" Marvin screamed. "I saved lives, which should count for something. Please give me a chance to prove myself. Let me help make sure that no one gets poisoned again."

There was an argument over this, but eventually they agreed to let Marvin stay under strict supervision. Marvin did an examination of the surrounding plants, and realized that there was only one person who could have had access and knowledge to get the plant: The doctor.

Marvin realized, however, that no one was going to believe him if he accused the doctor of this. So he gathered some herbs and told the townspeople, "I have found a way to immunize you. I need all of you to take this mixture, but I need your doctor to take it first so that if anyone else is affected, he's safe for sure."

This was viewed with instant suspicion, of course. Marvin offered to take the mixture himself and he did. He seemed to be unaffected and so the doctor consented, thinking that Marvin had no reason to harm him. Instead, they were both dead within minutes. Marvin had sacrificed himself to save everyone else and thus tried to make amends even with his dying breath.

Victoria finished the story and Conner's words came back to her. He had written this ending before the Day of Natis, which meant that he was prepared to sacrifice himself for the others, and thought that he would, too.

Victoria put the book down and got up. She walked out to the square and looked at the statue there. It had been recently reconstructed, and showed a boy, not yet a man, standing with his arms on his waist. The saviour of Levion was actually supposed to be this age. However, if one looked closely at his face with the slight smile, it reminded them of an author that briefly passed through the town, changing their lives forever.

However, it was the eyes that most reminded one of that author. They seemed to be soft and looking far off, into a much brighter future and those eyes helped people to believe that that future was well within reach.

-- The End --

Acknowledgements

Not every family in our country would accept a boy taking Arts and dreaming of being a writer, but my family did, and for letting me pursue my dreams, I thank them deeply.

I've got very few close friends, and when it comes to my writing, each one of them has read my work and encouraged me when I needed encouragement the most. I would like to mention Rehan, though, for years of literary companionship and friendly rivalry; and Gigi, for the years of close friendship.

There are two particular teachers I would like to thank - Mrs. Daruvala, for seeing my potential and giving me the confidence to go down this path, without which I might never have reached this point; and Miss Jasmin, for innumerable life lessons and support.

Lastly, but definitely not the least, I would like to thank the brave women who are out there every day, fighting and sometimes winning their personal battles against oppression, and especially those women that helped contribute to the character of Victoria.